Coffeehouse Angel

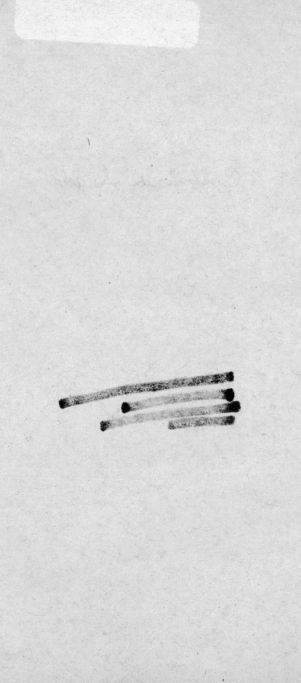

Coffeehouse Angel

SUZANNE SELFORS

SCHOLASTIC INC.
New York Toronto London Auckland
Sydney Mexico City New Delhi Hong Kong

ISBN 978-0-545-23687-4

12 11 10 9 8 7 6 5 4 3 2 1   10 11 12 13 14 15/0

Printed in the U.S.A.   40

First Scholastic printing, January 2010

Book design by Nicole Gastonguay

For my little sister, Laurie Selfors,
who likes her coffee ultrastrong
and her marathons ultralong.
She amazes me each and every day.

Coffeehouse Angel

Be not forgetful to entertain strangers, for thereby some
have entertained angels unawares.
Hebrews 13:2, The New Testament

For a single good deed, one will be rewarded tenfold.
6:161, Al-An'am, The Koran

Do you believe in signs?

Lightning striking a car you just stepped out of, a black cat crossing your path, a piece of frozen toilet waste falling from an airplane and crashing through your living room ceiling—that kind of thing? Happenstance, maybe. Or maybe something bigger than you is well aware of your existence and trying to tell you something. I never used to believe that kind of stuff.

But then I met him.

One

The first time I saw him, he was lying in the alley behind my grandmother's coffeehouse. I figured he was some sort of bum.

The yellow bulb above the back door cast an eerie light, pooling around his brown hair like melted margarine. What was he doing out there? Homeless people didn't hang out in Nordby. Too much rain. No public shelters or bus stations. Was he dead?

I took a cautious step out the door, leaning to get a better look. His chest rose with slow, deep breaths, but the way he was stretched out on his back, his arm flung over his face, I couldn't tell if his eyes were open or closed. Maybe he was passed out drunk, or waiting for me to get closer so he could grab me—another sixteen-year-old girl, gone.

Problem was, I had forgotten to take out the trash the night before and I needed to get it into the Dumpster or it would stink up the coffeehouse. But he blocked the way.

He was dressed in a khaki kilt and a ragged sweater. His bare legs were pale against the cobblestones and his toes stuck out past the ends of his sandals. December, in my part of the world, is way too cold for sandals.

"Hello," I called. "Do you need help?"

"Sleepy," he mumbled. That was all he said.

Who wasn't sleepy at 6:00 a.m.? I would have loved another hour in bed, but as usual, I was working the early shift—alone. Suddenly, I wished I hadn't said anything to him. If he turned out to be some kind of murderer, there was no one around to hear my screams. None of the other shops had opened yet. The employees of Java Heaven, our next-door neighbor, didn't show up until seven. That's right—two coffeehouses, side by side. Maybe that's not unusual in the coffee-drenched world we live in, with coffeehouses sprout-ing up as fast as cavities after Halloween. But we were here first!

Anyway, no one would be out walking a dog on such a cold morning, or window-shopping in the dark. Even though Grandma Anna was upstairs in our apartment, she'd have her radio on full blast, which would drown out my cries if that guy strangled me.

Maybe I was overreacting, but normal, safe, sane people don't usually sleep in alleys.

He rolled over.

I dropped the bag of garbage, ran inside, and locked the door. Then I did what I always did when I didn't know what to do. I called my best friend. We were both early birds—me because of my job, Vincent because of swim team practice.

"Vincent," I said, clinging to the ancient rotary phone my grandmother kept in the kitchen. "There's a guy lying in our alley and he's freaking me out."

"Maybe you should call the police."

That wasn't such a good idea because my grandmother Anna Svensen, owner of Anna's Old World Scandinavian Coffeehouse, had gotten a stern warning from Officer Larsen just a few days before. "You can't keep calling the department for every little thing," he had lectured after pulling his head out of the freezer.

"But it's groaning. I thought it might be dangerous," she had explained. "Maybe it's a fire hazard. You want this place to burn down?"

"If you're worried about a fire hazard, then for God's sake, Anna, call an electrician. Groaning freezers are not part of my job. Or lost keys, or late deliveries, or tourists who forget to tip." He tucked his thumbs under his belt. "There might come a day when you've got a *real* emergency and you'll want me on your good side."

Grandma Anna didn't like people telling her what and what not to do. And because her husband had served as a Nordby police officer for most of his life, she believed that the local force should be at her disposal, end of story.

"I don't want to call the police," I told Vincent. "It's not a *real* emergency. But can you stop by?"

"Sure," Vincent said. "I'll be right over. Hey, don't go into the alley, just in case."

I hung up the phone, feeling a bit less worried. It wouldn't take Vincent long to shoot down Main Street on his bike. I checked the back door again, to make certain I had locked it. Then I began my morning chores.

Every morning before school I worked at our coffeehouse, getting things ready for Grandma Anna, who would hobble downstairs at seven to open the doors to her loyal customers. I didn't mind the early hours. I liked the darkness, the way all the shops slept, the way the seagulls called from the docks. Vincent often stopped in before swim practice to grab a scone or Danish. We'd sit at the counter and share the quiet, as if we were the only two people in the world. For a few minutes he'd forget his single-minded goal—to earn a swimming scholarship to a top university and go to the Olympics. And I'd forget my single-minded goal—to, well, I didn't have one.

Vincent had known that swimming was his thing from the moment he had accidentally toddled off the edge of the Nordby public pool. What was my *thing*? My life was an ode to failure—the closet at the end of our hallway held the proof. A guitar, a harmonica, a recorder, a chess set, a fencing mask, a dried-out box of clay, skating boots, sheets of choir music, a microscope, and some boxing gloves— evidence of things started but not finished. Desired but not achieved. Okay, I admit it. I lost interest the moment those projects went from "fun new idea" to "oh crud, I actually have to practice." But I kept hoping that something would flow, something would come as naturally to me as swimming had come to Vincent.

Each of us is supposed to be good at *something*. Maybe that's one of the big lies they feed us in school, like telling us that Columbus discovered America, or that your vote actually counts, or that girls and boys are equal. Hello? Ever heard of biology?

Maybe the horrid truth is that some of us aren't meant to be good at anything. But I wanted to be able to say, *This* is what I'm good at, it's what I was born to do. *This* is my thing.

Even if I had discovered some God-given talent like

Vincent's, I wouldn't have had much time to pursue it. The coffeehouse supported Grandma and me, so my working there was a matter of survival. I may sound like I'm complaining, but I really love the place. It had been my home for as long as I could remember. I fit right in with my pale blond hair and hand-knit sweaters. *Look at the Norwegian girl in the cute embroidered apron. Take a picture of her and stick it on a postcard!*

I slipped an apron over my head and poured coffee beans into the grinder. Fog drifted past the front picture windows. The guy in the alley would definitely be cold. Didn't homeless people usually carry blankets around with them? A shopping cart filled with extra shoes, a poncho or two, maybe a tarp?

I measured the coffee and dumped it into a huge percolator. A smaller percolator was saved for decaf. Only a few of Grandma Anna's customers drank decaf. Scandinavians like their coffee strong and jolting—a craving for caffeine that is embedded in their DNA after all those centuries of darkness and cold. That's my theory.

My thoughts kept drifting to the homeless guy. Had he tried to rob the place? Was he a drug addict who needed quick cash? Nothing seemed disturbed. Maybe he was just down on his luck. I peered out the back window. His arm had fallen to his side. The yellow light cast a jaundiced hue on his sleeping face, which seemed young. Maybe he had run away from home.

"Meow." Ratcatcher, the coffeehouse cat, rubbed against my leg, whining for breakfast. Her belly often collected dustballs because it hung all the way to the floor. "Meow." She nipped my ankle.

"Good morning to you too." I tore off the corner of a day-old Danish and dropped it. Ratcatcher inhaled the morsel. She was supposed to keep the rats in check. We had never seen a rat in the coffeehouse, but they scurried along the nearby docks. Ratcatcher once caught a field mouse, but she didn't eat it. She preferred pastries.

I started to bag up the day-old pastries. Ralph, one of our regulars, usually took them down to the dock to feed to the seagulls. The pastries were perfectly good, just a bit dry. I ate them all the time. What if the homeless guy was hungry? What if he had to pick food out of garbage cans? He probably needed the pastries more than the spoiled gulls needed them. And on such a cold morning, he would probably like something warm to drink too.

Vincent had warned me not to go out there, but I could just slip the food out, real quickly. I wouldn't have to go near the guy. I poured some coffee into a large Styrofoam cup, dropped in a sugar cube, stirred in some cream. Then I grabbed a packet of chocolate-covered coffee beans—a free sample from our supplier. As quietly as possible, I cracked open the back door. Reaching, I set the Styrofoam cup on the stoop and placed the bag of pastries and the packet of coffee beans next to it. Then I closed and locked the door, my heart beating wildly. Maybe I shouldn't have risked it. He could be an escaped lunatic. He could have a gun. I would be blamed for the sugar and caffeine rush that led to Nordby's worst crime spree.

I nearly had a stroke when Vincent pounded on the front door. He leaned his bike against the picture window. Vincent's a big guy. "As big as a barn," my grandmother liked to say. He has one of those wide, V-shaped swimmers' bodies. It's like his upper half got switched with someone else's lower half.

Vincent had been my best *guy* friend since the fourth grade. Don't worry, this is not one of those "I'm in love with my best friend" stories. 'Cause I wasn't. But my grandmother couldn't seem to get that through her head. She thought that boys and girls couldn't be best friends because it went against nature. She didn't know what she was talking about. This wasn't the *Old World*. Boys and girls are best friends all the time.

I liked Vincent right away because he was different from the other fourth-grade boys. He never traveled in a pack. He never tried to pull up my skirt to see my underwear. He never, ever told me that I was too tall, or that I was stupid, or that my salmon sandwiches were gross. We became best friends. Just like that.

"Hi," I said, letting him in. He threw his gloves and knit hat onto a table. His black hair was flattened against his forehead.

"Is he still in the alley?"

"Yeah."

Vincent pulled a piece of paper from his coat pocket. "I looked up shelters in the phone book, in case he's homeless. There's one over in Kingston. I wrote down the address." He walked to the back door and unlocked it. "I'll give him some change for the bus. Your grandma won't want him hanging around. It's not good for business." He hesitated a moment, then grabbed a rolling pin off the counter.

"What are you doing?" I asked.

"You never know." Vincent had this way of keeping a level head, no matter what happened. I think it was all that swimming, lap after lap, like underwater meditation. He was like a floating Buddhist.

He opened the back door and stepped onto the stoop. I peered over his shoulder. The guy was gone. The goodies and coffee cup were also gone. Vincent handed me the rolling pin. "Guess you won't have to worry about him." He scrunched his nose and picked up the garbage bag. "This is rancid." He carried it to the Dumpster at the end of the alley. "You sure you didn't imagine that guy? Maybe you just saw some shadows." He nodded toward a pile of crates.

"I didn't imagine him," I insisted. "I left some coffee out here, and some pastries."

"You talked to him?"

"No. But the bag and the Styrofoam cup are gone, so that proves I didn't imagine him."

Back inside, Vincent washed his hands. "I'll be late for practice."

"Thanks for rushing over."

"No problem. I always have your back, Katrina. See you at assembly." He grabbed his hat and gloves. I handed him a scone, half of which he stuffed into his mouth. He could eat an entire meal in the time it took me to butter my bread. Ratcatcher watched enviously.

I stood on the sidewalk as Vincent pedaled his way up Main Street, past the dark shops and empty parking spaces. Off to perfect his talent. "Bye," I called.

He waved, then disappeared around the corner.

I was glad that the homeless guy had gone. It was hard enough to get all my chores done and still get to school on time without adding a possible murderer to the mix. He had looked young, maybe even my age. He probably wasn't a murderer. I hoped that he'd gone back home—to someplace nicer than an alley. Maybe that coffee would keep him warm on the way.

I picked up the newspaper and was about to go back inside, when a flash of white caught my eye. A small something, glowing like a paper lantern, rolled down the quiet street. It rolled past the trinket shop, past the hand-knit sweater shop and the candy shop, and then, caught by a breeze, bounced up onto the sidewalk. It rolled past the bookstore and the barbershop and came to an abrupt stop at my feet.

It was a large, empty Styrofoam coffee cup.

Two

Last year, this guy named Aaron started calling me Coffeehouse Girl. At least it wasn't Hurricane Girl, the obvious choice, since my name is Katrina. And it was better than being called Lard Ass, or Crater Face, or Homo—delightful titles bestowed on some of my classmates.

"Hey, it's Coffeehouse Girl."

"Wanna take my order, Coffeehouse Girl?"

"Hey, Coffeehouse Girl, why don't you introduce Lard Ass to the concept of nonfat milk?"

His teasing wasn't a big deal. Neither the popular girl nor the shunned girl, I existed somewhere in the mundane middle—the perfect place for the untalented. Fortunately, the nickname hadn't spread beyond Aaron and his buddies. And it didn't feel like a malicious nickname. It was just a factual statement. That's who I was—the girl who worked in that weird old-lady coffeehouse. And that's what I smelled like, not like an old lady but like freshly ground coffee. Sometimes the grounds got caught in the hem of my shirt or on my shoes. Sometimes the percolator's steam scented my hair. Aaron's buddies would sniff me.

"Coffeehouse Girl smells *gooooood*."

"I'd like to drink her up."

"I've got a grande for you, Coffeehouse Girl."

I wonder if it's a universal law that boys become annoying turds around age eleven and slide downhill from there?

But they never said those things to me when Vincent was around.

Vincent didn't have a nickname. He could have, the way he always smelled like chlorine, the way his goggles left imprints around his eyes, the way he shaved his legs before races. But no one bothered Vincent. He had broken every swimming record held by Nordby High. Though swimming didn't draw the same kind of frenzy as basketball or football, the line of swimming trophies in the gym's trophy case couldn't be missed.

His size didn't hurt either. Half Native American, half Norwegian, he looked like the offspring of Geronimo and Conan the Barbarian, minus the killer attitude and weaponry. In other words, he was an absolute hunk. So while others bore the weight of Freak or Loser, Vincent got left alone, which was exactly how he liked it.

Vincent and his dad belonged to the Suquamish tribe, as did about a quarter of the students at Nordby High. The most famous member of the tribe was Chief Sealth, also known as Chief Seattle. The tribe owned most of the land to the east of Nordby, and it had plans to build a huge casino and resort. But until the resort's completion, there was little tribal money for higher education. And Vincent's dad didn't bring in much from his job as a security guard. So Vincent needed that swimming scholarship.

Monday morning always began with an assembly in the gym. Paper coffee cups with Java Heaven cloud logos overflowed from the trash can. Kids hung out at Java Heaven because it offered the trendy stuff like smoothies, energy drinks, and iced espresso. Senior citizens hung out at Anna's because it offered the stuff senior citizens prefer, like percolated gut-eating coffee, nondairy creamer, and sugar that comes in cubes.

Elizabeth, my best *girl* friend, waved from the bleachers. I sat between her and a freshman I didn't know. Vincent sat with the swim team a few rows lower. If this had been a picnic, or a movie, or that God-awful monster truck rally he had dragged me to, then Vincent would have sat next to me. But in high school, you gather at the watering hole with your herd. Vincent's herd all wore matching Nordby Otters Swim Team sweatshirts.

I didn't have a herd.

"Face is sitting down there," Elizabeth informed me. She always knew exactly where Face was sitting. You'd think she had stuck a GPS unit up his butt or something. "Face is *soooo* cute."

She said that at least four times a day.

Face was Elizabeth's code name for David Cord. She didn't want anyone to know that she had a killer crush on him. Face was not a member of the mundane middle. His herd wore polo shirts and spent most rainless afternoons at the Nordby Golf Course.

"Good morning, students," Principal Carmichael greeted from center court. "As you all know, winter break begins next Wednesday." Screams of glee erupted. Students stomped their feet. Mr. Rubens, the phys ed teacher, jumped out of his chair and blew his whistle. The enthusiasm settled back to boredom.

The principal cleared her throat. "We have a lot to accomplish before winter break, but guidance counselor appointments are of the highest priority. Yellow notices have been placed in lockers to remind those students who have not yet met this requirement. These appointments are mandatory."

Someone behind me hollered, "Fascist!"

Carmichael scowled. "The yearly consultation with the guidance counselor is an important part of your education, especially for those of you who are planning to go to a college or university." She adjusted the microphone. It shrieked like it always did. Elliott, the school's technical genius, ran out to fix it like he always did. No one yelled "Nerd!" Elliott was going to bring teleportation to the masses or invent liquid time or something and we all knew it.

"Thank you, Elliott." Principal Carmichael adjusted her glasses. "And now Heidi Darling has an announcement, so please give her your undivided attention."

Elizabeth and I groaned as Heidi strode to the microphone. It was the whole perky thing that made us cringe. Natural perkiness is digestible in small amounts. But she was too wide-eyed, too smiley, too bouncy. What kind of a carbon fingerprint does a person leave after maintaining that level of energy?

"Listen up," Heidi said in her clipped way. "This year, my dad's coffeehouse, Java Heaven, is sponsoring the Winter Solstice Festival, so that means that it's going to be the biggest and best festival ever." She paused expectantly. No one applauded, but she kept on smiling. "So the thing is, we need help, people. The decorations don't get set up on their own." Groans filled the gym. Heidi planted her hands on her hips. "My dad said he'll give Java Heaven coupons to those who volunteer, good for a free sixteen-ounce Mocha Cloud Frappe, which is organic because we care about the environment."

"Hey, Coffeehouse Girl." Aaron, the annoying turd, sat behind me. "You got anything free to give out? I'd like to taste your frappe."

Elizabeth jabbed him in the shin with her pencil, then leaned close to me. "Maybe I should ask Face to go to the festival."

"Go for it," I said encouragingly, even though I knew she would never ask him. Elizabeth could jab guys with pencils, she could intimidate them with her big boobs and her in-your-face attitude, but she had no idea how to ask one out. We were both pretty pathetic when it came to guys. Neither of us had ever been on an actual date.

Heidi waved one of the Java Heaven coupons. "If we show our school spirit, we can make this the best Solstice ever. *Gooooo* Otters!"

Heidi Darling was like a virus, the way she invaded everything—every school club, every committee and event. Last spring she had painted a mural on the cafeteria wall with the theme "school spirit." Why would a person want to do all that stuff? And who really cares about "school spirit"? What's the point?

"I highly advise each of you to volunteer and help with the festival decorations," Principal Carmichael said, taking the microphone from Heidi. "Volunteering will look good on your college applications."

And there's the point.

Our main focus as teenagers, according to just about

everyone, is to jam-pack our lives with activities so that we can get into an Ivy League college and therefore succeed in life. Because that's the way it works. Weak application= crappy college. Crappy college=crappy job. Crappy job= crappy life. In other words, poverty, alcoholism, obesity, and depression. It's enough stress to make your hair fall out. By the time Heidi Darling graduated, her college application would be the size of an encyclopedia. She was on the fast track to Har-friggin'-vard.

"Thank you, Heidi," Principal Carmichael said. Heidi speed-walked back to the bleachers. "So students, remember to see your guidance counselor before—" The principal stopped speaking as the gym's double doors slammed open.

A strange guy entered. He wore a khaki kilt, a ragged sweater, and sandals with no socks. A satchel hung from his shoulder and his long brown hair was all messed up, as if he'd been *sleeping in an alley*.

"May I help you?" the principal asked. "Young man, may I help you?"

"I apologize for the intrusion, madame." He walked toward the bleachers. Maybe he was a new student, but that still didn't explain why he had been sleeping in our alley.

"He's *sooo* cute," Elizabeth whispered. I usually ignored Elizabeth's declarations of "cute." With each boyfriendless month that passed, her standards lowered. She was dangerously close to substituting "cute" for "alive." However, the guy did look much better under the bright gym lights than that yellow alley light.

"Excuse me," Principal Carmichael said. "You're not a student here. We have strict security codes."

"I won't be but a wee moment." He stopped walking and

scanned the bleachers. "I've come seeking a lassie. I mean, a young lady." A roar of student laughter broke the tension.

"You're not *seeking* anyone until you check in at the office," the principal said. "Mr. Rubens will show you the way. Mr. Rubens?"

Mr. Rubens put his hand on the guy's shoulder. "Come with me, young man."

The guy calmly slid from Mr. Rubens's grasp and walked right up to the first row. "I must reward her good deed." Then he pointed. "There she is."

Oh God.

Three

Is it ever a good thing to have the entire population of your school turn and stare at you? If you've just scored the winning touchdown—yes. If you've just broken a swimming record—yes. If a weird guy in a skirt starts yelling your name in the middle of an assembly—*never*.

He cupped his hands around his mouth. His voice echoed off the walls as he aimed his words at the eighth row—my row. "Katrina, could you come down? I've a delivery to make, so if you'd just come down, I can reward your good deed and be on my way."

I don't know what laws of physics are involved, but if you fill a gym with teenagers and tell them to stare at one object, heat is actually produced. I half expected to spontaneously combust.

Stuck between a snickering freshman and a wide-eyed Elizabeth, I couldn't escape. I wanted to slide between the bleacher benches. Pull my sweater up over my head. Evaporate.

Mr. Rubens grabbed the guy's arm. "It's time for you to leave."

The guy cocked his head. A puzzled expression spread across his face. "There's no need for violence. You have my word that I am a pacifist. I just need a bit of time with Katrina."

I sank as low as I could without giving myself a spinal injury. I focused on Elizabeth's patent-leather boots. How did she keep them so shiny? Why had she chosen red laces? Why was that guy making a scene and *how did he know my name*?

"You'll have to wait until three o'clock when school has ended. Then you can speak to Katrina," Principal Carmichael said. "Perhaps that's not the rule at your school, but it's our rule."

A long pause followed, during which I kept my head down. "I'm not supposed to break any more rules," the guy said thoughtfully. "I shall wait for her at three o'clock." Footsteps faded and the gym doors slammed shut.

Elizabeth elbowed me. "He's gone."

Everyone started talking. Principal Carmichael excused us to our classes. "Who was that?" Vincent asked as we left the gym.

"That was the guy who was sleeping in the alley." I kept my voice low as students streamed past, smirking at me. "See, I didn't imagine him."

Elizabeth pushed between us. "Huh? What are you talking about?"

"I didn't have time to tell you—"

"He's our age," Vincent interrupted. "I thought he was an old homeless guy. Why did he come to the assembly? Is he going to go to school here? What did he mean when he said he wanted to reward your good deed?"

"He's gorgeous," Elizabeth said. "I wish he'd reward me."

Principal Carmichael sped toward us. Though she could only manage small steps in her high heels, she picked up momentum like a crazed tap dancer. "Katrina," she called, motioning me aside. Vincent looked at his watch, shrugged apologetically, then continued to class.

"I'll tell you everything at lunch," I assured Elizabeth.

"You'd better." She wandered off.

The principal smoothed her short hair and caught her breath. "Katrina, please explain to your friend that this is not an open campus and that in the future he must check in at the office. We can't have that kind of disruption again. In our post–9/11 world, we must be steadfast and firm with our procedures."

"He's not my friend." I turned my back on some eaves-droppers.

"There's no need to lie." She sighed. "You're not in trouble. He's very handsome and I can see why you'd want to go out with him." She fiddled with her blouse. "Just make certain it doesn't happen again."

"I don't want it to happen again," I said. "I don't even know him."

"Well, he obviously *knows* you."

I made it to World Mythology just before the bell rang, taking my seat behind Vincent, next to the windows. Whispers buzzed around the room. I looked out the window to avoid the curious stares. A row of naked cherry trees lined the parking lot. The winter sky was thick with clouds, turning our little corner of the world gray.

I must reward her good deed.

I didn't expect to be rewarded for the pastries and

coffee. And those chocolate-covered coffee beans had been an afterthought. I didn't even expect a thank you, but not making a spectacle would have been nice.

He'd be waiting for me at three o'clock.

"Vincent, do you still have that shelter address?"

Vincent reached into his sweatshirt pocket and handed over the torn piece of notebook paper. "I'm guessing he's not homeless," he said. "I bet he just got messed up at a party and ended up passing out."

"Yeah, that makes sense. But just in case."

If I ran into him, I'd say "You're welcome, but don't worry about rewarding me," and he'd go away, never again to walk into the middle of an assembly and point at me. Soon the incident would disappear from the collective conscience, replaced by someone else's embarrassing moment— maybe a tumble in the cafeteria or a fart during study hall. But the World Mythology teacher, Mr. Williams, was not ready to let my embarrassing moment evaporate.

"Katrina," he said as he plunked some books onto his desk. "Your visitor this morning, what was that he said?"

My cheeks heated up. "He wasn't my visitor. I don't even know him." I pretended that I had something to erase.

"But didn't he say he wanted to reward your good deed?"

Some of the other kids laughed and repeated, "Good *deed*."

"I bet it was *goooood*," Aaron said, wiggling his eyebrows at me.

Great. Give a stranger a free cup of coffee and suddenly everyone thinks you're a slut.

"Well, this is quite a coincidence because today we begin a chapter about good deeds." Mr. Williams picked up a text and sat at the edge of his desk. His thighs spread out like corduroy logs. "The good deed is a common theme in mythology. Sometimes the doer is rewarded with fortune, fame, or power. But sometimes the good deed leads to the doer's *downfall*."

Winter air seeped under the classroom windows. I shivered. I was too young for a downfall, wasn't I?

"We begin this section with a fable called 'Androcles and the Lion.' "

I only half listened as Mr. Williams read the story about the escaped slave who finds a lion in the jungle and removes a thorn from the lion's paw. As a reward for the good deed, the lion spares the slave's life when they later encounter each other in the Coliseum. I fiddled with a yellow reminder slip that someone had stuffed into my locker: *Guidance counselor appointment, Wednesday, 8:00 a.m.* My vision blurred across Vincent's sweatshirt, which was damp around the collar from his wet swim-practice hair. Vincent didn't need a guidance counselor. He knew exactly what he wanted and where he was headed. Likewise, Elizabeth's dream to open an art gallery in New York City guided her every move. They knew.

I didn't know.

Mr. Williams closed the book. "One of the major themes in these good deed stories is that we should never underestimate those who appear to be inferior, like when a lowly slave helps the King of the Jungle. Sometimes the small, meek creature surprises us. Your assignment this week is to write your own good deed story, three to five pages, based on personal experience, and bring it to class on Friday." He smiled at me. "We shall await yours, Katrina, with bated breath." The bell rang. "Oh, and read the next story for tomorrow."

For the rest of the morning I endured the questions. *What did you do? Where did you do it?* No one cared about truth. Rumors were set free to roam the hallways like hairy tarantulas.

Elizabeth and I ate lunch in her car, hidden behind tinted windows. I pulled my lunch bag from my backpack and told her everything. "That's it? Coffee and some pastries?" She unwrapped a hummus sandwich.

"And some chocolate-covered coffee beans."

"Again, that's it?"

"Sorry to disappoint you." I peeled back my yogurt's foil cover. Grandma Anna had shoved one of her Old World sandwiches into my bag—a pickled herring and onion creation. Try eating that for lunch and maintaining a position in the mundane middle.

"Hey, maybe you can ask him to Solstice. And I'll ask Face and we can double-date."

"What? I don't even know him." How many times would I have to repeat that?

"So? He's cute."

"Cute? Yeah, he's cute," I admitted. "But he wears that stupid kilt."

"What's wrong with a kilt? At least it's different. Nordby guys wear sweatshirts and jeans. Boring!"

"But he was sleeping in our alley. Don't you think that's weird?"

Elizabeth peeled the crust off her sandwich. "There's probably a good explanation."

Elizabeth had been my best girl friend since seventh grade, when we had each started our periods for the very first time on the exact same day and had ended up in the nurse's office, crying and confused. Well, I had been the one doing most of the crying, while she had simply been pissed off. "It's not fair!" she had screamed when the nurse handed us each a pad with wings. "How am I supposed to wear this thing with jeans? Everyone will see it." I had assured her that no one could see it, and she had assured me that no one could see it. Best friends, just like that.

"How come Heidi's in charge of the decorations for the festival?" Elizabeth complained. "I should do it. She's not an artist."

"Heidi's in charge because she wants to be in charge."

"Right. Well, I should volunteer this year. It would look good on my college applications."

"Yeah, it probably would."

Elizabeth opened a bag of potato chips. As I reached in for a handful, Vincent and Heidi walked past. Why was he walking with her? Sure, they were both on the swim team, but he didn't usually hang out with the girl swimmers. And Vincent knew that I didn't like Heidi Darling. He knew that her father's coffeehouse had stolen most of our business. He knew how much I despised Mr. Darling. Heidi laughed at something, tossing her ponytail from side to side. Vincent smiled at her.

"Did you see how she was fake laughing?" Elizabeth asked, stuffing chips into her mouth. "What's up with that? I bet she likes him. I bet she'll ask him to the festival."

"No way. Really? You think she *likes* him?"

"Why not? What's not to like? Why don't you *like* him?"

"Because he's my friend." And because I knew everything about him. I knew that he sometimes got a little pimple on his earlobe. I knew that he got really bad gas if he drank milk. And I knew that he sometimes had nightmares about drowning. Our relationship was way beyond liking. We *knew* each other.

But if Heidi *liked* him, then that would be a total nightmare. If my best friend was dating my enemy's daughter, then I'd have to listen to him tell me how wonderful she was and I'd have to act nice because that's what best friends do. I'd have to hang out with them. I'd become the third wheel.

Heidi and Vincent walked into the science building. Just before the door closed, he touched her arm. A fire alarm went off in my head.

In the grand scheme of things, touching someone's arm is nothing. An arm is just an arm. But I didn't go around touching people's arms. Touching someone's arm is definitely a gesture of fondness. Fondness can lead to all sorts of things.

No way. Never. Not in a million years would I hang out with Heidi Darling. Forget it. Vincent would have to choose between us. And he would choose me because we had been best friends since the fourth grade.

Wouldn't he?

Four

Three o'clock arrived, right on schedule. No way was I going out the front school doors. Weird kilt-wearing guy might be waiting.

So, after grabbing homework from my locker and creeping out the art room's back door, I hurried past the tennis court and onto the sidewalk, completely avoiding the front of the school. No sign of him. Phew.

I didn't like to ride the school bus home because its designated Main Street stop was right in front of Java Heaven. The students who piled out always headed straight into Mr. Darling's coffeehouse. Never did they walk the dozen extra steps to Anna's Old World Scandinavian Coffeehouse. Only I walked those steps, and that always made me feel like the only kid not invited to a birthday party. Mr. Prince, our school guidance counselor, once gave a speech at an assembly about how everyone secretly feels like an outcast, even popular people. How could Heidi Darling feel like an outcast with so many people crowding into her father's shop?

Sometimes I caught a ride with Elizabeth, but on Mondays she had to stay after for math tutoring. Even though I was sixteen I didn't have my own car. Unlike Elizabeth, I didn't have rich parents, or any parents, for that matter. Fortunately, Nordby was small enough to get around on foot or bike.

Nordby is an odd sort of place. The bay is home to a small fishing fleet and a marina. At the water's edge, two seafood restaurants balance on pilings. Main Street, which is crowded with little shops, runs parallel to the water. The buildings are brightly painted and sweetened with gingerbread trim and folklife murals. A sign at each end of the street reads: VELKOMMEN, which is "welcome" in Norwegian.

In its early years, Nordby was all about Norway—hence the grand Sons of Norway Hall that sits at the north end of Main Street. But over time things got mixed up. Someone built a Swiss cuckoo clock tower next to the bakery. Someone erected a Dutch windmill on top of the shoe shop. Someone else installed a bronze statue of a little boy in Bavarian lederhosen. I guess the city planners just wanted Nordby to look like a fairy-tale town. And so it does.

The downhill walk from the edge of school to Main Street usually took about fifteen minutes. I passed the new Java Heaven billboard. A picture of the Darling family, made up of Heidi and her mother and father, smiled at pedestrians, golden halos shining above their heads. VOTED MOST HEAVENLY ORGANIC COFFEE IN NORDBY. Who had voted? No one had sent me a ballot.

We didn't have a billboard for our coffeehouse. My grandmother didn't do modern things like advertise, which is one reason we weren't making much money. To top that, we had unknowingly lost a coffee election. My brain went into "I am such a total loser" mode as I stared up at Heidi Darling's perky face. She could add "Billboard Model" to her list of accomplishments.

"Lovely day."

"Jeez!" I clutched my backpack straps. The guy from the alley was standing next to me. "You scared me."

"My apologies." His sweater was beginning to unravel along the edge and his kilt had a few grass stains. I expected someone who slept in an alley to reek, but a nice scent drifted off him, flowery but not familiar. He noticed me looking him over. "Excuse my appearance. I'm usually not so disheveled, but I just came from a celebration in Scotland. Did you know that they toss trees up there? It's a beautiful country. I hope they send me again, but I doubt they will. I stayed much longer than I was supposed to."

Maybe I should have felt scared. He was a stranger, after all—a very handsome stranger. I'd never seen eyes that dark blue—the kind of blue you'd find on a chart of primary colors. When he blinked, thick lashes brushed against his cheeks. An odd sense of calm washed over me.

A clump of students passed between us. A few pointed at his kilt. No one at Nordby High wore a kilt, not even the president of the Comic Book Club.

"What do you want?" I asked, calm turning to embarrassment.

He folded his arms "What I want, Katrina, is to meet my obligation."

"Oh. You mean you want to *reward* me? You don't need to pay me."

"Pay you? I'm afraid I don't carry currency." He smiled. "I'm here to give you what you most desire."

Okay. Weirdo alert. I pulled Vincent's slip of paper from my pocket. "Do you need a place to sleep? Here's the address for a shelter. I don't think you need *currency* for a shelter. It's just that you can't sleep in our alley again. Believe me, if my grandma finds you out there, she'll call Officer Larsen. She will. She calls him about everything."

He ignored the paper. "I have no plans to sleep in your alley again, but it's not my choice. My job dictates where I sleep. One day I might wake up in the Maharajah's guest bed and the next day I might find myself in a London sewer pipe." He shrugged. "Fortunately, wherever I end up, I absorb the language. Makes things so much easier."

"Uh-huh." The guy was crazy. No matter how nice he smelled, or how charming his smile, he was nuts. I shoved the paper into his hand. "Well, the shelter will probably be a lot warmer than a London sewer pipe. Okay, good-bye." I quickly walked away.

Don't follow me, don't follow me.

Of course he followed. Once you're on a crazy person's radar, forget about it.

"I don't have any money, if that's what you want," I said, trying to keep some distance between us.

"What *I* want is irrelevant. I'm here to discuss what it is that *you* want."

"Could you please stop following me?"

"But I must reward your kindness."

"Don't worry about it." I shifted to power-walker pace.

"I'm not worried. But there are rules regarding these matters. Your good deed had no selfish intent behind it.

That is an extremely rare occurrence." His sandals made *flop-flop* sounds as he matched my pace. "Even if I wanted to, I couldn't ignore your unselfish good deed. They'll just keep sending me back until I reward you."

Who were "they"? Voices in his head?

"There's no need. Really, it was nothing." At the intersection I punched the crosswalk button. A car crammed with jocks drove by.

"Hey, it's Coffeehouse Girl and Skirt Boy!" Aaron yelled.

The guy from the alley didn't seem to hear the insult. He just kept staring at me. I punched the crosswalk button three more times, but the walk sign didn't light up. What if he had a knife in that satchel of his? I could be in real danger.

A school bus drove past, filled with swim teamers on their way to a meet. Vincent smiled at me from a window, then froze in mid-wave when he noticed the guy from the alley. Would Vincent be the last witness to see me alive?

The guy was still staring.

"If you follow me any more, I'm going to call the police." I punched the button again. *WALK*. Pumping my arms, I crossed that road at record speed. If he tried anything, I'd flag down a passing car and scream "HELP!" When I reached the sidewalk, I turned to warn him again, but he wasn't there.

He had disappeared.

Adjusting my backpack, I started down the steep hill, glad to have gotten rid of him. He had *issues*.

A cold breeze carried the bay's salty scent up the hill. Winter came to Nordby in October and hung around until

April. Week after week of clouds and wind was the norm. I shoved my hands into my pockets. Had that been the shadow of a ponytail next to Vincent on the school bus? What was wrong with me? Why was I worried about Heidi and Vincent? They had the swim team in common, that was it. Just the swim team.

The nice thing about the Nordby High Swim Team was that most anyone could join. You didn't have to be a record-breaker. All you had to do was swim four lengths of the pool without resting in between and without any kind of flotation device. So, if you could do that, you were in. But if you got a side cramp and sank like a rock after the second lap, like I had, then you were out—even if you had bought a brand-new pair of goggles and a subscription to *Swim Magazine* because you had hoped that swimming would be your *thing*.

"Hello." The guy from the alley was sitting on a bus bench just up ahead. When had he passed me? "I just want to make it perfectly clear that I'm *not* following you. I'm just resting a spell." His long brown hair danced across his shoulders as the breeze kicked up. "You didn't give me the opportunity to explain."

My inner voice screamed, "Run! He's a freak. Get away from him." If I had listened to that inner voice I would have saved myself a whole lot of trouble, that's for sure. But heeding one's inner voice requires confidence, which I totally lacked. Fortunately an older man sat on the bench, reading a newspaper while waiting for the bus, so I felt safe—for the moment.

"How do you know my name?"

"It's part of my job." He reached into his satchel and

pulled out a small black book. It was titled, *The Law*. "I'm afraid I'm not handling this well. You see, I've not been in this situation for a rather long time. I usually just deliver messages."

"You're a messenger?" I hadn't heard of any messenger services in Nordby.

"That's correct." He showed me the side of his satchel. Golden letters read: *Messenger Service*.

I decided that he was probably around my age, maybe a year older. Where did he go to school? Had he escaped from a mental institution? I looked at my watch. "I've got to get to work."

"Wait." He leaned forward. "Just listen." He opened the black book and read. " 'If it doth come to pass that during the course of thy travels, an unsolicited, unselfish act of kindness is bestowed upon thee, then thou must reward the act by granting to the bestower that which the bestower most desires.' " He placed the open book on his lap. The pages were blank. "I must obey what is written in this book."

The man with the newspaper looked at the blank book, then scooted away to the far edge of the bench.

"RUN!" screamed my inner voice.

If I ran, he'd probably follow. But if I let him reward me, then this crazy game might end. He could go on his crazy, freaky way and I could get to work. "It was just a few old pastries," I said nicely. "They weren't worth much. You can give me that pencil and we'll call it even." I pointed to a pencil that stuck out from one of his kilt pockets.

He narrowed his eyes at me, then continued to fake read from his book. " 'Be wary, for the bestower, being neither of selfish nor greedy disposition, may attempt to persuade you that a token or bauble would suffice.' " He cocked his head. "A pencil? I think not. Pencils are quite common in this century."

A young Hispanic woman strolled up the hill and sat between the man with the newspaper and the guy from the alley. I recognized her from the drugstore where she worked as a cashier. She set a bag of groceries on her lap. Peering over a stalk of celery, she stared at alley guy with a shy smile.

He returned the smile, then turned his attention back to me. "Well, what will it be? What do you most desire?"

I wasn't about to tell a complete stranger that what I most desired was to not feel like a loser all the time. What I wanted was to be good at something, like Elizabeth with her art, or Vincent with his swimming. Forget good—how about exceptional?

"I want that pencil."

"I don't believe you. You're being dishonest."

"Fine. Then how about that book?"

He hugged the book to his chest. "You can't have this book. It's only for messengers."

"Look, I don't have time for this game." I pointed to my watch. "I'm going to be late. Why don't you just give me whatever you want to give me so we can both get to work?"

He shrugged. "If I knew what you most desired, I would have given it to you already."

I felt like a swimmer with one fin, going round and round and round. *I'm outta here.* "Good-bye."

But just as I took a step, he jumped to his feet. This was it, the moment between life and death. The flash of a knife blade, the click of a trigger. I opened my mouth to scream.

If Elizabeth were here she'd kick him right in the balls. Should I kick him in the balls? Is it easier to kick a guy in the balls if he's wearing a kilt? The man with the newspaper tensed. The woman with the groceries clutched her bag tightly.

But he didn't attack. He just scratched his head. "All right then. If you won't tell me, I'll figure it out myself." His gaze swept my body. "You appear to be dressed in the same fashion as the other students whom I observed at your school. Nothing out of the ordinary, so I'm guessing that you consider yourself to be an average sort of person."

He was getting on my nerves. "Please hurry up."

"Being an average sort of person, you probably desire the same thing that other average people desire."

"Whatever." Grandma Anna would start to worry. She'd probably call Officer Larsen, which might be a good thing, considering the circumstances.

He fanned the pages of his book, looking for something. "Now, what does the average person desire? That is the question."

The Hispanic woman spoke. "I think that it is peace for the world."

Alley Guy shook his head. "Only a few ask for world peace. And they are as rare as a sunny day in Nordby. There's a chart in here somewhere. Here it is." He ran his finger down a page. "I should have known. Fortune is what most people desire." He returned the book to his satchel and looked at me, his eyes widening hopefully. "Is that what you most desire, Katrina? Do you want fortune?"

Play the game, get rid of the crazy guy. "Fine. I'll take it."

I stepped away as he fumbled in his pockets. "Now to

find the perfect object in which to contain the desire." He pulled out a roll of twine, a handful of bottle caps, all sorts of junk. Then he pulled out the packet of chocolate-covered coffee beans. "A wee bean will do. That's how they say it in Scotland, you know. *Wee* this and *wee* that. Wid ya be likin' a wee bit a magic wit yir coffee bean, lassie?" Smiling, he shook a single bean onto his open palm.

The woman leaned close. "A coffee bean? I love coffee, but so expensive. I do not buy."

"I'm sorry to hear that," he told her. Then he pinched the bean between his fingers and held it at arm's length, way too close to my face. "I contained your desire in this coffee bean. Clever of me, don't you think?"

I raised my eyebrows, feigning amazement.

"Go on. Take it."

"If I take it, will you leave me alone?"

"I suppose I must. I have a message to deliver." I held out my hand and he dropped the bean into it. "Go on. Eat it."

As if I'm going to eat a bean that's been sitting in a crazy homeless guy's pocket. Who knew what kind of germs lurked in there—maybe a few from that London sewer pipe. If I ate it, I'd get E. coli or dysentery or a huge tapeworm.

"Go on."

His wonderful, unidentifiable scent blew over me— spicy and flowery at the same time. But even the world's best scent can't kill E. coli germs. I pretended to pop the bean into my mouth but kept it in my hand, an old trick from childhood when Grandma Anna used to give me cod liver oil capsules. While chewing air, I secretly slid the bean into my jean pocket. Then I fake swallowed.

Alley Guy scratched his head. "Well, since I have no more business with you, I guess I should be leaving."

"Okay. Good-bye."

He collected his satchel and, to my relief, started up the steep hill. "Farewell," he called, his kilt swaying with each step. "Have a long and healthy life, Katrina Svensen."

Along with the man reading the newspaper and the woman holding the grocery bag, I watched as he walked away. No doubt about it, that had been the strangest encounter of my life.

"His eyes shine like the moon," the Hispanic woman said. Then she reached into her grocery bag and pulled out an enormous tin of coffee. She looked at the tin as if she had never seen it before.

Five

Why do we drink coffee?

As kids we hate it. It's disgusting. But somewhere along the way we learn to accept the bitter flavor, even crave it. When does that happen exactly? I think it happens right around the time we realize that maybe nothing exceptional will ever come our way. That maybe we should just forget about Shirley Temples and pineapple punch and limeade, throw away the festive paper umbrellas and the maraschino cherries, and settle for a mug of brown liquid.

On that winter afternoon, condensation coated the picture windows at Anna's Old World Scandinavian Coffeehouse. A wave of muggy air hit me as I stepped inside.

"There you are," Grandma Anna called. She stood behind the counter holding an armful of wet towels. "I was worried about you. I almost called Officer Larsen."

"Sorry."

"Hello, Katrina." Four men waved from the corner table—Ingvar, Odin, Lars, and Ralph. Burly, wind-worn men who had captained fishing boats in the years when king crab had ruled the Bering Sea. Ralph was the only Native American in the group, and though an occasional argument arose about Native fishing rights, they were a solid bunch of friends. Retired, they met every other day to play an ancient Viking board game called Hnefatafl, which means "King's Table." My grandmother called these men *The Boys*.

"Why's it so warm in here?" I asked.

"Dishwasher went kapoot," Ingvar explained, an unlit pipe hanging from the corner of his mouth. "Spewed steam like a farting dragon."

"Made a real mess," Odin said, moving one of the white pieces across the board. "Hey Anna, where's those sandwiches?"

I followed my grandmother to the back room, where she dumped the towels into a basket. Her loafers squelched, soggy with sudsy water. "You didn't call Officer Larsen about the dishwasher, did you?" I asked.

She smoothed her short gray hair. "Officer Larsen doesn't understand appliances. Ralph looked it over. He said it blew a pump and I'll have to order a new one. That's two dead appliances this month. I don't know how I'm going to pay for them." She sighed, then gave me a hug as she always did when I came in after school, squishing me with her big soft stomach.

"Are we still broke?"

"Now don't you worry about that." Grandma Anna shook a finger at me. "That's my concern, not yours."

"Anna!" Odin cried. "You want a man to starve to death?"

"You're too fat to starve to death," she yelled back. She grabbed the mop from the corner. "Could you make The Boys some sardine sandwiches? There's still a puddle to clean."

Sardine sandwiches.

Since we catered to the Scandinavian crowd and to tourists who wanted a taste of the Old World, we served open-faced sandwiches on dense dark breads, layered with things like red onions, pickled herring, and tomatoes. And sardines. Those little fish are supposed to be good for you and they don't taste too bad, once you get used to the fact that you're also eating skin and bones.

I set my backpack on a shelf and pulled an apron over my head. After washing my hands, I grabbed a loaf of pumpernickel and joined Irmgaard at the counter. She had worked at Anna's for as long as I could remember—always there when we opened, always there when we closed. Other than myself, Irmgaard was the coffeehouse's only employee. We knew that she lived alone in an apartment complex at the edge of town. We knew that she could make great soup. And we knew that she was heart-stoppingly beautiful even though she never wore makeup; only wore plain, dark clothes; and kept her hair cut super short. Her beauty was the reason, I suspected, that The Boys spent so much time at Anna's Coffeehouse.

But no one knew where she had lived before coming to Nordby. No one knew her age—we guessed about forty. And no one knew why she had taken a vow of silence.

Irmgaard dropped a block of butter into a tall soup pot, then stirred gracefully while I built the sandwiches. She dumped two handfuls of chopped onions into the pot. They sizzled and filled the coffeehouse with their aroma. I didn't mind her silence. It never felt awkward, the way it can with other people. It seeped into me, in a hypnotic way.

Odin bellowed again. I stacked the sandwiches onto a tray and hurried to the corner table. Big calloused hands grabbed the salty treats.

"Thanks," The Boys said.

I gathered their mugs and filled them at the percolator. "Would you like anything else?" I asked a woman whose little boy was writing "poop" on the foggy window. Other than The Boys, they were the only customers, typical for a December afternoon. Tourist season didn't start until May, when pleasure boats began to chug into the marina.

"We've finished," the mother replied. She paid her bill, then gathered her coat and purse. Her kid had picked out all the onions from his soup and had piled them on the table.

"So, Katrina, what's new in school?" Ralph asked.

"Not much." I wiped the table's oilcloth as the mother and son left. "Hey, did you guys know that Mr. Darling is sponsoring the Solstice Festival?"

"Well, he'd better not come in here and ask for a donation," Grandma Anna said, sticking her head out the pantry curtains. "I've already given him most of my customers. I'm not about to help him decorate his shop!"

Ingvar chuckled, sliding his pipe across his mouth.

"That man's shop is a blight," Odin said, claiming one of Lars's game pieces. "All those kids hanging out there all the time, crowding the sidewalk. You can barely get past the place. Thank God no kids hang out here."

Odin's comment drifted back toward the pantry and I waited for my grandmother's reaction. Financial worries came in second to her constant worries about my social life. What's wrong with having only two friends? At least I didn't have to buy their friendship with Mocha Frappe coupons.

"Katrina." My grandmother emerged from the pantry. I took a deep breath, preparing myself for the onslaught. "Why don't you ask a nice boy to go to the Solstice Festival with you?" She wiped her hands on her apron. "You're such a pretty girl. I'm sure there are lots of nice boys who would love to go. You just pick the best one and ask him."

Grandmothers can tell you that you're pretty, and they will. They can tell you that you're talented and special and the best darn thing that ever walked on two feet. That any boy would be lucky to breathe the same air that you breathe. But those comments don't count. Grandmothers have to say those things.

Here's what a grandmother probably won't tell you. That it's great to be blond if you're perky and outgoing, but if you tend to be untalented and shy, it doesn't help much. That sixteen-year-old boys don't like to date girls who tower over them. And that those same boys steer clear of girls who hang out with only one particular guy, even if he's just a best friend, because they figure that something else is going on.

Then throw in a bunch of rumors about a guy in a skirt and a "good deed," and you might as well just slit your wrists.

"Forget about working, Katrina. We can manage one night without you. This year you should go out and enjoy the festival."

"I'll think about it." I wasn't going to think about it. Who would I ask? The only boy I ever did anything with was Vincent.

Five o'clock came, closing time at Anna's Old World Scandinavian Coffeehouse. The Boys rolled up their game

mat, put on their coats and hats, and bid good night to
Grandma Anna and me. Then, with especially tender
voices, they bid good night to Irmgaard. She smiled shyly
but didn't look up from her soup pot. The Boys headed off
to the pub for a "snort," which is what they called a shot of
whiskey.

Just as I was about to flip the open sign, Mr. Darling
sauntered in. Like his daughter, he kept his hair in a ponytail, only his didn't bounce. It hung kind of limp and thin.
He snickered at the word "poop," still etched on our front
window. "New item on your menu?" he asked.

"What do you want?" my grandmother asked between
clenched teeth.

He smoothed his navy sweater with its Java Heaven
cloud logo and surveyed the empty room. "I'd be happy to
send a few of my customers over if you need the business,
Anna. What's a neighbor for?"

I hated the way he called my grandmother by her first
name, as if they were friends. "We're closed," I told him.
"That's why we don't have any customers."

"I see. Just offering my help."

My grandmother rose to her full five feet three inches.
"I've been in business for over forty years," she said. "And
I've managed quite nicely without your help."

"Over forty years?" He acted as if he didn't know that
fact. As if he hadn't bothered to read the sign above the
door: *Anna's Old World Scandinavian Coffeehouse, Bringing
the Old Country to Nordby for over forty years.*

He pointed a finger at me. "Say, don't you go to school
with my daughter?"

I'd gone to school with Heidi since the first grade. We'd

played in the same piano recitals, had joined the same Girl
Scouts troop, had read poetry in the same school pageants.
But Mr. Darling never seemed to remember me. Which
brings me to another thing a grandmother won't tell you—
You just aren't memorable, sweetheart.

"What's your name again?"

"Katrina."

"Hmmm." He looked doubtful. "Well, I'll try to remember that." Then he sat on one of our stools and folded his
hands on the counter. "Forty years is a long time to run a
business, Anna. And every business has its life span. I bet
you're tired of this place."

My grandmother closed the back curtains, hiding the
mess of wet towels. "Why would I be tired of this place?"
Then she busied herself with the percolator, emptying the
grounds into a bucket we kept under the sink while I cleaned
the tables and Irmgaard worked on her soup. A group effort
at snubbing.

Once a month, Mr. Darling came over to rub our noses
in the fact that his coffeehouse, which had only been in business for two years, overflowed with customers. The laptop
crowd liked the hip music. The at-home moms liked the
whipped, iced coffee drinks that were basically milkshakes.
And everyone on the planet liked his organic fair-trade coffee. Our coffee wasn't organic. Nor did it come with a fancy
label that said it had been picked by a native cooperative,
that the bags were recyclable, and that 10 percent of the
profits went back to the coffee farmer.

No sireeeee.

Our coffee came in a big plastic bag from Bulk Supply
Company. The label just said *Coffee.*

Mr. Darling cleared his throat. "Anna, I've made a decision that affects both of us."

"I'm too busy to talk right now," she snapped, dumping the remaining coffee down the sink. "Unless you're here to buy something, I'd like you to leave."

Irmgaard grabbed some potatoes from the pantry and began chopping. I wished that Mr. Darling would leave. I always felt self-conscious when he visited, well aware of our total lack of trendiness. Organic coffee is a great thing. We should have served it too. But Grandma Anna said nothing was wrong with the regular coffee, plus she didn't want the additional expense.

"As a matter of fact, I would like to buy something." Mr. Darling pivoted on the stool. "You see that wall?" He pointed to the wall that separated our two businesses. A portrait of the King and Queen of Norway hung there. They had once visited Nordby. "I've decided to tear down that wall so that I can expand my business."

Irmgaard gasped. A few potatoes rolled off the counter.

"What?" I cried.

Mr. Darling smiled. "I'll need you to vacate as soon as possible."

Six

"Vacate?" My grandmother dropped the old percolator into the sink.

Mr. Darling fiddled with his ponytail. "It's progress, Anna. Nothing personal."

"Of course it's personal. I own this business."

"You can't tear down that wall," I said. "She has a lease—a lifetime lease."

"That's right. I have a lifetime lease. When my husband sold this building, we were guaranteed this space and the upstairs apartment at a fixed rent for life. And I'm fit as a fiddle."

Like a gunfighter in a Western, Mr. Darling took his time rising from his stool. He towered over my grandmother, and I'm not just referring to his height. While he prospered, we eked out a living. While he met the growing demand for earth-friendly products, we handed out styrofoam coffee cups. While he marketed, we waited and hoped for a crowded tourist season. Crossed fingers don't work as well as coupons, team sponsorships, and a "flavor of the week."

"You'll find, if you reread your contract, that *life* refers to the life of your business, not the life of its owner. Only as long as your business is in operation do you receive the fixed rent." He folded his arms confidently. "And let's be honest. Your business is dying. I spoke to the landlord this morning and she said that if you vacated, remodeling could begin without delay. Once I rip out the kitchen and open the back room, I figure I can squeeze in two dozen more tables. I'll give you a fair price to leave. It will certainly be more money than you're making now."

My grandmother's face ignited. She gripped the edge of her embroidered apron. "My income is none of your business."

As much as I despised Mr. Darling, perhaps his offer was not such a bad thing. Grandma Anna was seventy and she always said she couldn't afford to retire. And she wasn't fit as a fiddle. She kept seven different bottles of pills on her bathroom counter. I knew about the high blood pressure and arthritis, but she hadn't told me what the other pills were for.

Mr. Darling cleared his throat. "Think of the money, Anna. This place is falling apart. Look at those old percolators and that old stove. The countertops are peeling and the single-pane windows are fogged. I'll give you a nice sum to move out. Take a vacation. Buy a condo in sunny Florida. Wouldn't that be nice? My mother is moving to Florida. Florida's a great place to retire."

As my grandmother stomped around the counter, her loafers—still soggy from the dishwasher explosion—made little farting sounds. "I'm not buying a condo in Florida. Nordby is my home. My husband took his last breath in this town. And I have employees who rely on me." Irmgaard hung her head, avoiding Mr. Darling's intimidating gaze. "I'm not selling. Not to you. Not to anyone."

"Oh, I think you'll change your mind," he said, smugness pushing at the corner of his upper lip.

"You can think whatever you want to think, but I won't change my mind."

The lip fell. "We'll see about that."

Grandma Anna put her hand to her chest. "Is that a threat?"

"My heart is set on expanding my business. I don't like to be disappointed."

I stood close to my grandmother. Her shoulders trembled slightly. "You will leave," she told him.

He did, but he made us wait while he cleaned a spot off his shoe. Once he had gone, my grandmother slammed the door, turned the closed sign outward, then crumpled into a chair. Irmgaard and I hurried to her side.

"Are you okay?" I asked.

"I should call Officer Larsen and report that man." She slapped her palm on the table. Then she sighed. "But he's right. How am I going to fix everything that's falling apart? The Boys buy a few cups of coffee and sandwiches. That's not enough to keep us going during the winter months."

"We'll make some money during the Solstice Festival," I said. "We always have a long line for our hot chocolate."

"Not last year."

"Oh, right." Last year the line to get into Java Heaven had been so long that it had blocked people from entering our shop to buy my grandmother's famous Norwegian cocoa.

"We can't rely on the festival," she mumbled.

"We'd get more people in here if we got an espresso machine," I suggested for the millionth time. Irmgaard nodded.

"I'm not getting an espresso machine. This is a Scandinavian coffeehouse, not a French bistro. Espresso machines don't make egg coffee."

I thought about saying *That's the point*, but didn't. Norwegian egg coffee is a disgusting combination of boiled coffee grounds, sugar, and a beaten egg. Yep. A beaten egg. It's an Old World recipe and that's who asked for it—old people. Didn't much matter, anyway. Good espresso machines cost thousands of dollars.

My grandmother patted my hand. "Don't you worry, Katrina, or you'll get worry lines all over your face, just like me. You should be thinking about your grades and about college. That's your future. That's what a sixteen-year-old girl should be thinking about. And finding a nice boy to take you to the festival."

"I'm staying here and working the festival, with you. We'll bring in good money, I know we will. I'll make sure that Mr. Darling's line doesn't get in the way this time."

With a grunt, my grandmother pushed herself from the chair. "You spend too much time in here." She patted my cheek. "It's all my fault. Your parents, rest their souls, wouldn't want you working so much. Maybe I should close for good."

I didn't know what to say. The coffeehouse was my home and, in many ways, it was my sanctuary. I may not have loved all its odd flavors, but its dusty charm was a part of me. Outside, I was an average student, with average grades and average looks. My name did not grace any trophies in the gym case or any murals on the school walls. Five years from now, no one would even know that I had been at Nordby High. But once I stepped inside our coffeehouse, I knew exactly what to do and exactly who I was.

I was an important part of Anna's. I worked the cash register, ordered supplies, made sandwiches, and chitchatted with tourists. As my grandmother slowed down, I sped up, taking on more responsibilities. Sure, it was not an ideal situation. Ideal would be going back to when we had lots of customers, more employees, and fewer demands on my time. When locals came in and I knew exactly what they were going to order. When business was conducted at the counter, and book groups and knitting clubs met on set days of the week.

I didn't want to see Anna's close down. That would be like losing my family all over again.

We finished our evening chores. I opened the door that led to our upstairs apartment. Ratcatcher waddled down the stairs. She wasn't allowed in the coffeehouse during the day. I crouched and scratched her head. She pawed at my jean pocket, the one holding the coffee bean. I had forgotten all about it.

"Grandma, if you could have what you most desired, what would it be?"

"I'm not sure."

"Someone told me that fortune is the most common thing people ask for."

"Well, money sure would help."

"Is that what you most desire?"

She looked at me, the creases in her face relaxing.

"What I most desire is for you to have a long and happy life, sweetheart."

Irmgaard collected her coat and purse.

"Why don't you stay and have dinner with us?" Grandma Anna asked, as she always did. "There's no reason to eat alone." Irmgaard shook her head, as she always did, and left to catch the bus, a Tupperware container of extra soup tucked under her arm.

Our apartment sat above the coffeehouse. It would have been nice to have a yard and a garage. I had both when I was three, the year my parents were killed in a car crash. But those memories were just vapors—the sound of a lawn mower, a bowl of Cheerios, a woman's scarf, soft and red.

Grandma Anna went to bed earlier than usual, upset by Mr. Darling's visit. I slipped out of my clothes and stood in front of my bedroom mirror. The first thing I always noticed when I looked in the mirror was my height. Five foot eight seemed crazy tall to me. What was good about being so tall? Supermodel tall, maybe. Basketball player tall, totally. God help me, but if I grew another inch I'd become an honorary member of the Masai tribe.

Pajamas on, homework spread across my bed, the phone rang. "Hey, I saw you standing on the sidewalk with that guy. What did he want?" It was Vincent. He was eating something crunchy.

"He just wanted to thank me for giving him some coffee. How was the meet?"

"Okay." Genuine modesty was one of the things I really liked about Vincent.

"How did you do?"

"First in the fifty backstroke."

"How did Heidi do?"

"Heidi?" The crunching stopped. "Why are you asking about Heidi?"

"No reason."

Because I saw you hanging out with her and now I'm thinking the worst. Because at some point you're going to get a girlfriend, aren't you? Of course you are. You're amazing. And then I'll have to scoot over so she can sit next to you at the movies. And what if she wants butter on the popcorn, after you and I agreed that movie theater butter tastes rancid? That could be a real problem.

"It's just that Heidi's dad was here today and he wants to give us money to vacate so he can expand Java Heaven. He's such a jerk. He was really mean to Grandma. I wish the Darlings would just move away."

"Mr. Darling's a jerk, that's for sure. But Heidi's not so bad. She can't help the way her dad is. You know she does a lot of good stuff for the community. She volunteers at the food bank and I was thinking about helping her a few times. Anyway, don't worry. Her dad can't force you to leave."

Oh God! How could he say that Heidi wasn't so bad? Why was he defending her?

I lay back against the pillows. "Mr. Darling said that he didn't like being disappointed. I think that was a threat."

"Just keep boycotting Java Heaven. What more can you do? You know I'll never buy their coffee. Hey, you sure that guy with the skirt wasn't bothering you?"

"He's gone."

"Good. Okay. I'll come by in the morning."

I stared at the ceiling for a long time. What was bugging me more—the idea of Vincent going out with Heidi, or the idea of him going out with anyone? Would I be so worried if he started dating someone else? I'd be fine with it, wouldn't I?

He can't force you to leave. I thought about that as I opened my World Mythology textbook. It seemed like Mr. Darling could do whatever he wanted. He had gotten the space next door, even after Grandma had begged the landlord not to rent to him. I wrapped my bathrobe tighter and stuck my feet under the quilt. Our apartment felt colder than usual. The furnace was probably on the fritz again.

The next story in the good deed chapter was "Jack and the Beanstalk." I yawned. Did I even need to read it? Everyone knows that story.

This kid named Jack trades a cow for a bean that grows into a beanstalk. Or maybe it's three beans. His mother gets mad at him. Or maybe it's his father. But I knew that they were poor. Something about a golden harp and a man-eating giant. Okay, so maybe I didn't remember the whole story. I glanced at the bottom of the page and read: *"Take this bean," the strange man said. "It will bring you fortune."*

Huh? What a weird coincidence.

The phone rang again. It was Elizabeth.

"So, did he wait for you after school?"

"Yeah." I pushed the book aside and told her all about the guy and the bean.

"Did you eat it?"

"No."

"You should eat it."

"What? That's crazy. Why would I eat it?"

"Maybe it's crazy, but you never know. I wish someone would give me a magic bean. I'd wish for Face to notice me.

Crap, I gotta go. My dad's flippin' out because I dented the car. It's just a little dent but he's going ballistic. See ya tomorrow."

My jeans lay on the floor. I slid out of bed and plucked the bean from the pocket. The chocolate had worn away, staining the pocket's lining. I held the little bean in my fingers. Fortune would solve everything, wouldn't it? We could fix up the shop, buy an espresso machine, and hire more employees.

As if. No way was I eating that thing. Alley Guy was a lunatic.

And yet, I didn't throw it away. Why? For the same reason that I make a wish before I blow out my birthday candles, and look into the sky for the first evening star, and pull extra hard on the wishbone. Because, deep inside, like a Scandinavian craving caffeine, I craved change. I had been living a quiet life in the mundane middle, hidden in my two friends' shadows, but that wouldn't work much longer. When they left Nordby to pursue their dreams, I'd become visible, exposed for what I was—nothing much at all.

I set the little bean on top of my dresser.

Seven

Tuesday morning came, but you wouldn't know it without a clock. On days like that, the sun became almost mythic. People would say things like: "Remember when it was warm? When was that exactly?" After I had finished my cereal, a rainstorm descended upon Main Street. I peered out the back window. Fat drops rattled the Dumpster's lid. The alley's yellow lightbulb hummed. No one slept on the wet bricks. Hopefully he had gone home—back to his family and some *medication*.

I made the coffee. Just as I was filling the jam pots, Elizabeth, a breathing kaleidoscope of patterns and colors, blazed through the front door. Her artistic expression was not limited to canvas.

"Thought I'd give you a ride. It's like a typhoon or something." She brushed the rain off her striped raincoat. Then she sat on one of the stools and helped herself to a day-old pastry. Cinnamon icing oozed between her fingers.

Elizabeth had a thing for sweets, and I mean *a thing*—daily doses of white flour and glazed icing to the extent that, if stranded on a desert island, she'd go through withdrawal pains that would put a heroin addict to shame. She kept a platter of cookies near her easel and you could always find a candy bar or package of Ding Dongs in her glove box. Her particular favorite, marzipan, she ate straight out of the tube. Total junkie.

Fortunately, Elizabeth was one of those perfectly proportioned plump people, like an hourglass. "Hourglass figures are classic," she often said.

I'm one of those perfectly proportioned skinny people, like a flagpole. Flagpoles are patriotic. That's about the nicest thing I can say about flagpoles.

"So, did you eat it?"

"No."

"Let me eat it. Maybe it will work for me." She wiggled on the stool. "Why let it go to waste? If it works, I'll share the money with you. Come on." There was no use in arguing with her. She wouldn't give up. That's how she had gotten her father to give her a car—two weeks of nonstop whining. Her dad deserved some credit, having lasted two weeks. I tended to fold quickly.

"Come on. Give me the bean. Please? At least let me see it."

"Fine." I went upstairs and collected the little bean from my dresser. Ratcatcher followed, batting at my ankles along the way. The faucet gurgled in the bathroom as my grandmother got ready for the day, her radio blaring down the hall.

"Yuck," Elizabeth said when I showed her the bean. "You said it was covered in chocolate."

"It melted off."

"But it's plain. I can't eat it plain. It'll taste disgusting."

"I didn't say you could eat it."

"Are you going to eat it?"

"No."

We stared at it, as if we'd never seen a coffee bean. As if something about it would be different. "Hey," she said. "Let's grind it up and drink it."

Okay, so I was curious about the bean. Of course nothing would happen because nothing ever happens after the birthday candles go out or after the wishbone snaps. But maybe something *would* happen. Though it wouldn't. But what if?

"Come on. Let's do it," Elizabeth begged. "Don't worry about those stupid jam pots. Irmgaard can fill them."

I poured coffee into a mug. Then I washed the bean with soap and hot water, just in case. I dropped the bean into the electric grinder. A short *whirrr* later, a dusting of grounds appeared in the basin. Elizabeth pressed against my shoulder, watching as I pinched the grounds, then sprinkled them into the mug. They floated, shimmering like golden sequins.

"I've never seen coffee grounds shimmer like that," I said.

Elizabeth leaned closer. "Me neither."

We jumped as the front door slammed. Vincent hurried over to the counter, water dripping from his knit hat. "It's dangerous out there. The wind almost knocked me over, twice."

"Watch out, you're getting water on me," Elizabeth complained as Vincent shook his head. "Jeez, what are you? A dog? Where's a towel?"

"In the back room," I told her. She stomped off.

"Can I get some toast?" Vincent asked.

"Yeah." I dropped some bread into the toaster, then got some butter from the refrigerator. Vincent liked his toast dark, with enough butter to lather a sunbather.

"That coffee tastes bad," Vincent said.

Coffee? I had only turned away for a moment. I pointed to the mug of magic coffee. "Did you drink that?"

"I just took a sip. It's got a weird aftertaste."

Uh-oh. Does E. coli have a weird aftertaste? What about botulism or cholera? Can you taste those diseases, because I'm fairly certain that those are the kinds of diseases that would be hanging out in a London sewer pipe. Or any sewer pipe. Had I poisoned my best friend?

Elizabeth emerged from the back room just as Vincent poured our magic coffee down the sink. She grabbed the empty mug. "Hey, we were going to drink that."

"He took a sip," I told her.

He rubbed his red nose. "Sorry. I just wanted something hot." Elizabeth and I stood side by side, watching for signs of fortune—diamonds raining from the ceiling, gold coins pouring from Vincent's ears, that sort of thing.

"Why are you staring at me?"

We waited for changes—for his wallet to swell, for gold chains to appear around his neck. Nothing. The toast popped. He buttered it and ate it.

"Oh well," Elizabeth said with a sigh. "Better get to school."

Vincent put his bike in the alley, then we piled into Elizabeth's car. Her window wipers squeaked as the blades fought the downpour. Up the hill we went, past the Nordby

Veterinary Clinic and the Chevron station. "Sorry about the bad coffee," I told Vincent. I kept asking him how he felt, worried he might turn green or spotted. "You're not getting a fever, are you? Do you feel like you're going to puke?" Stuff like that. He told me to "quit it already."

Just as we passed the nail salon, the black car in front of us veered right, left, then right again. "What's he doing?" Elizabeth asked, slowing. The car took a sharp left and crossed the opposite lane, right in front of an oncoming truck. The truck veered into our lane.

"Watch out!" I cried, covering my face. I was going to die in a car crash, just like my parents. We were all going to die! Elizabeth slammed on the brakes as the truck swerved and narrowly missed us.

I dropped my hands, watching in silent shock as the black car drove up on the sidewalk, then crashed into a bus bench. Vincent threw open the door and raced across the street. Other people got out of their cars, but Vincent was the first to reach the crashed car. He opened the driver's door and a man tumbled onto the wet sidewalk.

Traffic came to a standstill. My heart thumped wildly as I got out of the car and ran toward Vincent, who was crouching over the driver. A siren wailed in the distance. Rain bounced off the bus bench.

"Oh my God," Elizabeth said. "That guy looks dead."

Eight

Turned out the driver wasn't dead. Just almost dead.

Vincent knew CPR because he'd worked as a lifeguard at the Nordby Community Center Pool last summer. Elizabeth and I huddled in the rain as he rhythmically pushed against the man's chest. He searched for a pulse in the man's neck, then pushed his chest some more. When the ambulance arrived, the medics shook Vincent's hand. Officer Larsen drove Vincent to the police station to answer some questions about the accident. Drenched to the skin, Elizabeth and I got into her car and drove to school. "That was amazing," Elizabeth said.

The fact that Vincent had saved an old guy's life didn't surprise me one bit. If anything bad was going to happen, you'd want Vincent around. Everyone else would be freaking out, screaming "Earthquake!" or "Alien invasion!" but he'd figure out how to get to the nearest exit, or how to build a ray gun.

Thanks to Elizabeth, the story spread quickly. When Vincent returned from the police department, Principal

Carmichael congratulated him over the loudspeaker. Students swarmed him. Teachers asked him to recount the event. The first news van pulled up at noon. Then CNN showed up. Then FOX. Turned out the old man was some kind of software developer—a mega-billionaire who had come to Nordby to buy property. He had had a heart attack while driving, and Vincent's CPR had definitely saved his life. So, from his hospital bed he made an announcement. He would reward Vincent with—drum roll, please . . . a full scholarship to whatever college or university Vincent chose to attend.

Amazing.

That was the best news ever.

"Oh my God," Elizabeth said as we stood in the cafeteria, watching throngs of reporters shove microphones at Vincent's face. "I just remembered, he drank the magic coffee. He got *fortune*."

"He gave a man CPR," I reminded her. "He earned that reward. It had nothing to do with the bean."

"Really?" She narrowed her heavily lined eyes. "I suppose you think this was just a coincidence."

"Yes."

"Katrina, there are no coincidences. It's all part of something bigger."

"That's crazy. Of course there are coincidences. You and I are both wearing green shirts. We didn't plan that."

She sighed. "You believe what you believe and I'll believe what I believe."

I didn't feel like arguing. Something else caught my attention. Heidi Darling had squeezed her way through the reporters and was standing next to Vincent. "We're on the same team," she told them with a dazzling smile. She wore the latest trendy jeans, dyed in all the right places. She looked pretty. My old jeans were still wet from standing in the rain. Soaked to the skin, my butt kind of itched.

Principal Carmichael glowed with pride, or maybe from the heat of the camera lights. "We promote good values here at Nordby High. In fact, I personally created our values-centered curriculum. It's no surprise to me that one of our students acted heroically."

Vincent's bleary-eyed dad showed up. He worked nights as a security guard at the marina and never seemed to get enough sleep during the day. Even though he walked around in an exhausted stupor, usually unshaven, he was pretty good-looking for a dad.

"He's always been a good kid," Mr. Hawk told the reporters. "Real good."

Mr. Darling made an appearance, handing out Java Heaven coupons to the reporters and their crew. "Our coffee is one hundred percent organic. One hundred percent free trade." He shoved a poster in my hand. "Put this up in your window."

Unbelievable. I unrolled the poster, which advertised the "Vincent Mocha." What? He had named a drink after Vincent? And had printed up posters? Could he do that? Could he name a drink after someone without asking that person?

The swim team gathered for a photo. Heidi Darling put her arm around Vincent for the picture that would be plastered all over the Internet. Someone shoved a microphone in her face. "What do you think of your teammate?"

"Vincent's the best," she replied. "He's a great guy. I've always known he's a great guy."

"She definitely *likes* him," Elizabeth whispered in my ear.

Okay, hold on just a moment. I knew that Vincent was a great guy, long before Heidi knew it. I knew it when he walked me to the nurse's office in the fourth grade, after I had split open my lip on the monkey bars. I knew it when he didn't tease me after Elizabeth and I got a horrid case of head lice from trying on wigs in a costume shop. I knew it because whenever I called him in the middle of the night, when I couldn't sleep or was worried about something, he never got mad at me.

But Heidi acted like it was something she had discovered. Like she was letting us all in on a secret. They looked so chummy with their chlorinated hair and matching sweatshirts.

"Vincent and I spend every morning together," Heidi said.

Elizabeth squeezed in next to a reporter. "If you want to know about Vincent, you should ask Katrina." She pointed at me. "She's his best friend."

"Shhh," the reporter scolded. "That girl with the ponytail is still talking."

Heidi pressed against Vincent's shoulder. "My dad owns Java Heaven and he created a special drink called the Vincent Mocha." She held up one of the posters. "The best cocoa, the best coffee, the freshest milk. Vincent loves it."

Well, if you knew Vincent half as well as you claim to know him, you'd know that he wouldn't drink that in a million years because he's lactose intolerant!

Vincent looked totally surprised when he read the poster. But Heidi didn't give him a chance to say anything because she kept talking to reporters about how amazing

Vincent was. Elizabeth fake gagged. While she had no real reason to hate Heidi, other than the excessively perky thing, she hated her on my account because that's what real friends do. "Did you notice that her hair is turning green?" she whispered in my ear.

Heidi's hair wasn't the only thing turning green. Jealousy had invaded me and I was pretty sure I looked exactly like the Incredible Hulk.

"Can I have that poster?" Elliott stood next to me. Principal Carmichael had put him on technical duty. He'd been providing extension cords to the camera crews. I gave him the poster. "I'm going to get Vincent's autograph, then sell it on eBay." He smiled at Elizabeth. "I like your striped raincoat." She ignored him.

Vincent didn't make it to any of his afternoon classes. He sat in the cafeteria, answering the same questions over and over. When I passed by, between Geometry and English Composition, he waved, looking totally bored. I never got the chance to congratulate him or ask him about the poster. But I knew that he hadn't agreed to the "Vincent Mocha" because my friends and family had a longstanding pact to never buy Java Heaven coffee, to never taste Java Heaven Coffee, and to never, ever, step inside Java Heaven.

By the end of the day the rain clouds had cleared, but colder air moved in. I walked home, a hand-knit scarf wrapped around my face, trying to disappear into a cocoon of yarn. I should have been skipping merrily down the street, celebrating my best friend's fortune, but I had let the Darlings worm their way under my skin. I concocted the following conspiracy theory: that Heidi and her father were working together. She would take away my best friend so I'd be miserable, and in my misery, I'd convince my grandmother that we should move to Florida.

"I'll never move to Florida," I snarled.

"I wouldn't move to Florida either. Too humid."

I gasped, inhaling a mouthful of yarn. I stopped walking and pushed the scarf off my face. "You said you were leaving."

"I've been trying to deliver a message here in Nordby." He patted his satchel. "But I haven't been able to deliver it."

"Look . . ." I paused, weighing my options—run away or deal with him. "What's your name anyway?"

"I don't have a name." He wore the same kilt and sweater. That flowery scent swirled around us. "But if you'd like to call me by a name, you can call me Malcolm. That's what they called me in Scotland. I spent a long time there. So here's a thought—if you're going to move, you might consider Scotland."

"Look, Malcolm, I've got a lot on my mind."

"You've got a lot on *your* mind? I've got a lot on *my* mind."

God, those eyes were blue. If Elizabeth had been there, she would have wanted to paint them. I felt a rush of inspiration. Maybe I should try to paint them, but I had about as much artistic talent as that elephant at the Seattle Zoo. Every Sunday, a zookeeper gave her a canvas and she painted with her trunk. I don't care how many people raved about that elephant's paintings, they were terrible. Just a bunch of splotches. That's what my paintings always looked like. That's why there was an easel and a jar of paintbrushes in my Closet of Failure.

Malcolm kept right on talking. His skin was perfectly clear. He exfoliated, no doubt about it. And his long brown hair wasn't an everyday brown. Close-up, I could see dozens of shades of brown and red and copper—like one of Elizabeth's palettes. "Are you listening?" He waved in my face. "Katrina, I wish you'd listen."

I snapped out of it. "Okay, I'm listening. But just for a minute because I've got to get to work. I don't have time to play that coffee bean game again."

"That's the problem." He pushed his hair behind his ears. "You thought it was a game. You weren't supposed to give the bean to someone else."

"Huh? I didn't give it to someone else."

"You did. You allowed your friend to drink the coffee that you made from the bean, and your friend received fortune."

How could he know that? Had he been spying on us through the window? Was he some kind of stalker? The cold air tickled my nose. I wanted to hide behind my scarf again. "Vincent got a scholarship because he saved a man's life."

"After he drank the coffee. That bean was for you, to give you what you most desire."

"Well . . ." There had to be some way out of this conversation. "Obviously what I most desired was for Vincent to get a scholarship. So now everybody is happy."

But I wasn't happy. Something else had caught my attention, something even more annoying than Malcolm and his delusions. The Java Heaven billboard stood across the street. A new message had been painted across the top: *Stop in and try a Vincent Mocha, in honor of our hometown hero.* How had Mr. Darling managed to do that so fast? Did he have a legion of little elves working for him, running around painting things here and there, printing up flyers and coupons at elf speed?

Only one thing to do. Anna's Old World Scandinavian Coffeehouse needed a special Vincent drink. So what if we didn't have a billboard? We couldn't just sit back and let Mr. Darling turn Vincent into a commodity. He was *my* friend. If anyone was going to turn him into a commodity, it would be me!

"Katrina? You've got to listen."

"I gotta go. Bye!" I pulled the scarf over my face and ran down the hill, my backpack lunging with each step. We'd make a special Vincent drink and sell it at the Solstice Festival. Better yet, Vincent could help us sell it. That would bring in tons of customers. We'd have so many customers that they'd line up and block Mr. Darling's door. Sweet revenge. Vincent could autograph the cups. What would we call our drink? What's the Viking word for hero? Probably something unpronounceable—something that sounded like you were trying to clear a wad of phlegm from your throat. Forget that.

I rushed into the coffeehouse. The chairs were empty— no real surprise since The Boys didn't come in on Tuesdays.

"What an exciting day," Grandma Anna said, giving me an extra-tight hug. "We heard all about Vincent saving that man's life. Some of those news station vans pulled up. I got to meet Brad Stone. You know, the anchor from channel seven. He came into the shop with his crew."

"Really?" I unwound my scarf and took off my coat. "What did they order?"

My grandmother stared at her sensible shoes. Silence filled the space between us like poison gas.

"Grandma?"

"They didn't order anything. They thought this was the entrance to Java Heaven. They had some coupons."

Coulda put money on that one.

"Okay, we've got a situation." I leaned on the counter. Irmgaard stopped stirring her carrot soup. "Remember last Solstice, how Mr. Darling gave out those heavenly cloud cookies and all those people lined up?" Irmgaard and Grandma nodded. "This year it could be even worse."

"What do you mean?"

"I mean, this year Mr. Darling will be selling coffee named after Vincent. Our Vincent."

"Oh dear." Grandma Anna rubbed the back of her neck.

"So, I think we should create a Vincent drink of our own. Only, it's got to be better than Mr. Darling's. And we'll have the real Vincent here, in the shop, handing out the coffee."

"We will?"

"Of course. I haven't asked him yet, but he'll do it. He loves us."

"He's a good boy."

"But someone has to go next door and buy one of those drinks so we can see what it tastes like. We need to know what we're up against." It would be difficult enough to try to outbrew Mr. Darling, but we first had to get our hands on the drink itself, and we lived by the law of never setting foot inside Java Heaven. "What about one of The Boys?" I asked.

"Oh no." Grandma Anna cleaned carrot peelings from

the counter. "They're my friends. I won't send them into that horrid place. I'll call Officer Larsen. Tell him it's an emergency."

"But it's not an emergency." I drummed my fingers on the counter. I wouldn't ask my friends to go in there either. My two friends. It was a matter of pride, but I also secretly feared that they might never emerge, once they had tasted the *dark side*.

"We could just ask a stranger. Someone walking down the street," I suggested.

"And what if that stranger told Mr. Darling that it was one of us who wanted the drink? Over my dead body. I won't give him the satisfaction." Grandma Anna tightened her apron. "Not a drop of his coffee will ever touch my lips!"

"I'll be the one to taste the Vincent Mocha," I said, a martyr to the cause. "But we've got to figure out how to get one."

I peered out the front picture window. A Java Heaven employee strolled the sidewalk, handing out tiny sample cups to passersby. His apron, with its cloud logo, was as crisp and white as a brand-new bedsheet—quite blinding beneath the somber late-afternoon sky. He called out to someone, then walked right past our windows. I cracked open the door to eavesdrop.

"Hey buddy. Would you like to try our new drink? It's called the Vincent Mocha, named after our local hero."

"I'll give it a wee taste."

Oh, I knew that voice.

Nine

I shoved my head out the door and peered up the sidewalk. There he stood in his kilt-wearing glory. The Java Heaven employee handed him a sample. "Hope you like it."

"Thank you," Malcolm said. "I'm quite fond of coffee. There was a particular blend in Egypt that was only picked by moonlight and only served to the pharaohs. I wasn't around then, but I've been told that the moon's reflection could be seen in the brew."

"Wild. Well, have a nice day."

I pretended to clean the window as the employee returned to Java Heaven. Then I hurried up the sidewalk. "Um, hello again. Malcolm, right? Um, what's that? It looks like coffee. Yep, that looks like a sample cup of coffee. Is that what it is?" *Smooooooooth.* Throw acting into the Closet of Failure.

He held the tiny cup. Chocolate shavings adorned a miniature dollop of whipped cream. A peppermint stick stuck out the top. It looked like a candy straw. Would those evil Java Heaven elves stop at nothing? Who in their right mind could resist such a concoction? Malcolm cleared his throat, breaking my hungry stare.

"You seem to be wanting this." He balanced the cup in his palm.

"Oh, careful." I tried to snatch it, but he moved out of reach.

"You want this, that's for sure." He frowned. "Why should I give it to you? You wouldn't listen to me."

I looked over my shoulder, to make certain that no one from Java Heaven was eavesdropping. Irmgaard and Grandma Anna, however, pressed their faces against the picture window. "If you give that to me, then you'll have given me what I *most desire*." Excellent answer. "That's what you want, right? That's the law, right?"

He shifted his weight. The cup wobbled precariously. "You told me that fortune was what you most desired."

"I was confused. I didn't know. But now I know. What I actually desire is that cup of coffee." My fingers twitched. I just wanted to grab it. Would the coffee be flavored with something exotic like organic Ecuadorian free-trade rainforest-saving cinnamon?

"A wee cup of coffee is what you most desire? But you work in a coffeehouse. Why would you want this particular cup? Is it special in some way?"

"Just give it to me," I said between clenched teeth. "Please."

"I suspect you're trying to trick me, just like you did with the pencil." His expression remained serious.

"I'm not."

"I'll give it to you under one condition."

"What?"

"That after I complete my delivery, you will tell me what you most desire. No deceptions."

"Fine. Whatever." I took the cup.

"I'll be back." He switched his satchel to the other shoulder, then walked up the sidewalk, his kilt sashaying with each long step. His calf muscles bulged. Messengers probably needed strong legs. And his legs had just the right amount of hair. Probably soft hair, not prickly like Vincent's legs when the hair started to grow back after a swim meet.

"Oh my God, did you see him?"

"He's so cute."

"Who is he?"

Heidi Darling rounded the corner, arm in arm with a couple of girlfriends. Matching lime sherbet earmuffs clung to their bobbing heads. Honest to God, if Heidi Darling wore a grocery bag on her head, then a bunch of other people would start wearing grocery bags on their heads. Elizabeth once made a vest out of grocery bags for a recycling project. She wore it a few times but it never caught on.

Standing there, red-handed, my brain kind of froze. But Heidi's legs didn't freeze. She sped down that sidewalk, a smirk taking up half her face. "So, Katrina, I see you're drinking *our* coffee now. I don't blame you. The Vincent Mocha is the best."

"I'm not drinking it."

"Why are you holding it, then?"

"I'm not holding it." I marched over to the garbage can and tossed the sample cup and its contents. What else could I do? It was one of the most embarrassing moments of my life. Like when a vegetarian gets caught with a hunk of prime rib.

Heidi followed me. So did her clones. "Well, it's sure to be a hit. Vincent's famous. We're such good friends."

That really got me. I wanted to say, "He's not your friend, he's *my* friend." Imagine if we all went around telling people exactly what we were thinking—we'd all sound like a bunch of third graders. *MY Vincent drink will be so much better than YOUR Vincent drink.*

Instead, I pretended not to care. "Whatever," I mumbled, hurrying back to the safety of Anna's, right into my grandmother's overly curious gaze.

"Do you know that boy?" Grandma Anna asked.

"What boy?"

"The one who gave you the coffee?"

"No. I don't know him."

"Oh. That's too bad. I thought maybe he was a new friend." She limped toward her desk. Her legs always stiffened at the end of the day. "I don't know how they expect people to buy such small cups of coffee. Who would buy such a tiny cup? Maybe someone with anorexia."

"Those are sample cups," I explained. "They're free."

"Free?" Grandma Anna shuffled through the mail pile. "How can they afford to give away so many samples? Organic coffee is expensive." She shook her head as she examined each envelope. "Oh dear."

"What?"

"Never you mind."

"Grandma?" Maybe she'd finally talk to me about our finances. Maybe she'd let me help. "Grandma, I know we're having troubles. I've heard you talking to the bank."

"That's none of your concern. I can manage." She pursed her lips as she opened one of the envelopes. A cold breeze passed through the room, rustling the mail. "Irmgaard?" Grandma Anna called. "Close that door. It's cold out." The mail rustled again. "Irmgaard?"

I went back to the kitchen. The coffeehouse's front door stood wide open. Irmgaard was outside, looking up the sidewalk.

"Irmgaard?" She wore a dazed, unblinking expression and fiddled with a cross that hung from a long chain, the only piece of jewelry she ever wore. "Irmgaard?" I tapped her on the arm. She blinked, then ran back into the shop. "Irmgaard?" I said, following. "What's the matter?" She shook her head, then grabbed her coat and purse, nearly knocking over Mr. Darling on her way out.

"Why won't somebody close that door?" Grandma Anna complained, limping into the kitchen. "What do you want?" she snarled.

Mr. Darling leaned against the door's frame. "Just checking to see if you've given my offer any more thought. I'm anxious to get started on the remodel before tourist season begins."

"Well, good for you." She tried to close the door, but his big head was in the way.

"Here's what I'm willing to pay. It's a generous sum." He held out a piece of paper.

"I'm not interested."

He continued to hold out the paper, but she just folded her arms and glared at him, her neck straining for height. I folded my arms and glared at him too—a unified front against his invasion. He raised his eyebrows, then tucked the paper into his pocket. "You'll change your mind, one way or another."

After he had left, Grandma Anna deflated back to her soft self, but she was in no mood to talk. "Go upstairs and do your homework. I'll finish up down here."

"You sure?"

"Yes." She headed back to the office. "I can't imagine what got into Irmgaard. She never leaves without hugging me good-bye."

I grabbed my backpack and headed upstairs, cursing Heidi Darling with each step. One more second and I could have escaped with the sample cup. At least I knew some of the ingredients. I still needed to call Vincent, to ask if he'd come and sign cups for the Solstice Festival. And I needed to call Elizabeth. She'd design a great logo for our version of the Vincent Mocha. We'd use double the whipped cream and buy peppermint straws the size of walrus tusks!

No one answered the phone at Vincent's house. I left a message. "Hey, congratulations. I didn't get to talk to you today. You're so famous. Can I have your autograph?" I laughed self-consciously. "I'm really, really happy for you. You've got it made. A full scholarship. That's great. Really, really great. Um, I've got this idea and I'm hoping you can help. So call me."

No one answered at Elizabeth's either. I dumped the contents of my backpack onto the bed. I did a page of geometry, memorized the parts of a cell for Biology, then stared at a blank piece of paper. Mr. Williams wanted us to write a good deed story, three to five pages, for Friday. If I wrote about giving Malcolm some day-old pastries I risked coming off as a braggart. *Oh, look at me, I help homeless people.*

Or I'd come off as really cheap. *Why didn't she give him something that wasn't day-old?* I decided to write about Vincent's good deed.

I wrote a paragraph, but the incident with Heidi kept intruding. I kept seeing that smug look on her earmuff-framed face. Me, just standing there, holding that cup. Like all embarrassing incidents, this one took on a life of its own. "Relive me," it whispered, over and over. "Are you starting to get somewhere with your homework? Well, we can't have that, so it's time to relive me again." Why, why, why had I just stood there, watching Malcolm walk away, staring at his legs like an idiot? If only I had gone straight into the coffeehouse.

The phone rang. Before I could say *hello*, Elizabeth screamed, "Turn on channel seven! Vincent's on the news!"

Sure enough, there he stood, in his swim team sweatshirt, calmly answering Brad Stone's questions. His straight black hair looked extra chlorine shiny on TV. I might have noticed that he spoke eloquently and that he seemed more mature than his sixteen years. I might have noticed that he looked happier than I'd ever seen him look.

But all I noticed was the Java Heaven coffee cup that he held in his right hand.

Ten

Wednesday morning found me waiting in my guidance counselor's office for my mandatory appointment. I picked a few Ratcatcher hairs off my sleeve while Mr. Prince finished a phone call.

Thumbtacked posters covered every inch of wall space. Most of the posters were motivational—*Reach for the Stars, Be All That You Can Be, Go for It!* That kind of thing. The rest dealt with serious subjects like drugs, suicide, and school shootings—the ugly realities of the teenage world. Each poster was the exact same size. He had probably torn them out of some guidance counselor catalog. Or maybe he subscribed to a Crisis-of-the-Month Club.

I tapped my feet. Get off the phone already. I wanted to get to class and talk to Vincent. He hadn't returned my call last night and he hadn't stopped by the coffeehouse before practice that morning. Maybe he was feeling bad about holding that cup on TV. He had to know that I'd be fuming. Java Heaven didn't exactly need free advertising.

If I carried around a little black book with the words

The Law written on the front cover, I would insist that the first law in that book be: *Thou shalt never, ever partake of Java Heaven coffee!*

But I didn't need a little black book because my friends—my two friends—already knew that law. And to break that law would mean disloyalty and serious hurt feelings on my part. Anyway, Mr. Darling had probably shoved that cup into Vincent's hand just before the interview. But, then again, Vincent could have dropped it. He *should* have dropped it. Law #2: *If a cup of Java Heaven coffee is shoved into thy hand, then thou shalt drop it.*

"Okay, Katrina, let's get started." Mr. Prince slid a pair of glasses onto his long nose. "How are you?"

"Fine." I smiled sweetly, unclenching my hands. The last thing I wanted was to get into a conversation with Mr. Prince about *feelings*. "Everything's fine."

"Good." He cleared a space on his desk. "The purpose of this meeting is to check your progress and make sure that you're on the right track."

"Okay."

"You're a sophomore this year," he said as he opened a file.

"Yeah."

He pulled a piece of paper from the file, looked at both sides, then frowned. "Surely I'm missing some pages. Your file is awfully thin. What kind of activities are you involved in?"

"Uh, nothing really."

"Clubs? Sports? Basketball?"

"I work."

He sat back in his chair. "Working is admirable, Katrina, but surely you have time to get involved here at school."

"I work every morning and every afternoon."

"I see. Is that necessary?"

"My grandmother can't afford to hire any more employees."

"Ah. Well, have you given any thought to what you'd like to do after you graduate?"

"Not really. My grandmother wants me to go to college."

"Exactly." He pointed to a poster behind his head. *Education Paves the Road to Success.* "Nordby High has an excellent rate of college acceptance. Sophomore year is the time to start getting serious. It's no longer just about grades. Competition for all the top schools is intense. Admissions committees want students who are involved on many levels. Let me show you something." He heaved a notebook onto his desk. "I've been working closely with Heidi Darling. You know Heidi, don't you?"

"Yeah." Ugh. Was it too early in the morning to vomit?

"This is a work-in-progress, mind you, but her achievements are impressive—the exact thing every admissions committee is looking for." He spun the notebook around. "I have her permission to share this with other students. In fact, I'm going to put it on display in the hallway."

I expected a spotlight to appear and a choir of angels to descend as Mr. Prince opened the notebook to reveal its glory. Would I be blinded by its brilliance? I should have brought some sunglasses. And so, on that Wednesday morning, when I could have been in World Mythology class asking Vincent about the coffee cup incident, Mr. Prince shared the supremeness that was Heidi Darling.

Mrs. Darling is one of those mothers who loves to submit photos of her kid to the newspaper. Not every now and then. It's more like her second career. Heidi's entire life had been documented in the *Nordby News,* from her first tooth (*Local Baby Bites Grocery Clerk*) to her Girl Scouts cookie sales (*Local Girl Declares New Peanut Butter Flavor Yummy*), to her signature ponytail (*Local Middle School Student Cuts Hair for Cancer Patients*). You get the point. I'd been in the paper once, when the king and queen of Norway came to Nordby. You can pick me out of the crowd if you look for the tall girl with the neon blond hair standing in the third row near the statue of Leif Erikson.

Mr. Prince flipped through page after page of personal recommendations. Then through page after page of activities: Pep Club, Yearbook Committee, Dance Committee, French Club, Sophomore Class Treasurer, Future Business Leaders of America, Honor Society, Sons of Norway, Swim Team, Nordby Chamber of Commerce Student of the Month. Dizziness swept over me. The average brain can't handle so much data.

"Heidi's a sure thing," he said, closing the notebook. "She'll get into her first-choice college, no problem. I want all the students here at Nordby to go to the college of their choice. But you've got to be competitive, Katrina. You've got to step up to the plate. Heidi's résumé is not all that unusual."

"It's not?" He had to be joking.

"Students your age are publishing books, creating Internet businesses, setting world records."

"They are?" I sat back and took a huge breath, picturing my Closet of Failure.

"That's why you've got to get involved. Right away." He handed me a slip of paper. "This will help you get started. It's a checklist of things that will give you a better chance at getting into college. Internships, apprenticeships, community service, those sorts of things. By the way, do you know what you'll major in?"

"No. Should I?"

He grimaced, as if thinking, *This one's a total loser, poor thing.* "It's never too early to set goals. What are you good at?"

Pouring coffee. Cleaning tables. Attracting weirdos in skirts.

"Nothing, really."

"Everybody is good at something."

"I'm not so sure that's true."

"Of course it's true." He pointed to a poster of a bunch of people dressed in various uniforms. *Everybody Is Good at Something.* "What about your friends. What do they like to do?"

"Well, Elizabeth takes lots of art classes. And she's won some awards."

"Excellent. You should take some art classes with her. Who else?"

"Well, Vincent swims and—"

"Vincent Hawk? Oh, he's a dream applicant, that's for sure. If he's your friend, then you should definitely get a letter of recommendation from him, before he gets too famous. In the meantime, why don't you take this aptitude test. It will only take about ten minutes. Answer the questions honestly or it won't do you any good. The answers are analyzed by a company in Seattle. We should get the results on Monday or Tuesday."

"Do I have to? I'd like to get to class."

"I really think you should take it. Only ten minutes."

So I took the test. It was a bunch of personality questions about what I'd do in different situations. Would I fold under peer pressure or would I stand my ground? Did I prefer large groups or being alone? If I answered all the questions honestly the results would be, *Aptitude: Zero. Dominant Characteristics: Boring. Top Career Choice: Coffeehouse Girl.* I already knew I wasn't good at anything. I didn't need to see it confirmed in writing.

But I answered honestly, just in case some miracle occurred and the test's analyzer uncovered a hidden talent— a diamond in the rough.

I handed Mr. Prince the test.

"Be sure to get started on that checklist," he told me.

"Okay." I shoved the checklist into my pocket and went looking for Vincent.

Eleven

It's too cold to eat in my car," Elizabeth said as I closed my locker. "The windows are icy."

Principal Carmichael had strict rules about not eating in the hall or in the gym, so that left us, on a nasty winter day, with one option. We stepped away from the locker and joined the hot, hormonal current of ravenous teens, pushed along like flotsam until we reached the cafeteria. I hadn't yet spoken to Vincent. He was still busy with interviews.

Students squeezed onto benches, shoulder to shoulder. Conversations erupted, utensils clanged, paper and plastic crinkled. The overhead fluorescent lights washed out everyone's food.

Elizabeth grabbed my arm. "Face is sitting over there. Look, he's eating french fries."

"Do you wanna sit over there?" I couldn't imagine sitting at the same table as the golf team. Besides looking totally out of place, what would we talk about? Golf seemed like the most boring game in the entire world.

"Sit by Face? Are you crazy?"

We found a spot in the corner, on the floor near the vending machine. Except for the constant clunking of packaged snacks, it wasn't so bad over there. A guy walked by with his hand shoved in some girl's back pocket. Elizabeth shot them a nasty glare. "That's so demeaning," she said. "Why don't we have boyfriends?"

I opened my thermos of carrot soup. "Because we don't talk to boys. Except for Vincent."

"Are we talking to Vincent? Shouldn't we be giving him the silent treatment?"

"Maybe." Soup steam drifted up my chin. "I want to know what he was doing with that cup."

"I'm telling you, it's all about Heidi. I still think she likes him." Elizabeth pushed her gold bangles up her arm and opened her lunch bag. "If I asked Face to go to the Solstice Festival with me, do you think he would?"

"I don't know." Seemed unlikely, but who was I to squash her fantasy?

"Why doesn't anyone ever ask me out? Look at me. I've got style." She lifted the hem of her denim skirt, exposing her hand-painted tights. "And I've got good breath. Don't I have good breath?" She blew in my face.

"Yep. Good breath." At that moment in my life, boyfriendlessness wasn't high on my list of worries. Last night, after my grandmother had fallen asleep, I had gone downstairs to snoop through the pile of bills. Quite a few were stamped *Past Due*. How do you pay past due bills if you don't have any customers?

"And I've got boobs. I'm overflowing with boobs. So what's the problem? I want to go to the festival with a guy this year." She stared across the cafeteria, longing filling every cell in her body. For a moment, her longing infected me and I pictured myself standing beneath the decorated Solstice tree, holding hands with a boyfriend. My boyfriend.

The Solstice Festival had long been my favorite holiday. It started with the decorating of an enormous tree, erected in the center of town. As a little girl I'd fill a pinecone with peanut butter and roll it in birdseed. Then all the kids would hang their pinecones on the tree. Each family would bring a worn pair of shoes and stick it under the tree—an Old World tradition to symbolize harmony throughout the year. St. Nick would come and hand out candy. And we'd sing carols and stroll the street, stopping at each shop for a special treat. Then we'd get dressed up and go to the grand feast at the Sons of Norway Hall. We'd eat some good stuff, like salmon and hot rolls, and I'd ignore the disgusting stuff like lutefisk and Jell-O salad.

I stopped filling those pinecones years ago, when I started working in the coffeehouse, but I still got caught up in the merriment. The little kids always came in for hot chocolate, extra excited if it had snowed. Anna's was the most popular stop for hot chocolate.

Until Java Heaven.

"I'll tell you what the problem is." Elizabeth unwrapped a cupcake. "The problem is that these stupid Nordby boys are shallow. They aren't ready to think outside the box, you know? If they'd just get their heads out of their butts once in a while they'd realize that I'm a great catch."

"You are."

"So why doesn't Face notice me?"

"Because you're sitting in the corner on the floor."

She sighed. "What's the matter with me? Why can't I just go up to him and talk? Why do I get so nervous?"

"I don't know." I kind of knew. Back in the seventh grade I'd been in love with a guy named Sean. I cut his photo out of our yearbook and tucked it into my jewelry box. It was still in there. But, like Elizabeth, I never did anything about it, just wasted way too much time longing. He moved away at the end of that school year, never knowing how I felt. That image popped into my head again—me, standing beneath the Solstice tree, holding hands with a guy. He was tall and handsome, but it wasn't Sean. He looked like . . . Malcolm.

"My feet start to sweat every time I think about talking to him," Elizabeth said. "Don't you think that's weird? Maybe I should go see a doctor."

"I wouldn't worry about it." I ate my soup, then unfolded the checklist that I had crammed into my pocket. "Mr. Prince gave me this."

"He gave everybody one."

"Yeah, but do you notice anything about mine?"

She shrugged, then licked frosting off her finger.

"Mine's full of blank spaces. There's nothing on it. You've got your art classes and your art awards. You want to go to the Rhode Island School of Design. You want to open a gallery in New York. What do I want to do?"

"Face is getting some ketchup." Elizabeth craned her neck to watch. She couldn't relate to my situation. Talent was wired into her. She exhaled it. It oozed out her pores. She probably even farted it. Had I been born without the talent gene? Sitting at the edge of the chattering crowd I felt like a freak with my naked checklist. Surely there

were others like me, born without an inkling of direction.
The wanderers, the amblers, the dabblers, united by our
purposeless mantra—*I have no idea what to do with my
life*.

I was a big blank space.

"What if I end up like Irmgaard?"

"Are you going to take a vow of silence?"

"No, I mean she's got to be forty. And she's making soup
and living alone. That's sad. Don't you think that's sad?"

Elizabeth unwrapped a sandwich. "Maybe she likes to
make soup and live alone."

"The point is, if I don't start doing something with
my life, then I'm not going to get anywhere." I waved the
checklist. "If I don't put some amazing things on this list,
no college is going to accept me."

"Just make a bunch of stuff up. I mean, who will
know?" Elizabeth ripped the checklist from my hand and
set it on her knees. "Activities. Activities." She pulled a pen
from her purse. "What is that stupid game those old guys
are always playing?"

"Hnefatafl."

"How do you spell that?"

I spelled it and she wrote: *Captain of the Hnefatafl Club,
a society dedicated to the preservation of Viking culture.* "Get
one of the old guys to write you a letter of recommendation." She scanned the page. "Look, there's a space for lan-
guages." She wrote: *Viking*.

"I don't speak Viking."

"You know some words, don't you?"

"I know 'Hnefatafl.' "

"Well, there you go. That's more than most people

know." She swept sandwich crumbs off the list. "Oh look, here's a space for volunteering. You're always helping those old guys."

"The Boys?"

"Yeah. Don't you make them sandwiches?"

"So?"

She wrote: *Eldercare Volunteer, helping senior citizens with daily activities.*

"You're totally exaggerating."

"Everyone exaggerates. You think I'm going to tell an admissions committee that I won first place in an art contest that only two other people entered? I'm going to say that it was open to national and international entries because it could have been. I mean, nowhere on the rules did it say that you couldn't mail in an entry from Tasmania. You need to get The Boys to write letters of recommendation. Oh, I know what else. You can come with me tonight to my Life Drawing class. The teacher doesn't charge for the first visit. Then you can add that to activities."

"I can't draw. You know that."

"Who cares? Katrina, you've just got to play the game."

"Whatcha doing?" Vincent stood over us.

I shoved the checklist back into my pocket. "Nothing," I said.

He knelt, greeting me with his usual chlorine freshness. "Hey, sorry I didn't call you back. I was really tired when I got home last night. It was kind of a big day, you know?"

"We saw you on channel seven," Elizabeth said, her mouth full of sandwich.

"I was on channel five too. And CNN and FOX." He

shook his head. "I still can't believe it. One day I'm worried about paying for college. The next day I've got a full scholarship."

I forced a smile. I should have thrown my arms around him, should have jumped up and down like a baboon. Vincent had saved someone's life and had been rewarded beyond his wildest dreams. But all I could think about was that stupid Java Heaven coffee cup.

Elizabeth elbowed me. "Tell him."

"Stop it."

"Tell him."

"Tell me what?" Vincent sat against the wall.

Elizabeth leaned across my knees and got right in his face. "We saw you, Vincent Hawk. We saw you holding that cup. You know how Katrina feels about Java Heaven. You've totally hurt her feelings."

Vincent shifted his weight. He looked away. He shifted again because guilt can be very uncomfortable. "I didn't mean to hurt your feelings, Katrina. I didn't buy that cup of coffee and I didn't drink it. You know I wouldn't do that."

"Then why were you holding it?" I asked.

"It was Heidi's cup. She asked me to hold it while she fixed her ponytail and then she walked off. I handed it to the camera guy right after the interview started."

"Oh." I had gotten so angry after seeing him holding that cup that I hadn't watched the whole interview. "What about the Vincent Mocha? Can he use your name like that? You should tell him that he can't use your name."

"Well . . ." Vincent looked away for a moment. "I didn't know anything about that drink, but I'm not sure it's such a bad thing, Katrina. Ten percent of the profits will go to the swim team. We need new lane dividers and new timers." He frowned. "It's just a stupid drink."

I stiffened. "It's more than that. Mr. Darling is trying to close us down. Your name will help him make more money. And . . ." I didn't want to admit how bad things were. Vincent knew what it was like to be poor, but Elizabeth didn't have a clue. Anyway, I'd been raised to believe that money matters were personal. It was embarrassing too. Every day we worked and worked, only to sink deeper and deeper into debt.

Vincent nudged me. "Don't be mad. What can I do?"

Despite his calm, steady voice, all my worries burst to the surface. Like an out-of-body experience, I watched myself from across the room, painfully aware that I was acting like a pouty child. But I couldn't stop.

"I want you to hate Java Heaven as much as I do. That's what I want. You're *my* friend, not Heidi's. I want you to help us, not them."

Vincent Hawk, best friend since the fourth grade, smiled sweetly. "I'll always be your friend. If you want me to do something for Anna's, I will."

"If I come up with a special drink, will you help serve it and maybe sign some cups?"

"Yeah, of course."

Of course. He was still the same old Vincent. Heidi could trick him into holding her stupid cup of coffee, but she'd never be his best friend. I felt a million times better.

The bell rang. Vincent wandered off. Elizabeth tossed her garbage, then pulled the checklist from my pocket. "What are you doing?" I asked.

She clicked her pen. "You said you were going to create a special drink, right?"

"Right."

She scribbled something, then smiled.

Vice President of Product Development.

Twelve

That afternoon, Principal Carmichael announced that *People* magazine would visit on Friday, which meant that Vincent's good deed would spread throughout waiting rooms and beauty shops everywhere. Maybe he'd sign a book deal. Maybe someone would buy the movie rights. The possibilities were endless. Fortune had cast its big golden net over the swimmer from Nordby.

Despite the chill, I felt kind of springy walking home—almost perky. It was one of those rare moments when I wasn't comparing myself to everybody else. Elizabeth had helped me see the ridiculousness of the checklist. And with Vincent in our corner, we would make tons of money at the festival. We'd call it Hero's Hot Chocolate, with the actual hero serving it. Our line would wind down the sidewalk, blocking the entrance to Java Heaven. I snickered, imagining Mr. Darling yelling at us to move the line. We'd donate 10 percent—no, make it 11 percent to a local charity. Sure, Hero's Hot Chocolate was a short-term answer, but one thing at a time.

Lars, the oldest of The Boys, sat on the bus bench, his ruddy face half-hidden behind an upturned collar. "How come you're not at Anna's?" I asked.

"Can't get down the hill. My legs are giving me trouble."

I sat next to him. "Did you take your arthritis medicine?"

"Can't remember." He scratched a tuft of white ear hair. "I might fall going down that hill. There's no dignity falling in public."

"I'll help you walk," I said. *Eldercare Volunteer.*

He pulled his knit hat over his ears. "I don't need help. I'm taking the bus."

"But Lars, you know your son doesn't want you to take the bus."

He narrowed his cloudy eyes. "My son needs to mind his own business. It's a public bus and I'm the public."

Lars's son was Officer Larsen. Officer Larsen had sent his father to a detox facility dozens of times, but he always went back to drinking. Last year, at age eighty-two, Lars had almost killed some joggers on his drive home from the Nordby Pub. The state took away his driver's license. A few days later he moved in with his son. The doctor said that Lars's liver was in terrible condition, along with high cholesterol, high blood pressure, and stiff joints. He needed to start exercising or he wouldn't live much longer. But Lars wanted nothing to do with exercise. So Officer Larsen hatched a plan. There would be no alcohol in the house. If Lars wanted to drink, he'd have to walk the mile to the Nordby Pub on Main Street. That way he'd be forced to get some exercise. All the locals knew not to give Lars a ride. Everyone agreed that it was for his own good.

According to the doctor, the walking had improved
Lars's health.

So every afternoon he walked the mile. He'd stop at
Anna's for coffee and soup (Officer Larsen kept a tab there)
and every other day he'd play a game of Hnefatafl. Then
he'd end each evening at the pub. His son would pick him
up on his way home from patrol.

But on that particular Wednesday afternoon, Lars had
mutiny on his mind. When the bus pulled up, he hobbled
forward. As the door hissed open he reached for the handrail.
Millie heaved herself from the driver's seat and blocked the
entrance. "Just what do you think you're doing?"

"I'm riding the bus today," Lars said. "So get out of my
way."

"Now Lars, you know I can't let you on." Millie would
have made a great drill sergeant, the way her voice slammed
right into your head.

"Look here, *woman*, this is public transportation."

"I promised your son. You know that."

"My son's an idiot. Move aside!"

"Walking's good for you."

Lars yanked his hat off his head and shook it at her.
"My legs can't take it. I'm gonna fall. Mark my words—I'm
gonna fall, and then I'll sue you and everybody else."

I felt embarrassed for him. Not because we all knew he
was an alcoholic, but because he knew that he wasn't as
strong as he used to be. That had to be one of the worst
parts of getting old.

"You need to get yourself a walker," Millie said. "My
aunt uses one and she can go up and down a hill, no problem."

"I don't need a walker."

"You need something." Millie leaned out the door. "Hey, Katrina. Help Lars get down the hill, will ya?"

"Sure," I said.

Lars shook his hat again. "You think I need help? Look here, *woman*, this body used to haul two-hundred-pound crab pots from the ocean. These legs have fought storms that would break you like a wishbone. I don't need help."

"Look, *old man*, don't you call me *woman*," Millie said. "Hey, Katrina." I ran to the door. "Stop in at the pharmacy on your way home and see if they have any walkers."

"Walkers?" Spit flew from Lars's thin lips. "I don't need a damn walker."

"You're a stubborn one," Millie said. "You won't use a walker and you won't take Katrina's help."

"Lars," I said gently. "You should let someone help you."

"I'd be happy to help."

Millie sucked in her belly as Malcolm squeezed past her and down the bus's steps. "Where'd you come from?" she asked. "I don't remember picking you up."

He paused on the lower step and smiled. "And I don't remember ever laying eyes on a lovelier bus driver."

If people could melt like ice cream, that's what would have happened—Millie would just be a big puddle of rocky road. As Malcolm stepped off the bus his kilt slipped up his thigh—muscular, just like his calves. Millie patted her hair, smiling as if she'd been sipping Lars's whiskey.

"Hey lady, I'm gonna be late," someone hollered from the back of the bus. Millie returned to her seat. Malcolm waved as the bus door hissed closed.

I shouldn't have been surprised to see him. He had told

me that he'd be back after he'd delivered a message. Maybe with Lars around, he wouldn't start in on all that good deed stuff.

We stood on the sidewalk as the bus drove off. Lars stuck his hat on his head, then gave Malcolm the once-over. "Whatcha wearing a skirt for?"

Malcolm slung his satchel over his hip. "I find I'm partial to it. Quite comfortable." He offered his arm. "I'm happy to help you down the hill."

"You some kind of *fairy*?" Lars asked, stepping back. "Is that why you're wearing a skirt?"

I rolled my eyes. "Lars, he's offering to help you down the hill."

"I assure you that I'm not a fairy. Fairies are fictional beings, manifestations of mankind's primal fear of nature. I am a messenger."

Lars narrowed his eyes. "Whoopdedoo. I used to be a captain. Everyone called me Captain Lars. Now I'm a drunk, but I've still got my dignity. I don't need your help." He started limping down the hill, his legs slightly bowed. We followed, flanking him like bodyguards.

"Did you know that Hemingway was a drunk?" Malcolm asked. Lars eyed him suspiciously. "So were Mozart and Dean Martin. But they had their dignity too."

Malcolm had a nice way about him—a gentleness I hadn't noticed until that moment. Maybe my happy mood had clouded my judgment, the way ice cream can mask a sore throat. But here's something odd. Though Malcolm had spoken to Lars, and though his pupils had been fixed on Lars's face, I had felt his gaze on me. *Felt* it. He wasn't looking at me the way we look at people walking down the street, or food on a plate, or words in a book. He was *seeing* me. I shivered.

"May I carry that for you?" he asked, pointing to my backpack. "It looks heavy."

I still didn't know much about him. Would he try to steal my backpack? My wallet was inside. I only had ten dollars, but still. Yet this time my inner voice didn't scream at me. It didn't say, "Run!" Part of me wanted to move closer to him—to feel him looking at me. "No thanks. I'm used to carrying it."

Lars's limp made the going slow. I thought about running ahead to tell my grandmother all about how Vincent was going to help us. But I stayed, lingering in Malcolm's flowery scent. Lingering in the strange sensation of being *noticed*.

"What's wrong with your leg?" Malcolm asked Lars.

"I'm old. That's what's wrong. Everything's falling apart. You'll find out."

"I won't get old." He said that without any hint of humor. What did he mean? Was he suicidal? One of Mr. Prince's posters popped into my head: *Know the Warning Signs of Suicide*. I hadn't bothered to read any further.

"Kids never think they'll get old," Lars grumbled. "But life goes by fast—real fast."

The sudden rush of emotion made Lars stumble. Malcolm caught him by the arm. "Let go," Lars snarled after regaining his balance. "I don't need help. And I don't need a walker. No dignity in using a walker. Bad enough the whole town knows I'm a drunk."

We started walking again, but this time Lars hobbled ahead.

"Katrina, you promised that when I returned, you would tell me what you most desire. I still need to reward your good deed."

Oh great, back to that again. I grabbed a tissue from my pocket. Cold air always made my nose run. What could I tell him?

"Hold on now." Lars stopped walking. He turned and peered up at Malcolm, his eyes half-hidden by his knit hat. "*You* want to give Katrina what she most desires?"

Malcolm nodded. "I've tried, but she won't tell me what it is."

Lars shook his head. "She'll never tell you. No woman ever tells. And no man's ever been able to figure it out. You'll be guessing for the rest of your life and you'll always guess wrong. Women like it that way because it gives them something to complain about."

"That's ridiculous," I said, crumpling the tissue and dropping it into a garbage can.

Malcolm gripped his satchel. "I can't guess for the rest of my life. That's not possible. And I can't be on my way until I reward her. She's imprisoned me, you see."

"Imprisoned?" Lars glared at me. "You should be ashamed, Katrina, playing with this boy's heart."

"What?" I just about choked on my own spit. They were *both* crazy.

"It's all in this book." Malcolm opened his satchel and pulled out the black book.

"You studying to be a lawyer?" Lars asked after reading the book's title. "I want you to sue the city for me. That's a public bus and I'm the public."

"I'm not a lawyer. I'm a messenger." Malcolm opened

the book and read: " 'If it doth come to pass that during the course of thy travels, an unsolicited, unselfish act of kindness is bestowed upon thee, then thou must reward the act by granting to the bestower that which the bestower most desires.' "

Lars scratched his head. "You don't say?"

"I don't want to guess. I've had some troubles in the past, made some guesses that didn't quite work out. I can't afford to make another mistake."

Lars screwed up his face. "Uh-huh."

Malcolm turned to a new page. "There's a handy chart in here. It says that the most common thing people ask for is fortune. But Katrina didn't want that. She gave it to her friend. The second-most common thing people ask for is fame." Lars and Malcolm turned and looked at me. Yep, that's right, I was still standing there. I don't know why. I should have left those two idiots in the dust. "Could fame be what you most desire?" Malcolm asked.

Fame.

Seemed like famous people were mostly miserable, spending their time denying rumors, punching photographers, checking themselves into rehab. What good were billions of dollars and a recognizable face if you couldn't even walk your dog in your pajama bottoms without some jerk following you and then plastering your picture across every grocery store tabloid so people in checkout lines could stand around and talk about you as if they knew you? *Look how fat she's gotten. She's not so pretty. She's so tall, she should join the Masai tribe.*

"Katrina?" Malcolm's inky blue gaze swept over me like a feather duster. I shivered again. "Do you desire fame?"

Vincent seemed to be enjoying his fame, and it couldn't hurt our coffeehouse if I became the world's most famous person. What would I be famous for? Filling jam pots? Not that I believed in the whole magic bean thing. But I'd never get rid of this guy if I didn't finish his game. "I'll choose fame."

He pulled the packet of chocolate-covered coffee beans from his satchel. "I've only got two left. They were very tasty." He picked out a bean, then closed his eyes. Everything went quiet—no cars, no seagulls, even Lars held his wheezy breath. The world froze. But I didn't freeze. My heart pounded. I looked left, then right. Nothing else moved. I stood there, out of sync with a world suspended. "What's happening?" I whispered.

Malcolm's thick lashes rested on his cheeks. He seemed frozen too. I stared at his face, my gaze drawn to his mouth. Some guys had pencil-thin lips, but his lower lip was as perfect as his upper lip. What would it be like to kiss him? That thought, which popped into my head without an invitation, surprised me with its vividness.

Malcolm's eyes flew open and he smiled.

I stepped away and the world came back to life.

"Here you go." He held out the bean. "And don't pretend to eat it like you did last time. I'm not stupid."

What had just happened? I felt a bit dizzy. And frightened. Maybe it was a blood sugar thing and I just needed to eat a cookie. I needed to get back to the coffeehouse and sit down. "If I eat this now, will fame come right away?"

"I believe so."

"Then I'd like to wait. I mean, look at me. If I'm going

to be famous, I'd like to fix my hair, maybe put on something nice."

"You should put on a dress," Lars said. "A nice dress. Girls don't wear dresses anymore."

"Yeah, I should put on a nice dress."

Malcolm frowned. "You won't eat it now?"

"I'll eat it later."

"You wouldn't be trying to trick me?"

"No."

"I'm freezing my nuts off," Lars said. "Take the bean."

I took the bean and put it into my pocket.

"Well then, I guess I'm done. I guess I won't be seeing you again." For a moment, his blue eyes, so deep and vivid, faded to gray. When he sighed, a cold breeze slid down my spine. "Time to be on my way or I'll get into trouble. I wish you a long and healthy life, Katrina Svensen. And to you, Lars Larsen, I wish you dignity." Up the hill he went, just like last time, except he stopped to look back, sadness clearly imprinted on his face. Then he was gone.

"I don't think that boy's right in the head," Lars said. "The pages in his book were blank."

Maybe I wasn't right in the head. The pharmacy sat across the street. "Wait here," I told Lars. They didn't have any walkers in stock. They'd have to order one and it was real expensive. I told the counter person I'd get back to him. I thought about asking if he knew anything about hallucinations, but decided against it. When I caught up to Lars, he was almost to Anna's. His limp had improved.

"Hey, Katrina." He held up a cane. "Isn't it a beauty?

Look, the handle's carved like a fish. And my name's right on it. Captain Lars."

"Where'd you get it?"

"I just found it." He waved it above his head and smiled. "Now, this has some dignity."

Thirteen

Odin sat alone at the corner table, staring forlornly at his game board. Ralph and Ingvar had abandoned him because Irmgaard was making krumkake—little rolled cookies flavored with almond, lemon, and cardamom. They watched as she poured yellow batter onto an iron. The batter sank into the iron's grooves, sizzling to a golden brown. The Boys waited with anticipation as she lifted the soft cookie with a spatula, then rolled it around a metal cone.

Irmgaard's silence and her graceful, repetitive movements could lull anyone into a trance. The steam from the hot iron had turned her cheeks pink. One might think that grown men would have better things to do on a Wednesday afternoon. But Ingvar would say, "What's better than a beautiful woman and a plate of warm cookies?"

"Katrina's got a boyfriend," Lars announced as we stepped inside.

"What? No I don't."

"What's that?" My grandmother barreled across the room, wiping her hands on a dish towel. Her lower lip actually trembled. "A *boyfriend*? Who is he?" Her enthusiasm was embarrassing. You'd think I'd discovered a cure for cellulite or something.

"No one."

"He's a foreigner," Lars said, unbuttoning his coat. "And he's not all there, if you know what I mean."

My grandmother pursed her lips. "He's not Swedish, is he?"

"He wears a skirt," Lars added, taking a seat across from Odin.

Odin raised an eyebrow. "A skirt?"

"You're dating a homosexual?" my grandmother asked.

"He says he's not a fairy," Lars said.

"What are you talking about? I'm not dating anyone." I dropped my backpack, then grabbed a krumkake. "And Malcolm wears a kilt, not a skirt. Lots of guys wear kilts. It has nothing to do with being gay."

"She's right. Romans wore skirts," Ingvar said.

"Romans didn't wear skirts. They wore tunics," Ralph said, crumbs falling from his mouth.

"They wore skirts," Ingvar insisted. "With pleats."

Ralph grabbed another cookie. "I'll tell you who wore a skirt. Mel Gibson wore one in that movie."

"Yeah well, he's an actor, and everyone knows that actors are *fairies*," Odin said.

The wisdom of the aged. I ate my cookie, then poured milk into a tall glass. The cookie helped me feel better after the whole "world freezing" episode. Maybe I'd just been tired, or hormonal.

"Where'd you get that cane?" Odin asked.

"Found it," Lars said.

Great, we were off the subject of boyfriends. My shoulders relaxed as I drank the milk. Why was it such a big deal whether or not I had a boyfriend? Of course, I wouldn't feel so defensive if I had purposefully chosen to be boyfriendless.

Lars moved one of the playing pieces. "Katrina's boyfriend said he was imprisoned. That's what he said. That Katrina had imprisoned him."

Everyone stopped eating and cooking and playing, and grinned at me. Goofy little grins as if I had just said my first word or taken my first step. My face felt like it was on fire. I bolted into the office, but Grandma Anna, despite her arthritic knees, stayed hot on my heels. "Is that what the boy said?" she asked, blinking excitedly. "Imprisoned?"

"I don't know." I looked around for the order sheets, trying to seem busy. One of my jobs was to place the orders for food and supplies. An unruly pile of papers covered my grandmother's desk. Shoe boxes overflowing with receipts lay on the floor. The desk drawers sat open. "What happened in here?"

She fiddled with some papers. "I'm trying to find the receipt for the television."

"The new one?"

She looked away. "I thought we could sell it on eBay. We don't really need it."

My stomach clenched. She loved that new television because she could watch two shows at once. Had we reached the point of having to sell our belongings? "Are things that bad?"

"We need a new dishwasher. It's a matter of necessity."

"Don't get rid of the television," I said. "We could have a garage sale. I've got all that stuff in the upstairs closet."

"We'll talk about it later." She turned her round face up at me, her eyebrows arched with hope. "Are you going to ask this boy to the Solstice Festival?" We were out of money and she was worried about my love life. Should I have been worried too? Does not having a boyfriend at sixteen put you on the fast track to spinsterhood? Did this mean I would spend the rest of my life alone, childless, dried up?

Aaron could start calling me Coffeehouse Crone.

"I'm not asking him to the Solstice Festival. I really don't know him." I picked up a bill from the power company. "Grandma, how much money do we need?"

"That's none of your concern." She whisked the bill from my hand. "How did you meet this boy?"

"He just showed up. He keeps following me."

She nodded. "That's what they do. Believe me, once a man falls in love, he follows you everywhere. He sends flowers, he calls, he takes you out to dinner, to the movies. He embeds himself like a tick." She sighed. "So romantic."

"Well, I don't want a tick."

Her dazed expression faded and her down-to-earth, commonsense nature reappeared. "Then you'll have to make that clear. If you don't love him, you don't love him. No good leading him on. Tell him that you appreciate his feelings, but you're just not interested." She patted my hand. "Your time will come." She went back to the kitchen.

I wouldn't have to tell Malcolm that I wasn't *interested*, because he had left Nordby. He had wished me a long and healthy life. Even if he turned out to be sane it didn't matter. He had gone.

I picked up another bill, this one from Acme Supply Company. Thirty days overdue. Another from Visa was also thirty days overdue. If only we could just throw them in the trash and be done with them, like bad sardines.

"Good-bye, Katrina. Good-bye, Anna. *Good-bye, Irmgaard*," The Boys called, the front door closing behind them.

"Grandma?" I went into the kitchen. "Did you see the late fees on these bills? They add up to hundreds of dollars."

She waved me away. "Not now, Katrina. I'm not feeling well. I'm going to lie down." She gripped the handrail and slowly pulled herself up the stairs. Going to bed at 4:30 in the afternoon wouldn't solve our money problems, but sometimes, crawling under the covers is the only thing a person can think to do.

I started to wipe down the counters, when Irmgaard opened her purse and took out her wallet. She held out two twenty-dollar bills.

"Oh, thanks, Irmgaard, but I'm sure things aren't that bad," I said. "We'll work it out."

She frowned and put the money on the counter.

"You know Grandma won't accept that." I picked up the bills and tucked them back into her purse. Irmgaard didn't have money to give away. No customers meant no tips.

I changed the radio station. Irmgaard never seemed to mind. Getting lost in the music always made cleanup go faster. As I hummed, the image of Malcolm with his eyes closed kept popping into my head. Did he know how perfect his face was? Did he know that even with those ragged clothes he was gorgeous? Watching him standing there, I had wanted to lean forward and kiss his lips. I didn't even know him and I had wanted to kiss him.

A sudden tap on my shoulder nearly gave me a heart

attack. Irmgaard stood next to me, her coat and hat on. "Closing time already?" I asked.

She bit her lower lip and looked away, uncertain about something.

"What's wrong?" I turned down the radio.

She pulled a small book from her coat's pocket—one of those little gift books that you find near a cash register. The gold foiled title was *Angels Among Us*. She waved it at me. "Is it for me?" Irmgaard had given me tons of gifts over the years, remembering every birthday and every holiday. On Easter she always brought a basket of chocolate eggs, on Valentine's Day she brought a bottle of drugstore perfume. She didn't have kids of her own, so I always figured I was sort of her surrogate kid.

She pointed to the image on the cover, one of those religious paintings from the Middle Ages. The person in the painting was robed, with large wings on his back and a golden halo radiating from his head. I took the book. "It's an angel," I said. She nodded eagerly, then motioned me toward the front door. She opened the door, then motioned again.

We stood outside the shop and Irmgaard pointed up the sidewalk. Then she pointed to her skirt. I was clueless. She tugged at her skirt. "I don't get it," I said.

We went through this all time. It was a game called *What is Irmgaard trying to say?* Vows of silence can be really annoying. Certainly they can create an aura of mystery and even reverence, for any kind of vow takes dedication, but if you're going to be silent, then you'd better develop a keen ability to play charades, or you'll drive everyone crazy.

She pointed—sidewalk, skirt, sidewalk, skirt.

"I still don't get it."

She sighed, walked up the sidewalk, then stopped. She held out her hand, palm up, as if balancing something. She pointed to her hand, then to her skirt, then to the sidewalk. Over and over and over.

Oh. "Do you mean the guy who was standing right here on the sidewalk, holding the sample cup? The guy wearing the kilt?"

She nodded, then took the book and opened it to the first chapter.

It was called "The Messenger."

Fourteen

I ate some of Irmgaard's clam chowder at our upstairs table. Why would she think that Malcolm was an angel? She was deeply religious, no doubt about that. She silently prayed before eating anything. I'd often seen her kiss the cross that hung around her neck, and she kept a travel Bible in her purse. But angels didn't stand around on sidewalks, talking to people. Or wear kilts or sleep in alleys. Did they? Unfortunately, I didn't have time to look through Irmgaard's gift book. I barely had time to squeeze in my geometry homework before Elizabeth came by at seven to take me to her art class.

"I called the teacher. There's an extra easel for you. This will be fun."

"Don't get your hopes up." I knew that I'd massacre whatever I painted. But at least the class would be something to add to the all-important checklist.

Grandma Anna lay on her bed, her radio tuned to a book discussion on NPR. "Can I get you anything?" I asked.

"No thanks, sweetheart," she said quietly. "I'm just worn out. You go and have fun."

"You sure? I don't have to go." She did seem more pale than the normal Norwegian pale.

"Go on."

Elizabeth and I ate the last of the krumkakes on the way to the community center. She had changed into her painting pants—an expensive pair of jeans with paint dribbled all over them. Sometime after school she had added a red streak to her hair. I slid into the passenger seat in my usual jeans and sweatshirt. Elizabeth talked about Face the whole way. She'd seen him in the grocery store buying a bag of potato chips, which gave her hope because she liked potato chips too. "Do you think I should sign up for golf lessons? Doesn't that just seem like the most boring game in the entire world?"

The parking lot was mostly full. The fat brick building that housed the community center used to be an elementary school. Flyers and notices wallpapered the hallway. "That's where the alcoholics meet," Elizabeth said as we passed a room with a donut- and cookie-covered table. She darted in and grabbed us a couple of pink iced donuts. "A bunch of divorced men meet over there," she said, continuing the tour. "They cry a lot."

In room 105, we collected two stools and two paint-splattered easels. Elizabeth gave me a piece of watercolor paper and some paints. All the other painters looked much older. They carried nice cases for their supplies. "You have to be sixteen to take this class," Elizabeth said, handing me a brush. Then she introduced me to the teacher, an anorexic-looking woman named Edna who must have had all the bones in her hand removed, because I'd never shook a hand that limp.

"What are we going to paint?" I asked as Elizabeth settled onto her stool.

A fat guy walked in, dressed in only a bathrobe. Elizabeth smiled wickedly. "This is Life Drawing."

"Huh?"

"Don't giggle," she said. "This is serious. The human body is a serious subject." She tied her hair back with a pink bandanna. "All the renowned masters painted nudes."

"Nudes?".

Fat Guy dropped his bathrobe.

They call it Life Drawing, but they should just call it Buck-Naked People Drawing or Let It All Hang Out Drawing. What's wrong with painting a bowl of apples or a vase of flowers? Look, I admit it. I'm just not mature enough to sit on a stool and paint real, naked people. It's beyond me. Especially naked guys.

I don't have brothers. Girls who have brothers are way ahead of those of us who don't. The only male in my house had been my grandfather, and he never walked around in anything skimpier than a pair of long red pajamas with baseballs on them.

The teacher and Fat Guy talked about his pose. The contrast between the two was shocking, her twiglike arms flying around as she explained her vision, his behemoth gut sagging as he listened. She kept talking, as if it was the most natural thing on earth to talk to a completely naked guy. He said that his back was acting up, so she suggested a reclining position. And then he reclined, in all his glory.

Elizabeth scooted her easel until it touched mine,

creating a screen to hide behind because she was . . . giggling. Ms. Sophisticated Artist was losing it. She cupped her hands over her mouth. "Oh . . . my . . . God . . ." She almost knocked over her water jar. "Ha, ha, ha, ha, ha."

"What's the matter with you? I thought you did this all the time," I whispered.

"That's my dad's caterer."

I peeked over the top of my easel. Fat Guy was plugged into his own music, his pink feet tapping merrily. No way was I going to paint his private parts. Forget about that.

Elizabeth dabbed her eyes with her sleeve and finally got it together. We kept our easels side by side so we could talk, which didn't seem to bother anyone, since everyone was plugged into their own world.

With a few strokes, Elizabeth outlined Fat Guy, the proportions perfect. I tried to copy her painting, but his feet ended up looking like blocks of wood, and his head was way too big. Elizabeth dipped a brush in magenta. Magenta? I didn't see any magenta on our model. I mixed white and red into a sickening shade of pink.

"I'm going to ask Face to the Solstice Festival. I'm just going to do it."

"Really?"

"Yes. I'm making myself sick with all this nervous crap. I'm acting so meek. I'm not meek."

"No, you're definitely not meek," I told her.

"Being meek never got anyone anywhere."

"Aren't the meek supposed to inherit the earth?"

"I hope not. Can you imagine how boring that would be?" She scowled at my puddle of paint. "What are you doing?"

"Making skin color."

"You need to add less red and more yellow."

Despite the addition of yellow, my nude looked like a Pepto-Bismol explosion. Edna, the art teacher, strolled by. Through tight lips, she pointed out that my perspective was all wrong, that my subject lacked emotion, and that I needed to add more yellow to my skin tone. "Thanks," I said. And then, so she wouldn't think I actually cared, I added, "I'm just doing this because my guidance counselor wanted me to."

"How are you going to ask him?" I asked after Edna had praised Elizabeth's work and moved on.

"In person. Face-to-face."

I was awed by her courage, but I always felt that way about Elizabeth. It's something my two best friends had in common—once they knew what they wanted, they went for it. A perfectly simple philosophy. I understood the concept but could never quite put it into motion. Like swimming four lengths of the Nordby pool. I knew what it took to do it, I just couldn't quite manage it.

"He gave me another bean," I said.

Elizabeth nearly poked her eye out with her brush. "No way! Let me have it this time. Please."

"You don't even know what I wished for."

"Oh. What?"

"Fame."

She sat up straight. "Why did you wish for fame? You don't want to be famous." She peered around the side of her easel. Closing one eye, she held out her brush the way artists do, measuring something. "I'm the one who wants to be famous. If I were famous, then my gallery would be the most popular gallery in New York City."

I added more pink to his gut. "Maybe I do want to be famous."

"No way. You hate it when people stare at you, and that's what happens to famous people. They stare at you, they follow you everywhere. I'd love it."

"What do you think I should have wished for?"

"Well, it was supposed to be what you most desire, right?"

"Yeah."

She tapped her brush against her knee. "Um. I don't know. You don't really have any interests." She shrugged. "Maybe your biggest desire is to have your parents back."

Why hadn't I thought of that? Of all the things I could have thought of, why hadn't that popped right into my head? Not that it mattered, because you can't bring people back from the dead, but shouldn't that have been what I most desired? It's just that my parents were like a dream, long faded from my memory, just two faces in a photo near my bed. I missed the *idea* of them, but an idea is not the same thing as an actual memory. It lacks emotion. So I didn't spend my days longing for two people I couldn't remember. Of course, my grandmother's grief was an entity unto itself.

"If you don't eat the bean, will you let me eat it?"

"It's at home." It wasn't. It was melting in my jeans pocket, but for some reason I didn't feel like sharing. Elizabeth was so good at getting her way, whether it was help with math homework or choosing what kind of soda we'd split at the movies. I knew that if I showed her the bean, I'd never see it again. "Want to hear something really weird?"

"Yeah."

"Irmgaard thinks that Malcolm's an angel."

Elizabeth just about fell off her stool. "NO WAY!"

We got into trouble after that outburst and Edna separated us. I had to struggle with my skin tones alone. More yellow made things worse. He looked like he was made out of Play-Doh. Then those stupid watercolors ran down the page, so it looked like he was leaking. The teacher wasn't impressed.

The end result of the Life Drawing class had nothing to do with technique but had everything to do with attitude, which illustrates the core difference between the way Elizabeth deals with the world and the way I deal with it. She painted Fat Guy in his entirety, even his private parts, and added all sorts of decorative elements, like a climbing vine and a Grecian urn and splashes of magenta and turquoise. I painted a lump of flesh and avoided all the . . . *details*. I never even considered adding my own touches. It never crossed my mind that we would be allowed to do that.

"What about the bean?" Elizabeth asked as we walked down the hall. "Please?"

I wished I hadn't told her. She'd never give up. "Fine. Let's grind it up and drink it tomorrow morning."

"Tomorrow's not good. I'm going to be gone all day. Mom's taking me to this special dermatologist in Seattle. It takes a year to get an appointment with her."

"Okay. Then we'll do it Friday morning?"

"Definitely."

"Hey, when are you going to ask Face?"

"Friday. At lunch. Don't let me chicken out, okay?"

"Okay."

"I mean it, Katrina. I'm going to do it. I'm going to walk

right up to him. Because being meek doesn't get a person anywhere."

I crumpled up my painting and threw it into the trash.

If the meek do inherit the earth, at least they'll have something impressive to put on their college applications.

Fifteen

Thursday morning came and Grandma Anna still felt sick. "It's my stomach," she said, refusing a plate of toast.

"Do you have the flu?"

"I don't think so." She pushed back the quilt and sat at the edge of her bed. "It feels like indigestion. I must have eaten something bad."

"Maybe it's because you're so worried," I said, sitting next to her. "Why won't you let me help with the bills?"

"It's my job to worry about the bills." She patted my hand. "Your job is to go to school."

"But I think I should stay home and take care of you."

"Irmgaard will take care of me." She stepped into some slippers. "You go to school. Get good grades, go to a good college."

My grandmother used to be so strong. But age had crept up, and like Lars she didn't want to be treated differently just because her body was slowing down. Anna Svensen had her pride and she believed that her problems were no one's business. Like my grandfather's alcoholism.

No one knew that he used to drink himself to sleep every night. Lucky for us he'd been a peaceful drunk, but she never told a soul.

I ate the toast, then did my morning chores. I turned on the yellow light and peered out the back window. The alley was empty. Why would Irmgaard think that Malcolm was an angel? He worked as a messenger and had come to Nordby to deliver a message—so he said. Could be he was homeschooled. Could be he'd been partying that night and had ended up in the alley after getting real drunk. Weekend binge drinking was popular with a lot of students at Nordby High. He was probably no different.

So, if I thought about it enough, I could explain his sudden appearance, but how to explain his odd behavior? Crazy had already occurred to me, but if he wasn't crazy, then why would he be making up such a weird story about needing to reward my good deed? Why would he be following me around?

Could he be interested in *me*? What a concept.

Thursday was a total bore. Elizabeth wasn't at school and I didn't see Vincent because he spent the entire day off campus doing a morning talk show and then an afternoon talk show. I kept thinking about Malcolm, working it over and over in my mind. Could he possibly like me? What did it matter? He had said good-bye and I was back to my normal routine.

On Friday morning Vincent showed up extra early. He peeled off his coat and hat and sat at the counter. "Why are you dressed up?" I asked. He never wore button-down shirts.

"I've got that interview with *People* magazine today."

"Oh. Right." I sliced some pumpernickel and dropped it into the toaster. "You look nice." He did. He rested his chin in his hand and closed his eyes. He had spent most of his life since seventh grade exhausted. Swim practice every morning and afternoon, late nights keeping his A average. He helped his dad with the domestic stuff too. No one knew where Vincent's mom had gone. She had left ages ago, with a married man, and hadn't been back to Nordby. He never wanted to talk about her. Though his dad had given away all her belongings, Vincent had kept a few hidden in his room—a blouse at the very back of his closet and a necklace tucked in his bedside drawer. We had each lost a huge part of our lives, but in a way, his situation was worse. My mom hadn't purposely abandoned me. That had to hurt beyond words.

He yawned.

"You could stop swimming," I said.

He opened his eyes. "What do you mean?"

"You don't have to earn a swimming scholarship now."

"I don't want to stop swimming." The toaster popped. "No one from the Suquamish tribe has ever medaled at the Olympics. No one's even competed at the Olympics. I want to be the first." As always, he practiced that simple philosophy—if you want to do something, go for it.

Elizabeth burst in, her hair pulled into a conservative ponytail. She wore a tan trench coat and plain jeans. My two friends looked as if they'd become Young Republicans overnight. "*What* are you wearing?"

"I don't want to freak Face out," she said. "I thought I should turn down the volume."

"Who's Face?" Vincent asked.

"This guy that I like, if you must know." Her unlined eyes looked half their regular size. "I'm going to ask him to go to the Solstice Festival with me."

"Oh, great." Vincent cleared his throat. "Uh, by the way, this is probably a good time to tell you that I'm also going to the festival."

"Huh?" I stopped buttering the toast.

He forced a smile. "Heidi Darling asked me."

"What?" I dropped the knife.

"Well, you know, she joined the team this year and we've been spending lots of time together. She asked me yesterday and I said I'd go." He acted as if he'd shared something as innocuous as a fair weather report. I felt as if I'd been struck by lightning. "I can't remember the last time I went to the festival."

I remembered the last time he went. We were sixth graders and we felt silly making those peanut butter pinecones for the tree, but we did it anyway, somehow realizing that it was our last chance to be kids. We waited for St. Nick, holding out our hands for candy canes and licorice. We knew it was Ingvar behind the white beard, not just because his pipe was dangling from his mouth but because we were wiser and the magic of the holiday had begun to fade. After the Grand Feast, Vincent's dad let us hang out on the deck behind the marina office. Vincent and I curled up under a big blanket to watch the parade of Solstice ships. I remembered every minute of that night.

I grabbed the edge of the counter. "What do you mean you're going to the Solstice Festival with Heidi?"

"I know you don't like her, Katrina, but it's just a date.

I'm still not going to buy her dad's coffee." He grabbed a slice of toast. Elizabeth grabbed the other.

I could barely control my panic. "But you're supposed to be here during the festival, remember?"

"What are you talking about?"

"I asked if you would help hand out the special drinks and sign the cups."

"Oh, that. You never said it was during the Solstice."

"*Yes*, I did."

"*No*, you didn't."

I looked to Elizabeth for help. She shrugged. "Come to think of it, I don't think you mentioned *when* you needed Vincent's help."

"WHAT? Of course I did. When else would I need him?"

Vincent finished his toast. "Jeez, Katrina, don't get so mad. How was I supposed to know? I'm not a mind reader."

Panic turned my voice all screechy. "You have to help that night. We can't outsell Mr. Darling without you."

"But I already said yes to Heidi."

"So?" I glared at him. *He'll have to choose. Heidi or me.* "Why would you want to go out with her in the first place?"

He looked away. That single gesture revealed all I needed to know. Vincent Hawk, best friend since the fourth grade, was in love with horrid Heidi Darling, daughter of my worst enemy. Unbelievable.

He wasn't thinking clearly. Heidi had hypnotized him with her fresh-scrubbed beauty. I needed to warn him, to help him see the truth.

"She doesn't care about you. She's only doing this to get to me."

"What are you talking about?" He narrowed his brown eyes.

"Her dad is trying to pay us to close the business and move. If she ruins my life, then I'll want to move. Don't you see?"

"How is my going to the Solstice Festival with Heidi going to ruin your life?"

Elizabeth was wide-eyed as I struggled for words.

"Because . . . because . . ." *Because Heidi already has a perfect life and if she gets you, then she'll have everything. Because if you go out with her, then I'll feel like you stabbed me in the back and that will change things between us. And then we won't hang out and I'll be miserable.*

"Because it's about loyalty," Elizabeth said, punching Vincent's shoulder. "Katrina needs you to help her."

"I'm loyal! How can you say I'm not loyal? I do everything with Katrina. It's just a date. You're both acting like it's the end of the world." He slid off the stool. "Look, Katrina, maybe you should think of another way to compete with Java Heaven. You can think of something." He put on his coat. "And I'll help, you know I will. I just can't help during the Solstice Festival. Heidi's all excited about going and I'm not going to hurt her feelings." As calm as ever, as if he had titanium skin impervious to *my* feelings, he put on his hat and left.

It had been such a great plan, but Hero Hot Chocolate was nothing without the hero. Tears welled in my eyes. What was more upsetting—the fact that my plan to make some money had crashed and burned, or the fact that Vincent had chosen another girl's feelings over mine?

"Vincent's way too good for Heidi," Elizabeth said,

hugging me. "She'll lose interest as soon as she realizes that he doesn't have any money, except for that scholarship. He doesn't even have a car. She'll dump him after a few dates."

I nodded, finding comfort in my best friend's potential misery.

"But you know . . ." She paused, then brushed crumbs off the counter. "I feel like I need to be brutally honest."

I fought off more tears. "What do you mean?"

"This was going to happen eventually. Vincent's too cute not to have a girlfriend. You've had him to yourself way too long."

Not long enough. But she was right. How could Nordby's swim champion and life-saving hero stay single? He'd get marriage proposals from all over the country once that *People* interview came out. But of all the people . . . Heidi Darling.

"It's getting late," Elizabeth said. "If we're going to grind up that bean, we should do it now."

Right. That bean. That stupid bean. I'd show Vincent. I'd grind it up and drink it and get real famous and I wouldn't need his signature on a coffee cup. I ran upstairs.

"You're going to be late," my grandmother called from the bathroom.

Ratcatcher pawed at my ankles as I pulled last night's jeans off the top of the laundry basket. Inside the pocket, the chocolate-covered bean was all sticky. Ratcatcher wound between my legs as I hurried down the hallway. "Stop it," I scolded. She kept winding. At the top step, she got right under my foot and tripped me. I caught myself on the railing, but the bean flew out of my hand and rolled down the stairs. The cat bounded after it. "Ratcatcher!"

The bean bounced off the last step and rolled across the kitchen floor. Ratcatcher wiggled her rump, then pounced. She swallowed the bean whole.

Elizabeth looked up the stairs. "Why are you standing there? Where's the bean?"

What a totally crappy morning. "Ratcatcher just ate it."

"You've got to be kidding."

"I'm not."

She put her hands on her hips and frowned. "If your cat gets famous, I'm going to be so mad at you."

Sixteen

As I've said, Law #1 in my book of laws is *Thou shalt never, ever partake of Java Heaven coffee*. The recent addendum to that rule is *Nor shalt thou PARTAKE of anything from Java Heaven, be it a beverage, a food product, or THE OWNER's DAUGHTER*.

In World Mythology I shunned Vincent and took the desk next to Elliott, dreading the moment when Mr. Williams would call on me to read my good deed story. And he would call on me, because he had given me the eager eye when I had walked into class. But first he made us sit through three other stories that had the following things in common: each story had been written by a girl, each story was about Vincent, and each story made me sick.

Isabelle read: "It was a dark and stormy morning when the accident occurred. Fate looked down from his throne in the sky and said, 'I choose that man to die today.' Little did Fate know that Vincent Hawk was in the neighborhood."

Oh, please.

Ashley read: "Rain pounded against Vincent's face as he shouted, 'As God is my witness, I will not let this man die!'"

Give me a break.

Chloe read: "Vincent didn't think about his own safety. I mean, what if the man had collapsed from the bird flu? Vincent risked his own life in order to save another."

Whatever.

They read. They blushed. They smiled at Vincent. He soaked up the adoration in his button-down shirt and jeans. The perfect hero, maybe, but not the perfect friend. Enough with the whole good deed thing. Could we just move on?

"Katrina?" Mr. Williams called. "Do you have a story to share?"

"I didn't write about Vincent saving that guy."

"I didn't expect you to write about Vincent. I'm sure I speak for the entire class when I say that I'd like to hear about your own good deed, the one your visitor referred to on Monday."

"I didn't write about that either." A few people groaned. "I made something up."

"Oh." Mr. Williams frowned and tapped his fingers on his desk. "*Well*, let's hear it anyway."

I shouldn't have read it aloud because I wrote the story in a fit of anger while Elizabeth drove me to school. It's never a good idea to read something aloud that you wrote in a fit of anger.

I'd never been mad at Vincent before. Well, just over little things, like the time he had dumped his clarinet spit all over my shoe in sixth-grade band practice, and the time he had purposefully tipped the canoe because he knew murky water freaked me out. Little things, boy things— things that didn't matter.

I stole a glance at him, sitting over there, all dressed up. He had chosen Heidi's feelings over mine!

"Please stand so we can all hear," Mr. Williams said.

"There once lived this girl who was a potato farmer," I read. More students groaned, some fell back in their seats. No one cared, now that it wasn't a story about me and Skirt Guy. I continued. "She worked very hard every day digging her potatoes. On the weekends she took the potatoes to market and sold them. And everything was fine. But then a man bought the land next door and planted potatoes. And come summer, he bought a brand-new tractor so he could dig his potatoes faster. And because he dug faster, he was able to take double the amount of potatoes to market. And because he put them into fancy bags with fancy organic labels, the townspeople started buying his potatoes instead of hers."

I didn't look up. I didn't care if they were bored out of their minds. This story had a point and I was going to make it.

"The girl was desperate. Selling potatoes was her only way to earn money, and the potato festival was in a few days—the biggest sales day of the year. So she asked her best friend if he would help her dig so she could try to get the most potatoes to the festival and the friend said, 'Of course I'll help you because that's what best friends do.' The next day the girl got up early and started digging. But where was her friend?" I took a dramatic pause. Someone sneezed. "The roar of a tractor's engine approached. She looked up from her digging and saw that her friend was driving the neighbor's tractor, in the neighbor's field. She was shocked. 'Why are you driving that tractor?' she asked. 'You know it belongs to my neighbor and he is stealing all of my business.' And her friend said, 'I'm driving it because your neighbor asked me to drive it.' And the girl said, 'So? You're supposed to be helping me get ready for the festival today. I need you.' And the friend said, 'But you never said that today was the day when you needed my help and I really, really like this tractor because it's pretty and I don't want to hurt your neighbor's feelings by not driving it.' And the girl said, 'Whatever! BE THAT WAY! YOU TRAITOR!' "

I sat down.

No one applauded or anything.

Mr. Williams scratched his head. "Uh, Katrina, is that it? Where's the good deed?"

I folded my arms. "There is no good deed. That's the point. There *could* have been a good deed but because the friend was a total jerk, he missed the opportunity to do a good deed."

"But what's the moral?"

"The moral is that sometimes you have to help your friends, even if there are other things you'd rather be doing." I smirked, confident that I had made my point. I felt righteous, sitting atop my wave of truth.

Vincent cleared his throat. "Maybe the moral is that she shouldn't rely on her friend for *everything*. Maybe she should figure out how to save her potato business on her own. Maybe she should *get a life*."

When waves break they can really crush a swimmer, especially if they're carrying bits of broken shells and rocks. Especially if they're carrying hurt feelings.

I didn't go to the rest of my morning classes. As soon as the bell rang I fled World Mythology. Mr. Prince had filled the hallway display case with Heidi's accomplishments.

How to Get into the Ivy League. I caught my reflection as I hurried past, ghostlike with long blond hair and pale eyes. I swear to God it whispered, *"Get a life."*

I didn't care that Elizabeth's car was covered in frost. I yanked the hide-a-key off the back tire, climbed inside, and settled in for a long sulk. When someone tells you to "get a life," what that person is actually saying is: "Your concerns are stupid. They are trivial and beneath me." That's a really mean thing to say to a friend.

That Beatles' song ran through my head—*I get by with a little help from my friends*. Without Vincent, there was only Elizabeth. When had I stopped making friends? When had I decided that two were plenty? Time passed. I did nothing, which is the truth, because sulking is as close to nothing as a person can get. If you ever want to waste time, and I mean waste it in a way that adds not a drop of meaning to your life, anyone else's life, or to the universe itself, then sulking is your answer.

I got hungry. I slid down the seat until the parking lot disappeared and all I could see was Elizabeth's glove box. I reached in and grabbed a pack of Hostess Ding Dongs. How long would it take me to freeze to death?

The driver's door swung open. Elizabeth threw herself into the car, slammed the door, then slid down next to me. "I'm glad you're out here. I can't take that sweaty cafeteria today. Why are you hiding?"

"I don't want to see Vincent. Why are you hiding?"

"I don't want to see Face. I asked him."

"You did?"

"He said he needed to think about it."

"Oh." I tore open the Ding Dongs wrapper with my teeth.

Elizabeth clutched the steering wheel. "That's not bad, is it? I mean, if he didn't want to go with me, then he would have said I can't or something. But if he wanted to go with me, he would have said yes." Her knuckles turned white. "Oh God, he's going to say no, isn't he? This is totally embarrassing. He's going to make me wait and then reject me. I wore these boring clothes for nothing. I hate him."

"Maybe you just surprised him."

"Maybe." She reached over and snagged a Ding Dong. "How long do you think he'll think about it? Should I ask him how long he's going to take? Oh my God, that would look so desperate."

I had no insights to offer Elizabeth. Face was as alien to me as any other guy at Nordby High—including, it turned out, Vincent.

"He thinks I'm fat."

"Elizabeth . . ."

"Forget him. I'm not going to sit around and wait for him to reject me." She finished the gooey cake in two bites. "I'm going to send him a note telling him that I've made other plans. That'll teach him to make me wait." She smacked her hand on the steering wheel. Then she squealed.

A face peered down at us, through the windshield.

We sat up. Malcolm settled on the car's hood, cross-legged, his satchel resting between his legs. The golden letters of *Messenger Service* sparkled. Elizabeth stuck her key in the ignition so she could roll down the window. She leaned out. "Hey, will you deliver a message for me? I want it delivered to this guy at school. Have it say, 'Dear David, I regret to inform you that while waiting for your reply to my kind invitation, I received another offer. Which I accepted.

Regrettably'—no, 'Yours Truly'—no, 'Sincerely, Elizabeth Miller.' Can you do that? Like, right now?"

"I can't do that, I'm afraid. The only messages I'm allowed to deliver are sent directly from my employer."

"I'll pay cash. You won't have to tell your boss."

"I'm afraid that is against the rules." Malcolm tilted his head and looked at me, his expression dead serious. "Why didn't you eat the second bean?" Though the windshield muffled his voice, his question slipped right into my ear. It tickled.

"How does he know that?" Elizabeth whispered.

No way could he have actually known that I hadn't eaten the second bean. Even if he had been spying through the front window of the coffeehouse, he couldn't have seen Ratcatcher. She'd been in the kitchen when she devoured the bean. He was bluffing, playing at his weird game. I rolled down the passenger window and leaned out. "What makes you think I didn't eat it?"

"I'll show you."

Seventeen

Truancy can get you into a lot of trouble at Nordby High, but we left campus anyway, intrigued by Malcolm's promise to show us something. "What's going on?" Elizabeth asked, pulling into the only available parking spot on Main Street.

A big crowd had gathered outside Anna's Old World Scandinavian Coffeehouse, which would have been great had they been waiting to buy Norwegian Egg coffee. But that's not why the crowd had gathered. I recognized a bunch of Main Street shopkeepers and other locals. Joggers and dog walkers had stopped, as had toddlers and parents. Clutching expensive organic drinks, customers drifted out of Java Heaven's front door and squeezed their way into the crowd for a better view.

A better view of what?

Fear set in. Had something happened to my grandmother? Terrible thoughts ran through my mind, everything that can go wrong with an old person—a fall, a stroke, a heart attack. She hadn't been feeling well. Why hadn't I stayed home to take care of her? Why hadn't I paid better attention when Vincent gave that guy CPR? Where was the ambulance? Why wasn't anyone doing anything?

Officer Larsen stood at the edge of the crowd, near the shoe shop. I hurried over to him. "Officer Larsen, where's my grandmother?"

"She's in the coffeehouse, but you shouldn't go in there," he said, writing something on a notepad. His cell phone rang. He turned his back to me before I could ask more questions. "This is Officer Larsen. We've got a situation and it's not pretty."

I went kind of limp, like in those dreams when your legs won't work. *She's in the coffeehouse.* Lying in the coffeehouse? Dying in the coffeehouse? For a moment, panic shut me down.

"Come on," Elizabeth said. I followed in her wake as she elbowed through the crowd. "This is worse than an after-Thanksgiving sale. Let us through. We work here."

Malcolm had disappeared again, but I didn't dwell on that. All I could think about was losing my grandmother. As we forced our way through the crowd, the coffeehouse seemed out of reach. The odd thing was, the crowd wasn't silent the way a crowd is at an accident scene. Everyone was talking and even laughing. With my heart pounding in my ears, I only picked up fragments of conversation.

"Unbelievable."

"Is it dead?"

"Where'd they find it?"

Finally we reached the front windows. Grandma Anna stood inside, wringing her hands. Her apron had come untied. Other than that, she looked unhurt and very much alive. With a huge sigh of relief, my heart stopped its wild dance and my legs stopped shaking. I grabbed the doorknob, but the door was locked, the closed sign faced out. "Grandma?"

"Don't let any of those people in," she said after cautiously opening the door.

Elizabeth and I slipped inside. Grandma Anna locked the door after us. "What's going on?" I asked. Irmgaard stood behind the counter, clutching our big carving knife as if preparing to defend herself.

"What's that smell?" Elizabeth plugged her nose. A stench, a bit like sewage, a bit like a wet dog, polluted the room.

"It's the cat," Grandma Anna said.

"The cat?" I went into panic mode again. Add to my checklist under talents: *Panics Easily*. "What happened to Ratcatcher?"

My grandmother pointed. I gasped. Elizabeth gasped. Ratcatcher lay at the base of the picture window, stretched out in all her black-and-white glory. She turned her chubby chin up and meowed a greeting.

"Oh. My. God." Elizabeth grabbed my arm. "What is she lying on?"

"That's a wharf rat," Ingvar said from the corner table. "Wharf rats can grow to three feet in Norway. Never seen one that big, though."

A stiff black rat body lay on the floor, its long rubbery tail stretched to the wall. Its mouth had frozen in a grimace, its limp tongue hung over a row of sharp teeth. Ratcatcher stretched across the rat's midsection, purring like a proud lioness.

"Ratcatcher actually caught a rat?" I couldn't believe it. For a moment I felt proud of the old girl. Then I thought I might barf. Rats give me the creeps. I don't even want to touch them in a pet store, and those are the little ones. This rat was so big it could have been my dance partner.

"Caught it *and* killed it," Lars said, jabbing his cane in the air. "Look at it. I'm guessing it's a forty-pounder."

"I'm guessing it'll get into that book of world records," Ingvar said. "That cat's going to be famous."

Elizabeth pulled me aside. "Where'd Malcolm go?" she whispered. "We've got to find him."

"Why?"

"Look at what your cat did. Look at all those people." She squeezed my arm. "Don't you see what's happening? Fame."

"It wasn't the bean," I told her.

"Of course it was the bean." She bounced on her toes, her boobs nearly knocking me over. "Don't you get it? Those beans actually work. This is like a fairy tale. We've got to find him and get another one." She stopped bouncing. "Oh crud, I've got to get back for my last class because we have a quiz. If I flunk one more quiz, my dad is going to take away the car. And then I have to go to my mom's stupid holiday work party. Double crud. I'll call you as soon as I can." She started to leave, then came back and whispered, "If you get another bean, don't you even think about eating it without me."

Over the next few hours I learned a lot about rats. Never, according to a *Nordby News* reporter, had a rat that size been found in Nordby or anyplace in the entire world. Some museum in the Midwest owned a prehistoric rat skeleton, from the days when rats had shared caves with saber-toothed tigers. According to the *Guinness Book of World Records,* the largest modern-day rat ever found was a Gambian pouch rat, but it was much smaller than this rat. Our rat. The rat found in Anna's Old World Scandinavian Coffeehouse.

My pastry-loving kitty cat had brought home the World's Largest Rat.

My awe was short-lived. While catching a beaver-sized rat was great for newspaper sales, catching it inside an establishment that serves food and beverages was not so great for that establishment's sales. It was bad. Real bad.

With no curtains to draw or blinds to pull, we had to endure the onlookers. A menagerie of faces continued to press against the picture window—eager, fascinated, disgusted faces. Mr. Darling's face appeared. He smiled, then started talking to Officer Larsen. "Go out there, Katrina, and see what that horrid man is saying," my grandmother said.

Cold air cleared the rat's stench from my nostrils as I stepped outside. Mr. Darling spoke to Officer Larsen in a voice that reached the edges of the crowd. "The Health Department needs to be notified. Rats carry all sorts of communicable diseases—plague, botulism, mad cow disease."

"That place must be filthy," a local said.

"I'd never eat in there," her friend said.

You don't eat in there anyway, I wanted to say. *You lousy traitors. You turned your backs on us the minute Java Heaven moved in.* But instead I said, "It's not filthy. We don't know how the rat got inside." They shook their heads, burning holes through me with their disapproving glares.

Could I blame them? I'd be a bit hesitant to buy sandwiches at the home of the World's Largest Rat. Nothing worse than finding one of those wiry black hairs sticking to a tomato slice, or a rat footprint on your bread, or a rat turd floating in your soup. A beaver-sized rat makes a cockroach infestation seem like a walk through one of those butterfly gardens.

"Anna's is clean," I pleaded. "Very, very, very clean. There's no reason to—"

"Officer Larsen," Mr. Darling interrupted. "I insist that you close Anna's Coffeehouse before someone gets sick."

"No one's going to get sick," I said, but nobody was listening because Mr. Darling had started to pass out Java Heaven coupons.

"Come try our newest drink, the Vincent Mocha, in honor of our hometown hero." He beamed the most joyous smile I'd ever seen as he basked in our crisis. Just when he wanted to buy us out. How *coincidental*.

I followed Officer Larsen into the coffeehouse and he delivered the bad news to my grandmother. "I'm sorry, Anna, but I'm going to have to call the Health Department."

"Don't be such a nincompoop," Lars hissed at his son.

"Dad, I'm just doing my job."

"Why do you have to call the Health Department? That rat didn't live in here," Grandma Anna said, her face turning blotchy. Irmgaard shook her head furiously. "See, Irmgaard is my witness. No rats in here. There's never been a rat in here."

"She caught it outside," I lied, "then brought it in."

"Now, Katrina, there's no need to fib," Officer Larsen said. "I know you don't let your cat outside." He rubbed the back of his neck. "I'm sorry, Anna, but I have to call the Health Department. Besides, if I don't, Mr. Darling will. He's got everyone riled up about communicable diseases."

"There are no diseases in my coffeehouse. Ask The Boys. They've been coming here for twenty years. Have they ever caught a disease?"

Ingvar fiddled with his pipe. "I got nothing to report."

Ralph sipped his coffee. "Doctor says I got acid reflux disease."

Odin moved a game piece. "You don't get that from a rat."

I cleared my throat. "I think Mr. Darling put the rat in here."

My grandmother turned her worried face up at me. "Katrina? What are you saying?"

"He must have put that rat in here. It makes perfect sense. He wants us to close down and move."

"That's a serious accusation. Do you have any evidence?" Officer Larsen asked.

"No. But who else would have done this?" I searched the faces of everyone in the room, but no one nodded or backed me up.

The *Nordby News* photographer pressed his camera against the window and a flash of light lit up the shop. Officer Larsen made his phone call. After the call he told us not to move the rat. He hung yellow tape around, as if it were some sort of murder scene. "Someone from the Health Department will be here tomorrow. In the meantime, call me if you need anything. Dad, I'll pick you up later." Then he left. The Boys bade their good-byes and wandered to the pub. Evening, brittle with cold, crept down Main Street and the nosey onlookers drifted off.

"I can't stand looking at that thing," my grandmother said. She threw a towel over the carcass. Ratcatcher peeked out from under the towel, purring louder as Grandma collapsed into a chair. Irmgaard rushed over with a cup of coffee. "Put a little rum in it, will you please?"

As I stared at the long rubbery tail, my suspicion of Mr. Darling grew. How else could this have happened? He could have bought the rat from a circus. How could I prove that he was behind this? Can a rat be dusted for fingerprints?

Irmgaard started tidying in kitchen. "Why bother?" my grandmother asked. "Did you see the looks on their faces? No one will ever set foot in here again. Over forty years in this town." She took a long sip of her coffee, then sighed. "Go on home, Irmgaard. Take tomorrow off. I'll call you and let you know what the Health Department says."

After a long hug, Irmgaard left. I sat across from my grandmother. Surrounded by Ratcatcher's purring and the rat's stink, we sat for a long time, stunned. What had been most important to me that morning—Vincent's betrayal—seemed totally unimportant. We had a bigger rat to deal with. "Don't you think that Mr. Darling did this?"

Grandma Anna frowned. "You shouldn't say things like that, Katrina. He may be arrogant and a bit of a bully, but putting a rat in our shop would be below even his standards. I just can't believe he'd be capable of such cruelty. It's just bad luck, sweetie. Either that or . . ." She looked at the ceiling. "Or someone up there is trying to tell us something."

Eighteen

My grandmother didn't sleep much that Friday night. Neither did I. I kept thinking that the mutant rat might have some mutant friends with revenge on their minds. I swear that at one point during the night, something walked across my legs. The night-light stayed on after that.

They say it's always darkest just before the dawn. Here's how dark it got.

Saturday morning's headline in the *Nordby News* read: *Ratcatcher, the Coffeehouse Cat, Catches World's Biggest Rat*.

Thanks to the wonders of technology, that article spread all over the world with the click of a Send icon. Isn't that great? Readers in London and Cairo shivered when they read that a rat with a six-foot tail had been sleeping in our pantry. Of course there was no proof that it had been sleeping in our pantry, but an unnamed owner of a certain organic coffeehouse speculated that it had been sleeping there.

Readers in Paris and Moscow squirmed when they read that a rat with feet the size of a St. Bernard had been scurrying all over our counters. Readers in Monte Carlo and

Stockholm gagged when they read that a rat with droppings the size of peanut M&M'S had been lounging on the tables, probably licking the salt shakers. Again, speculation provided by an unnamed source.

Ratcatcher's kill launched all sorts of editorials about rats and disease. Did you know that it only takes a single flea from a rat's back to start an outbreak of bubonic plague? Stores worldwide ran out of rat poison. One ginormous rat meant that there might be other ginormous rats lying in wait to conquer the world. Some environmentalists blamed the rat's size on pollutants. An unnamed source blamed its size on an endless diet of krumkake and sardine sandwiches—weird Old World food that no one should be eating in the first place.

I wanted to dump sardines right on Mr. Unnamed Source's head.

When television stations picked up the story, the focus turned from issues of health to Ratcatcher herself. Her cute, chubby face, a welcome contrast to the gruesome death clench of the rat, was plastered everywhere. "Can we interview her?" a CNN reporter asked.

"She's a cat," I said.

"We'd love to interview her. Can we set up a time? Is she sensitive to bright lights? Has she ever used a microphone? Does she have an agent?"

"She's a cat."

Grandma and I hid upstairs. Since we didn't usually have Saturdays off, we weren't really sure what to do with ourselves. We ate some scrambled eggs and puttered around. I couldn't focus on homework. I wanted to call Vincent but didn't. Anyway, he should have called to say he was sorry.

But what if he wasn't sorry? What if he had meant those

mean words? I was just this bothersome friend without a life and our friendship had run its course. He had moved on to better and prettier things. I missed him terribly. Being accused of spreading bubonic plague would have felt a lot less horrid with Vincent by my side.

"What's this?" I asked, picking up a brochure that lay on the table.

"Mr. Darling sent that over." She waved it away in disgust. "He bought one of the units for his mother. Poor woman."

The brochure was for Retirement Universe, a sprawl of pink and yellow cottages in South Florida. Each cottage looked exactly the same, and so did the residents with their silver hair and leathery bronzed skin. Couples dressed in plaid shorts and polo shirts rode golf carts and laughed as if they were having the time of their lives. I'd never seen my grandmother in shorts. Face would probably retire in a place like that.

"So much sun isn't good for a person," Grandma Anna said. She glanced at the wall clock, then drummed her fingers on the table. "I wish the Health Department would show up and take that horrid thing away so we can get on with our lives."

"Grandma, what if they close us down?"

She rubbed her tired eyes. "I don't know."

"How bad are things? I mean, how much money do you owe?"

She took her dish to the sink. "You know I don't like to talk about money."

"But we have to talk about it. It's obviously a problem. I've seen the bills downstairs."

She didn't say anything. She leaned against the counter.

"Do you think that maybe we should go ahead and accept Mr. Darling's offer?" I hated to ask, but it was the obvious, though repulsive, solution.

Her shoulders stiffened. "I'd rather take money from the devil." Then her shoulders sagged as if her courageous facade had become too heavy to wear. "But we may have to." At that moment, her voice soft, her eyes weary, she seemed older than her seventy years. I'd gotten used to her slower movements, to the growing number of pills on the bathroom counter and to the more frequent naps. But then and there her vulnerability hit me hard. She was the adult. She was my family. Her vulnerability was my vulnerability.

Late Saturday morning, Ratcatcher finally abandoned her kill. After chowing down a piece of coffeecake, she retreated to my bedroom and fell asleep in my laundry basket, bored with the whole rat thing. To the disappointment of the gawkers who continued to gather outside the window, we kept the towel over the carcass. As ordered, we didn't touch the stupid yellow crime tape.

Elizabeth called a hundred times that morning to shriek about how famous my cat was and to ask if I had seen Malcolm. I hadn't seen Malcolm, but then again, I hadn't left the building since the rat incident. Vincent never called. Turned out the swim team was away in Eastern Washington for a weekend meet. I know for a fact that there are newspapers in Eastern Washington. Surely he had heard about our disaster. Guess he was still pissed about my story in World Mythology class—about my calling him a traitor. But I couldn't forget his comment. I had a life. It was falling apart, but it was mine.

The Health Department official arrived in the afternoon. Every time we asked a question he said, "I can't answer that question until I've run a full inspection."

"But what if someone else put the rat in here on purpose?" I asked. "Isn't that against the law?"

"I can't answer that question until I've run a full inspection."

"But doesn't this seem strange? Rats don't grow this big in Nordby."

"I can't answer that question until I've run a full inspection."

He got real snippy about the towel. He picked it up with a pair of tongs and stuck it into a garbage bag. His thick greasy hair was coated with some kind of gel. Who does that? And he kept a puckered expression on his face as if everything displeased him. "A rat this size is nothing to mess around with," he said, taking out a gas mask.

"I didn't mess around with it," Grandma Anna told him. "I just didn't want to look at it."

"Let's hope you didn't mess with it." He held up the mask. "Bubonic spores and other contaminants can be carried through the air."

Well, that's just great. Good to know, after we'd been breathing *the air* all night.

He put on the mask, then a pair of gloves. I turned away as he stuffed the dead rat into another garbage bag. When he had packed up all his gear he said, "I'll be back on Wednesday at ten a.m. to conduct a full inspection. Until then, this place is closed."

"What?" My grandmother spit the word. "I can't stay closed until Wednesday. I'm running a business."

"That's the best I can do. I'm the only inspector for this area." He tacked a sign to the door. *Closed by the Health Department Until Further Notice.*

"Do you have to put that there? People will think the worst," Grandma Anna said.

"I'm afraid they already do," I mumbled.

Mr. Health Inspector heaved the bagged rat over his shoulder. "Don't remove that sign or I'll fine you five hundred dollars. It's the law." He left.

My grandmother called Officer Larsen. "A sign. Right on the door. You come over here and take it down. Right now. . . . What do you mean you can't? My husband worked for the police department for thirty-five years. That ought to account for something." She slammed the receiver. "How can we survive if they won't let us stay open?" Then she called Irmgaard to tell her the bad news.

I vacuumed the carpet for fifteen minutes straight, then sprayed some air freshener. As far as I could remember, the coffeehouse had never felt so gloomy. That yellow Health Department sign might as well have been neon, the way it glowed. *Attention: Death Trap!* Grandma retreated to her bedroom. She told me that she needed some time to herself. With an entire afternoon looming before me, I packed up my things and took the bus to Elizabeth's to do homework. I put on my grandfather's huge goose-down parka to protect me from the winter's cold and the coldness of judgmental stares.

Millie was driving the bus that day. She asked about Malcolm. I told her I hadn't seen him. The bus hummed as it turned off Main Street and drove up Viking Way, past the school. The lady next to me worked her knitting needles. .

Would Malcolm show up again? What would I say if he offered me another bean? I shook my head. They were chocolate-covered coffee beans, nothing more. Acme Supply Company had given us ten sample boxes. I'd eaten three of the boxes long before meeting Malcolm, and nothing weird had happened. But still, my life had been anything but normal since meeting him.

Elizabeth lived on the hill above the school, in the only gated community in Nordby. A manicured green space wound around the cedar and river-rock homes. She had this bulldog that always tried to tear off my shoes when I walked through the door.

"Get off me, Mr. Big," I snarled.

"Elizabeth's in her room," Mrs. Miller told me.

Elizabeth sat at her computer, her hair wound in a tie-dyed scarf. "I've checked my e-mails all morning. Nothing. He hasn't called either."

"Vincent?"

"No. Face." She was still in her pajamas—pink, with Marilyn Monroe faces. "What's he trying to do, torture me? What did I ever do to him?"

I pushed aside a colony of velvet pillows and sat on her bed. Her feather mattress bore the weight of my worries effortlessly.

She stuck out her lower lip. "Maybe he wants somebody better and if nobody better comes along, then he'll settle for me. Maybe that's why he's waiting."

"Why don't you call him?" I asked.

"What? Then he'll think I'm needy."

We were both waiting for a guy to call, as if that would make everything right in the world. I felt even sorrier for myself than I had before. Elizabeth checked her cell phone. "If I call him he'll think I'm in love with him."

"You kind of are, aren't you?"

"Maybe. But he doesn't need to know that. What's the matter with you? Why are you talking so softly?"

"I'm depressed. The Health Department closed us down."

"Oh. That sucks." She clicked madly on the keyboard. "But here's the good news. Your cat is the most popular thing on the Internet. Look at this video." Someone had filmed yesterday's event. They got a real good close-up of the rat. And there I stood, looking dumbfounded as Mr. Darling advised Officer Larsen to notify the Health Department.

"Does my mouth always hang open like that?"

Elizabeth clicked some more. "It's got over three million hits. This is the biggest thing on the Internet since those naked guys made fish and chips."

Just great. I lay back and stared at the painted stars on Elizabeth's ceiling.

"Your cat is FAMOUS," Elizabeth sang. "If we had eaten the bean, Katrina, we'd be famous right now."

"It has nothing to do with that bean. Mr. Darling put that rat in our coffeehouse."

"Where would he get a rat like that?"

"Oh, he'd manage. He probably stole it from the zoo."

"If he stole it, then someone would be looking for it. And no one is looking for it. You can't ignore what happened— first to Vincent and then your cat." She threw a pillow at me. "Open your eyes, Katrina. Those beans are amazing. We've got to find Malcolm and get some more."

"Elizabeth, stop talking about those beans. I've got

serious problems." I sat up. "Business hasn't been good lately. That's why I was so excited about Vincent's help at the festival. Grandma's got a whole bunch of bills on her desk that she can't pay. And we can't make money if we're closed. And even if we reopen, who's gonna come to our coffeehouse now? That rat has ruined us."

Why did I feel so ashamed? Our failure was not due to laziness. Irmgaard, Grandma, and I worked hard every day. But I realized that I should have done more. I should have helped my grandmother keep up with the world outside our doors. When she had said no to wireless, no to going organic, no to paper instead of styrofoam, I should have insisted.

"The thing is, if the coffeehouse fails and we can't pay rent, then we'll lose the space and we'll never be able to find another space that cheap. We have an agreement with the landlord. It's the cheapest rent in Nordby."

If I'd been talking about anything other than money, Elizabeth wouldn't have looked so perplexed. Even quantum physics would have been easier for her to digest. But money had never been a concern of hers. She owned every high-tech gadget available. She had a closet filled with new clothes, some she would never wear. She ordered take-out whenever she felt like it.

"If your grandma needs money, my dad can loan her some."

"Thanks, but there's no way my grandmother would accept that. She'd die if she knew I was telling you this."

"Then we need to find your angel friend and get another bean."

"He's not an angel." I remembered Irmgaard's book. I hadn't had a moment to look at it.

"How do you know? Angels can appear any place, any

time. They help people when they need help. Seems to me that you need help, Katrina. How do we find him?"

"I don't know. He's just shows up."

She turned back to her keyboard. "He said that messages have to go through his employer. So we'll call his employer and have a message sent to ourselves. When Malcolm delivers it to us, we'll ask for another bean. What's his employer called?"

"It just says *Messenger Service* on his satchel. This is a waste of time, Elizabeth. I've got to figure out how to save the coffeehouse."

"That's what I'm trying to do." She typed madly. "Nothing's coming up. Is there some type of logo?"

"No. Just gold letters. I can't believe you're trying to find a guy who claims to have magic beans. Don't you think that's crazy?"

"I'll tell you what's crazy. My asking Face to the Solstice, that's what's crazy." She clicked madly. "No messenger services listed in Nordby. There's only one listed in Bremerton and it's called Lilly's Messenger Service and the logo is pink."

"Don't worry about it," I said.

"OH!" She slammed her hand on the desk. "I just figured it out. Of course. We can't find his employer because, if he's an angel, then his employer is . . . God. We can't send an e-mail to *God*."

I rolled my eyes and sank back into the pillows.

I couldn't sleep that night. At ten thirty Ratcatcher knocked over a glass. I went downstairs to clean it up. I tightened my bathrobe belt and hid in the dark kitchen as Java Heaven employees wandered by, having finished the late shift. Were they going to a party? If Vincent had been home and if we hadn't been mad at each other we might have gone to a movie. He liked popcorn with that fake cheese powder sprinkled on top. I liked Junior Mints. Vincent always said that they tasted like toothpaste, so I never had to share, which was perfect because I can eat an entire box. Last weekend we had gone to see a spy movie. Last weekend we had been on speaking terms. Last weekend our world had been without fortune and fame.

The dark pressed in on me but I didn't want to turn on the light, in case someone else wandered by. *Look at the Norwegian girl, sitting alone in that plague-filled coffeehouse. Take a picture of her and put it on a postcard.* The place felt doomed with its lingering eau de rat and the big yellow sign burning a hole on the front door. The king and queen of Norway stared from the wall. They'd never eat in a place like this.

No way would I be able to sleep. Maybe I could do some homework or read something to distract myself. My backpack sat on one of the stools. I pulled the little book from it. *Angels Among Us.* I opened it.

At the bottom of the inside cover, printed in little gold letters was: *Property of Sister Irmgaard. Abbey of St. Clare.* Wow. Irmgaard had been a nun?

The book was mostly a collection of old drawings and paintings. It was divided into three sections: "The Messenger," "The Guardian," and "The Fallen."

I flipped through oil paintings of winged creatures in white robes. I recognized some of the painters—Raphael, Michelangelo, and Caravaggio. Then I stopped flipping.

It was Malcolm. His perfect face, his electric eyes, his long brown and copper hair, his strong legs. The artist's name was Carlino Botolucci and his painting was called *The Messenger*, painted in 1845. A shiver darted up my spine. I'd rationalized all the strange happenings, but this portrait jarred me to my core. I ran to the back door. The alley was empty. Where was he? I ran out the front door and stood on the sidewalk.

"Malcolm," I whispered, wrapping my arms around my pink bathrobe as icy wind stung my bare ankles. Music drifted from the pub, but not a single person walked along Main Street. Darkness gathered in the distance where the streetlights ended. My bare feet went numb against the cold cement.

"Malcolm. Where are you?"

"You'd better come in." He stuck his head out our front door. "It looks like a storm is brewing."

Nineteen

Just a whisper and he had appeared.

How had he gotten inside the coffeehouse? That should have been the question on my mind, but all I could think about was the glow.

Though the sun had set hours ago, I could have sworn it was hiding right behind Malcolm's back, wrapping its golden rays around him in a bright hug. Light shot out of the doorway like one of those paintings in the angel book. Was that a halo hanging over his head?

I couldn't move. Was this real? Aren't people who see angels crazy? Maybe I had a brain tumor or maybe I was on the brink of a seizure.

"Katrina?"

As he stepped through the doorway, the glow faded back to its source—a light fixture above the kitchen counter. Not heavenly, after all. I let out a huge breath, feeling disappointed and relieved at the same time. Coming face-to-face with an otherwordly being would be amazing *and* freaky. I had jumped to an impossible conclusion. His resemblance to the painting was explainable. If I pulled back Elizabeth's hair, wiped off her makeup, and moved time forward ten years, she could look exactly like the *Mona Lisa*. Sort of.

"Katrina?" He held out his hand. A sudden gust slapped his kilt against his thighs. "You're not dressed properly for the cold. Come inside."

I thought about taking his hand but felt too self-conscious. The gust swept across my terry-cloth bathrobe. Why was I wearing that old thing? Why didn't I own one of those glamorous bathrobes made of silk with a boa hem? I needed to get one of those. And some matching high heels with boa tufts. Elizabeth had a bathrobe from France. My bathrobe was from Wal-Mart. And why had I taken off my mascara and pulled my hair into a knot? I probably looked like I had the flu.

He held the door for me. As I walked toward him, I imagined stepping into the balmy paradise of a tropical island, because that's what it felt like. The winter wind kept its distance, as if Malcolm stood in a bubble of summer. Once inside, eau de rat was replaced by eau de Malcolm. Did he keep a spritzer in his pocket? "Where did you go?" I asked.

"Business."

"Irmgaard, the woman who works here, thinks you're an angel."

"Does she now?"

He shut the door. We were alone, at night, and I still had no proof that he wasn't crazy—just a gut feeling. If he had any sinister plans, this would be the perfect opportunity. I walked behind the counter, using it as a shield.

"Why does she think you're an angel?"

"Because I delivered a message to her."

"You did? When?"

"After I woke up in your alley. You've no need to fear me, Katrina." He laid his satchel on a table, then stood in front of the portrait of the King and Queen of Norway. "Is this your family?"

"No. My parents' photo is over there." I pointed to the photo that Grandma kept near the cash register. My mother, the source of my pale blond hair, stood on a beach with my father on their wedding day. "They died in a car accident when I was three. Do you have a family?"

He ran a finger along the portrait's frame. "Messengers don't have families." He said it matter-of-factly.

"But who do you live with?"

"No one."

My first impression of him was true, after all. "You're homeless?"

"I suppose you could say that, since messengers don't have homes. We're nomads. We go where we're needed." He turned his attention to the counter, running his hand along its surface, stopping to examine the salt shakers, napkin containers, a vase of fake flowers—inspecting the items as if he'd never seen them before. I was looking at him in much the same way.

"How old are you?" I asked.

"I'm not sure." He opened the lid of a jam pot. "Young, though, compared to the others. What's this?"

"Loganberry jam."

He smelled it, then tilted back his head and dumped the entire contents of the pot into his mouth. I shuddered, thinking how sickly sweet so much jam would taste. He swallowed, then smiled. "That was quite good. I don't get much opportunity to try food. I'm not supposed to partake of local customs, but sometimes I can't help myself. In Scotland I tried a boiled pudding." He found another jam pot and downed its contents, and then another.

"Malcolm?" I leaned against the counter, my head spinning with questions. What was true and what was delusion? Did he really work for a messenger service? Did he really have no home or family? Why had Vincent gotten fortune and why had Ratcatcher gotten fame? And why did the portrait in Irmgaard's book look just like him?

"Why does Irmgaard think you're an angel?" I paused. "Are you?"

"Some call me that." He wiped his mouth with the back of his hand. "I don't think that last one was loganberry."

"Marmalade." I felt sweaty all of a sudden. "This is crazy."

"Sorry. Did you not want me to eat the marmalade?"

"No. You telling me that you're an angel. That's crazy."

He scowled. "I am many things, but in good faith I am not crazy."

"Angels are supposed to have wings and they wear white robes and fly around with harps."

He closed the jam pot and frowned. "Says who?"

"Says every artist that ever painted one." I held out the book.

He folded his arms. "I've seen that book and only two of those artists actually met an angel—Michelangelo and Botolucci, and they both decided to add halos and wings to the portraits because that was what the people of their time expected. I don't think that portrait looks anything like me."

It looked exactly like him. "Prove that you're an angel," I said.

"You mean you want me to make frogs fall from the sky? Or . . . make time stand still?"

Time stand still? That moment flashed in my mind, standing on the sidewalk, the world frozen around me, staring at his face and lips. Wanting to kiss him. "You did that? You actually made time stand still?"

He shrugged. "Don't expect me to do it again or I'll be getting demoted for sure. I don't want to go back to stuffing envelopes."

"What do you mean?"

He pulled a golden envelope from his satchel. The envelope's surface glittered like golden fish scales. "See this?" I nodded. "This is the message for Irmgaard." He dropped it onto the table. It landed with a loud *clunk*.

"But you said you delivered it."

"I delivered it, but she wouldn't take it. And she still won't. I've tried and tried. And each day that it goes undelivered, it gets heavier. Go on, try to lift it."

I walked over to the table and tried to pick up the glittering piece of paper. The envelope was heavier than a bag of cement. I only managed to lift a corner. How could it weigh so much? Then Malcolm reached out and whisked it off the table with his index finger and thumb. I stuck my hands into my bathrobe pockets to hide my trembling. Sometimes the truth sneaks up on you like a chill. "How'd you do that?"

"Do what?"

"Make it so heavy?"

"It does that on its own, to punish me for not delivering

it. It's my one and only duty as a messenger. But Irmgaard keeps refusing it."

"Why?"

"She's afraid of what the message might say." He tucked the envelope back into his satchel, as if it weighed no more than an envelope should.

"Is Irmgaard's message bad news?"

"I don't know. I'm afraid there's a Law of Confidentiality. Truth be told, I messed up. I let myself be seen, when I should have just slipped the message to her while she was sleeping. I'm always making a mess of things, just like I did by giving you two wishes that you obviously didn't want in the first place." He looked at me again, right through my skin and into my bones, seeing me like a guy with X-ray glasses. "I should have paid closer attention. I know what it's like to want something, yet not want to admit it to anyone."

Was he reading my mind? "If you still want to give me a reward, then you can give me a big pile of money."

"But you already asked for fortune."

"Yes, but I didn't get it. And now I really, really need it."

He shook his head. "You can't be asking for the same thing. If fortune was your true desire, then that bean wouldn't have gone to someone else. I'm not going to hand over another wish until I'm sure it's your true heart's desire. One more mistake and I'll have no chance of ever getting promoted." He slid off the stool. "You got anything more to eat?"

He walked into the kitchen, opened the refrigerator, and pulled out a cube of butter. Before I could stop him, he took a bite. He worked the butter around in his mouth, then swallowed. "Bit odd," he said, setting the rest of the cube onto the counter.

"Why can't I ask for fortune if it's what I want? You said you're supposed to give me what I want."

"There's a difference between what you want and what you desire. I'm sure you could list a hundred things that you want, like a new bathrobe, for instance. But desire is a deeper longing. It comes from the soul, not from the mind."

One moment he was eating butter like a child, the next he was speaking eloquently. The light from the kitchen bulb did that thing again, where it gathered at Malcolm's edges, illuminating him like an actor on stage. His aura seeped into me. It melted the half-eaten cube of butter. What was I feeling exactly? Why did I want to kiss him?

Someone knocked on the front door. Outside, Vincent leaned his bike against the picture window. The clock read midnight. "Why are you out so late?" I asked after opening the door.

"I just got back. The bus ride took forever." He pointed to the Health Department's sign. "My dad told me about the rat. Did they really close you down?"

Cold wind whipped through the coffeehouse. I pulled Vincent inside and closed the door. Eau de Malcolm gave way to chlorine freshness. "What's *he* doing here?" Vincent asked, pointing at my guest.

Standing in a beam of refrigerator light, Malcolm squirted ketchup into his mouth.

"He's . . . visiting," I said.

Vincent narrowed his eyes and his voice took on a fatherly tone. "Why's he here at midnight?"

Malcolm licked the inside of a mustard lid, then said,

"I'm here at midnight because I'm fulfilling Katrina's desire."

"What?" Vincent did a quick scan of my bathrobe. "Oh jeez, Katrina, you don't even know the guy."

"It's not like that," I tried to explain. How could he think such a thing?

"Whatever. Didn't mean to interrupt. I rode over here because I was worried about you. I'll be sure to call next time." Then he put his mouth next to my ear. "I thought you had better taste than that." He slammed the door on his way out. Or maybe the wind slammed it. I'm not quite sure.

I opened the door. "And I thought *you* had better taste!"

He gripped his chrome handlebars. "You need to get used to the fact that I'm going out with Heidi."

"Well, maybe I'm going out with someone," I said.

"Whatever. You can do what you want. I'd never tell you who you could or couldn't date. If you started going out with someone, I'd accept it. I wouldn't act like a total jerk about it."

"Oh, really? Then why'd you get so mad just now?"

"Because he's not right for you. Look at him. He's a weirdo."

"Well, Heidi's not right for you. She's a phony."

"She's not a phony."

"Well, he's not a weirdo." I didn't turn around to look at Malcolm because he was probably eating dish soap or mayonnaise or something.

Vincent frowned. "Are you actually telling me that you're going out with a homeless guy you just met?"

"Yes." The lie couldn't be stopped. Who was he to get

all judgmental? As if Heidi Darling, manic do-gooder, was better than a Real-Life Angel. "He's taking me to the Solstice Festival." I folded my arms, trying to look confident.

"I thought you had to work."

"What's the point, now that you're not helping us sell Hero Hot Chocolate?"

"Whatever." Vincent lifted himself onto his bike and pedaled away.

"That's right," I yelled. "Whatever!"

Inside, Malcolm leaned on the counter, his little black book propped in front of him. "It says in here that the third-most common thing people ask for is love." He raised his eyebrows. "Is that what you might be desiring? Love?"

Before I could deny anything, or get defensive, or even laugh, my grandmother appeared at the bottom of the stairs.

"Katrina!" She held her hand over her chest. "I . . . I . . . I—" Her face clenched in pain. She staggered, reaching for the counter.

Malcolm caught her as she fell.

Twenty

They wouldn't let me ride in the ambulance. There wasn't enough room or something stupid. The paramedic put a mask over my grandmother's face, which was my last image of her before they closed the ambulance doors. I tried to call out, tried to tell her not to be scared, but the words wouldn't come. How do you tell someone it's going to be okay when it doesn't look like it's going to be okay?

Would she die with a horrid plastic mask on her face—with only a stranger in a uniform at her side?

"You should have a bigger ambulance!" I yelled as it drove away.

I ran into the coffeehouse and grabbed my grandmother's car keys and purse. I felt light-headed. I couldn't breathe fast enough. From far, far away, Ratcatcher meowed, begging for attention. I stumbled for the back door. Nothing mattered, not the magic bean, not Vincent's love life, not the checklist or the Health Department or the unpaid bills. The weight of the moment crushed me as my grandmother lingered between this world and the next. A moment like that puts everything into perspective.

We kept the old Buick in the alley, next to Mr. Darling's hybrid. The starter motor churned as I turned the key. I'd gotten my license three months ago, after lessons from Vincent's dad, but had only driven the car a handful of times. I turned the key again. It didn't start. Why wouldn't it start? The tank was half full. "Start." I turned it, and turned it, and turned it. I slammed my hand on the steering wheel. "START!"

Malcolm slid onto the passenger seat. He closed the door, then wrapped his fingers around my hand as I desperately gripped the key. "Try it again," he said calmly. One more turn and the engine started. His hand lingered for a moment, then he pulled away and looked out the window. It felt right that he was sitting beside me, as if he belonged there. As if I'd always driven with him next to me.

I backed out of the alley, then turned onto Main Street. The nearest hospital was located in Bremerton, a thirty-minute drive from Nordby Harbor. I had only been to the hospital once before, when Irmgaard had slipped in a puddle of spilled coffee and had gashed her leg. During that visit I hadn't felt sick to my stomach—hadn't felt as if my world could disappear as easily as coffee grounds in a windstorm.

Don't let her die, I repeated in my head, over and over and over. "Malcolm, do you think she's going to die?" He didn't say anything. I nearly drove through a red light. "I don't want her to die. Do you understand? That's what I want more than anything in the world. That's what I most desire."

"I believe you. But I don't have the power of life or death." He pushed back his hair. "I'm sorry."

My stomach curled into a knot. Something bad was going to happen.

We drove into the city. Store lights and headlights rushed by in an endless river. I turned into a crowded parking lot. This was the only hospital for the entire county. *Emergency Room* glowed in red letters from across the pavement. An ambulance sat outside the automatic doors. I parked crooked, taking up two spaces, then I leaped out of the car and ran as fast as I could.

What is that smell that greets you when you step into a hospital? Cleaner? Formaldehyde? Vomit? Or is that what fear smells like, leaking out of the pores of the patients and their families? The overhead lights nearly blinded me. I squinted, looking for directions. *Waiting Room. Restrooms. Information Desk.* My anxiety doubled as I hurried toward the desk. A black woman sat there, her hair pulled into dozens of tight braids.

"May I help you?"

"I'm looking for my grandmother."

"Her name?"

"Anna Svensen." Tears pooled in my lower lids. Her name had never sounded so small, so delicate.

The woman typed, looked at her monitor, then typed some more. "She's not listed."

"They brought her in an ambulance."

"When?"

"Just now."

"It takes a while for the patient's information to show up on my screen. Please take a seat and I'll call you as soon as it becomes available." She spoke kindly, which struck me as miraculous at one o'clock in the morning.

"But where is she? Is she dead?"

"They're probably assessing her. As soon as her name pops up, I'll call you. Your name?"

"Katrina Svensen."

"And what is your relationship to the . . ." The woman stopped talking. Her brown eyes widened as she stared over my head. I didn't need to turn around. I knew that Malcolm stood directly behind me, not only because the hellish stench had disappeared, but because the receptionist looked like she might swoon.

"Hello?" I waved my hand until she blinked. "How long do you think I'll have to wait before her name pops up?"

"Not long. Please take a seat in the waiting room."

When a receptionist says "Not long," she actually means "Oh, somewhere between NOW and ETERNITY."

I immediately despised the waiting room, with its plastic blue chairs and cold linoleum floor. Waiting was not what I wanted to do. Waiting accomplished nothing.

Worried people sat in that horrid room, wringing their hands, trying to find distraction in copies of *Field & Stream* and *Good Housekeeping*. An enormous fish tank sat in the corner. Fish tanks are supposed to be soothing with their little *bubble-bubble* noises and their soft colors. But even the languid movements of the fish didn't calm me. The only place that felt safe was next to Malcolm, who stood in front of the aquarium. The tank's light danced across his face. Just a few days ago I had wanted him to go away, but now I was drawn to him, seeking that familiar scent and the aura of warmth that radiated from his body. Seeking the calm that I used to find in Vincent.

I clenched my jaw. Was she okay? Was she in pain? If Malcolm hadn't been there to catch her, she might have broken a hip or worse.

He leaned closer to the tank, his eyes darting with the fish's movements. "I understand this sensation."

"Swimming?"

"No. Captivity."

"You don't like being a . . . messenger?"

"It's not a matter of liking or disliking. It's what I've been chosen to do." He crouched, nose to nose with a clownfish. "I'm not supposed to feel this way."

"You mean, like you're stuck?"

"Yes." He whispered the word, then turned and looked up at me. Something had changed in his eyes. His gaze had intensified and I couldn't break away. I didn't want to break away.

For the first time since meeting him, I knew exactly what he was talking about. I had never said "Hey, I really want to spend most of my free time working in my grandmother's coffeehouse." But she needed me. So I worked. There was a time when I really enjoyed it, back when the place was crowded. I knew what the regulars wanted without even asking. I could work the phone and the register at the same time and keep all the orders straight. We'd all share stories and town gossip, like it was just a big communal living room. But now I felt imprisoned by a place that no longer fit, like trying to press a growing foot into last year's shoe.

A siren snapped me back to the waiting room. The entry doors opened and a paramedic rushed in, pushing an old man in a wheelchair. Another paramedic held an IV above the old man's head. They disappeared through a pair of double doors at the end of the hallway. *No Admittance*. My grandmother was somewhere behind those doors. Maybe dying. Maybe already dead.

"Katrina Svensen?"

I rushed to the reception desk. The receptionist smiled politely.

"Your grandmother is in intensive care. No visitors are allowed until they've stabilized her."

I clutched my grandmother's purse. She was unstable, like a three-legged chair, like Lars without his cane—like a person teetering between life and death. "Is she going to be okay?"

The woman piled some papers onto her counter. "These need to be filled out. Do you have her insurance card?"

"I'm not sure."

She placed a pen on top of the pile and raised her eyebrows. "Someone has to fill these out. Her insurance information is required."

I shuffled through the papers. So many questions: Social Security number, current medications, primary and secondary insurance. I didn't know any of that stuff.

"Can't I just see her and then fill these out?" I pleaded.

The receptionist shook her head. Her braids jingled. "I can't let you go back there until the nurse or doctor says it's okay."

"But I'm not a visitor. I'm her granddaughter."

"It's policy."

"I just want to know what's happening."

"And you will. Soon."

"How soon?"

"I don't know."

Newscasters often use the phrase "something snapped." The guy who walked into the post office and started shooting people, or the woman who ran her husband over with their car—they were both perfectly normal people until *something snapped*. What is that *something*? Is it actually a part of the brain that fills with frustration until it stretches to the point where it explodes?

Malcolm stood staring at the fish, lost in their watery world. I couldn't stand it one second longer. I ran for the double doors, burst right through them, my head whipping left and right. Where was she? The old guy in the wheelchair sat in the first room. He was moaning as someone in scrubs examined him. I gripped my grandmother's purse, scurrying down the hall like an escaped lunatic in my bathrobe and slippers. I found a pregnant woman who was breathing really fast. A doctor told her that they were going to take her to surgery for a C-section. The next two rooms stood empty. I found a supply closet and some blinking machines. WHERE WAS SHE? The hallway seemed to stretch on and on forever, reflecting the overhead lights like a nightmarish house of mirrors.

"Young lady, you're not supposed to be in here." A security guard grabbed my arm. "You'll have to wait in the waiting room."

"But . . ." I considered hitting him with the purse, but it was too light and flimsy to knock him out. I'd probably get arrested. "I just want to tell her that I'm here."

"We have rules." With a firm grip, he led me back through the double doors.

As we emerged into the lobby, I yanked my arm from his grip, totally humiliated and frustrated. A stress headache erupted in my temples. The magazine readers looked up from their magazines. The receptionist frowned. The security man pointed to a chair. Its blue plastic creaked as I sat.

The receptionist walked over and handed me the pile of papers, but as she did this, Malcolm slipped through the double doors, unnoticed. The receptionist and the security guy went back to the information desk and started talking about some new restaurant that had just opened. I stayed in that chair, quiet and obedient so as not to raise suspicion. I pretended to fill in the paperwork, but my peripheral gaze never left those doors. Malcolm would find her. I had failed, but I knew that he wouldn't.

Five minutes later, while the security guy and the receptionist blatantly flirted, Malcolm emerged. He sat next to me.

"Well?" Some of the papers slid from my lap.

"She had a wee heart attack."

"Oh my God." I let the rest of the papers fall away. "Is she . . . ?"

"She's alive." He placed his hand on my arm and my heartbeat slowed. "It's not her time, Katrina. She won't be leaving you."

That was the best thing that anyone had ever said to me. A wave of relief rolled down my body, then I burst into tears, disrupting all the important magazine reading. Malcolm reached out, hesitated, then scratched his head, clearly unsure what to do. "Are you unhappy?" he asked with a frown.

"I'm happy." I rubbed my eyes. "Very happy. Thanks for finding her. And thanks for catching her."

"You're most welcome. I wish I could do more for you, Katrina." He sat back in the chair and stretched out his legs, propping his sandaled feet on the coffee table.

That's when I saw it. Right behind his left ankle. It

appeared for just a moment and then disappeared. It had nothing to do with the fact that my eyes were still blurry with tears. I saw it. A tiny white wing.

And that's the moment when I truly let myself believe.

Twenty-one

Calling Irmgaard was always an odd experience. I knew she was there because she had picked up the phone and I could hear her breathing. I tried to remember exactly what the doctor had said. My grandmother had suffered a moderate heart attack and needed to stay a few more days for tests and observation. Irmgaard caught her breath a few times. Despite what little I knew about her, I knew that she cared deeply for my grandmother. Otherwise, why would she work such long hours and fill in whenever grandmother's arthritis acted up? Why would she bring in those little bouquets in the summer or make Grandma's favorite carrot soup on dark winter afternoons? Without ever exchanging a word, she had become part of our family. But while she shared our moments, we never seemed to share hers. She didn't let us into her life outside the coffeehouse.

I waited for her to hang up first, so I could be sure she had heard everything. Then I called Vincent. He'd want to know. Vincent and my grandmother had always been close.

When we were little, she used to plan his birthday parties, since his dad was always exhausted from his night shift at the marina. She'd make the cake and drive us to the swimming pool or the bowling alley. She was there when Vincent got chicken pox, when he crashed his bike and needed stitches, and when he swam in his first meet.

"Sorry to call so late but Grandma's had a heart attack," I told Vincent's message machine. "She's at Bremerton General." Someone picked up the phone.

"Katrina?" Vincent's voice was groggy. I looked at the wall clock. Two o'clock. "What happened to Anna?"

His voice brought tears to my eyes. Just like that. Because I could hear his worry and that brought my worry back to the surface. But I tried to hide it. I told him what had happened, though in shorter sentences than I normally would, trying not to reveal how scared I felt. Trying to put up a front, which I never used to do with Vincent. I wanted him to think that I was strong. That I didn't need him for everything.

"I haven't seen her yet because they have to stabilize her first."

"I'll be right there. I don't want you to be alone."

"I'm not alone. Malcolm's here."

Dead silence. When he spoke, his tone was icy. "I'll come anyway."

"No. Don't." Truth was, I was still mad at him. Grandma's near-death experience should have snapped me out of it, should have made me take stock of all the good things in my life. But I was exhausted, and stressed, and raw. If he cared about my grandmother, why would he have abandoned us for the festival just so he could hang out with

Heidi? Just so she could add *Dating a Hero* to her checklist. "It's late. They don't want her to have visitors. Not yet." I was trying to hurt him by keeping him away. Trying to make him feel left out. It was one of the biggest jerk moments of my life. "I'll call you later."

I leaned against the wall. Everything had changed. Friendships inevitably run their course. Even if he'd never started dating Heidi, there would have been something else to pull us apart. He would have gone off to college, probably out of state. But then we would have parted as friends. For a moment I felt as if I were drowning. He was right. I needed to get a life.

Malcolm walked up, carrying a plate loaded with gelatin. The orange and green squares wobbled like alien guts. At that moment he looked like a kid, the way he smiled as if he'd just discovered buried treasure.

"Where'd you get that?" I asked.

"There's a room downstairs filled with food. I've never laid eyes on this sort." He offered me the plate. I'm not usually a fan of Jell-O, not since someone told me that it was made from horse's hooves, but I was half-starved. I slurped down six green squares. "I can get more if you'd like. They let you take as much as you want."

"Uh, Malcolm?" He had left his satchel in the car. "Did you pay for the food?"

"Pay?" He threw a green square into the air, then caught it in his mouth. I sighed. A stolen plate of Jell-O was the least of my worries.

As we walked back to the waiting room, Malcolm handed out Jell-O squares to everyone we passed, wishing each a good morning. The receptionist stared at him over the top of a file folder. Despite the manila barrier, I could tell she was smiling. Who could blame her?

I felt worn out, worried about the coffeehouse's future, about Grandma's future, about my future. The only nice thing, at that moment, was the warmth that enveloped me when I sat next to Malcolm. A narrow gap separated my arm and his shoulder—an electrically charged gap. I felt so self-conscious, sitting there, looking like total crap. I'm sure it's some kind of sin to be attracted to an angel.

"Come on over here, Marge. It's nice and warm." A man waved to his wife and they came and sat next to us. "Something must be wrong with the heating system."

It didn't take long for the rest of the people in the waiting room to claim the chairs around Malcolm and me. They stretched out their bodies as if basking beneath a sun lamp.

"It smells so nice over here," a woman said. She flipped through a newspaper. "Says here that they closed down that coffeehouse where they found the giant rat. I'd never eat there." I was too tired to muster a defense. The woman flipped to another page. "Oh look, honey, Nordby is having its Solstice Festival next weekend."

Which reminded me. I turned to Malcolm. "I lied to Vincent. I told him you were taking me to the festival."

He set the empty plate on the coffee table. "Do you not want to go?" He sat up straight. "Do you not want to go *with me*?"

"No, that's not it," I said, well aware that the woman with the paper was watching us. As was everyone else. "I just don't want you to feel like you have to go *with me*." I pulled the edges of the bathrobe around my neck. "I don't want you to think it's a date or something. Because I wouldn't expect you to go on a date, being who you are." I whispered that last part.

He didn't say anything. Then he leaned closer, so that his arm touched my shoulder. A jolt ran down my body. Everyone in our little group watched, waiting for his response. "I would be honored to escort you, Katrina."

"Oh. Okay." I pulled the bathrobe collar as high as it would go to hide my flaming cheeks.

Malcolm slapped his hand on his knee, then turned to the man sitting next to us and said, way too loudly, "I'm taking Katrina to the Solstice Festival."

"Good for you, kid."

"Katrina Svensen?" a nurse called. "You can see your grandmother now."

The nurse led Malcolm and me to the Cardiac Care Unit. She told us that we could have a few minutes and then we'd have to leave because they were going to do an echocardiogram and an angiogram. My grandmother lay propped against some pillows; a tube dripped clear fluid into her arm. Her skin was as white as the hospital sheets, as if the IV had diluted all her color. The wrinkles in her face seemed deeper. Her gray permed curls hung limp on her forehead.

She's alive, I told myself. It was the only good thought I could conjure because there is nothing good about seeing someone you love weakened, sprawled out, drained. I didn't want to confront that horrible thought, the one that comes late at night.

Each of us will die. I will die. There's no getting around it.

And the other horrible thought: *When my grandmother dies, I will be all alone.*

My grandmother managed a weak smile and reached for my hand. "I'd been feeling so tired," she said. "I didn't realize it was my heart. I should have seen the doctor."

I barely hugged her, afraid she might break. I sat in the little space at the edge of the bed, holding back tears of relief. "You're going to be fine now."

"I'm sorry I scared you." Her gaze traveled over my shoulder. Her smile brightened as she spotted Malcolm. "You caught me when I fell. You're Katrina's friend."

"I'm Malcolm."

She sniffed. "What's that lovely scent?"

"It's the smell of the Scottish Highlands. I brought it back with me as a souvenir."

Grandma Anna motioned me close. "I thought you were going to tell him that you aren't interested."

"Well, I was, but—"

"I'm to accompany Katrina to the Solstice Festival," Malcolm announced. He stared at the IV, watching the fluid drip slowly into the tube.

"You have a date?" My grandmother struggled to sit up. It was too much. Her eyelids fluttered. She groaned. Was she going to have another heart attack?

"Grandma," I begged.

She fell back onto the pillows. "The doctor told me no sudden movements."

Malcolm followed the tube to the place where it entered my grandmother's hand. "Interesting," he murmured. "They used to take fluids from the body to cure ills, now they put them back in."

"You'll need a dress," Grandma Anna said, her breath settling.

"What?" I wasn't following her train of thought. Malcolm was examining a plastic bedpan. "Dress?"

"For the festival. You'll need a new dress." She sighed and closed her eyes. "I'll never forget my first time I went to the Solstice Festival with a boy. His name was Harold— Harry for short. My mother made me a velvet blue dress, with little pearl buttons." Her voice became whispery. Malcolm set the bedpan aside and turned his blue gaze on her. He cocked his head as she drifted into a world of memories. "Harry took me to the Grand Feast at the Sons of Norway Hall. We danced five dances." She smiled dreamily. "He only stepped on my feet twice. And then he kissed me." She opened her eyes. "I wonder where he is now."

"Corporal Harold Jorgenson died in combat in Vietnam on July 14, 1966," Malcolm said.

Before my grandmother could ask him how he knew that, the nurse returned. "That's enough now. She needs her rest. You can see her when the tests are done." She shooed Malcolm into the hall.

"I'll be right there," I told the nurse, then I gave my grandmother another gentle hug.

"Katrina." She stroked my hair. "I'll probably be here for a few days. Don't waste any time worrying about me. You go home and get some sleep. And don't you go missing school. You keep up your grades. I'll tell Irmgaard and The Boys to check in on you before school to make sure you've had a good breakfast, and after school in case you need anything. And you be sure to call me before you go to bed so I know you're doing fine."

"But Grandma—"

"There's two hundred dollars in my checking account.

Use that for groceries. There's a credit card in the top
drawer of my desk, for emergencies. Your grandfather's
pension check will come on Wednesday. Take it to the
bank and deposit it right away. Use it to get yourself a new
dress."

"I don't need a new dress."

"Of course you do. It's not every day that a girl gets to
go on her first date. And with such a handsome boy. I don't
know when I've ever seen such a handsome boy. A new
dress is an absolute necessity and I won't hear another word
about it."

"But we can't afford it," I said.

Grandma Anna waved the comment away. Then she
turned serious. "Tell Irmgaard that she should start looking for another job as soon as possible."

"But we can still save the coffeehouse," I insisted. "The
Health Department will see that it's all been a big mistake
and we can still do something for the Solstice. I'll stay and
work, and Elizabeth will help—"

"It's no use."

"But I'm sure I can do it, Grandma. I'm sure I can
come up with something."

"Sweetie." She patted my hand. "I love the coffeehouse
more than you can ever know. Your mother and father and
your grandfather are a part of that place. It holds so many
memories. I know your intentions come right from the
heart, but you can't save the coffeehouse."

Unspoken words hung between us. *You can't save the
coffeehouse because you always start things and never finish
them, which is why we have a Closet of Failure at the end of
our hall. You've never poured yourself into anything. Never*

gone beyond the moment when it just starts to get difficult. It's so much easier to say you're not good at something and then quit.

"You go to the festival with that nice young man. There's no need to worry about the coffeehouse, because I've made a decision." And then she said the words I never thought I'd hear her say.

"I want you to promise me that tomorrow you will tell Mr. Darling I'm ready to discuss his offer. I'm ready to close the shop."

Twenty-two

After leaving the Cardiac Care Unit, Malcolm and I went back to the emergency waiting room, where I had left all that paperwork. I wanted to pretend that I hadn't heard my grandmother's decision to close the coffeehouse but her words followed me, echoing off the elevator's walls. Could she have suffered brain damage? No. I knew in my heart that she had made the right decision. If only we didn't have to turn the space over to such a pig.

As we stepped off the elevator, Irmgaard walked through the hospital's automatic entry doors, a suitcase in her hand. In the distance, a taxi pulled out of the load/unload lane. Dressed in a gray wool coat with a black shawl wrapped around her shoulders, she could easily have been Sister Irmgaard. Her eyes widened when she noticed Malcolm. She dropped the suitcase and rushed back outside.

"Irmgaard?" I called, rushing after her. "Where are you going?" I caught up with her at the edge of the parking lot. "Irmgaard?"

She stopped walking and looked toward the hospital, her eyes wild.

"Is it the message?" I asked.

She nodded furiously.

"You don't want it?"

She shook her head.

"Why don't you want it? What do you think it is?" Of course, she said nothing. "Irmgaard, you were right. He's an angel." I paused. "Are you a nun? *Were* you a nun?" It would explain the extra-short hair, the plain clothing, and makeupless face. And the lack of jewelry, except for the little silver cross. Perhaps the oath of silence was required at St. Clare's. But why would it be required in the outside world?

She took a step back and her eyes filled with tears. What was the matter with her? Shouldn't a nun or an ex-nun be thrilled about meeting an angel? Wouldn't this be the biggest moment of her life?

"Oh, Irmgaard," I said, taking her hand. "Don't worry. You don't have to read the message. I'll tell Malcolm that you don't want it. Please come inside. I need your help with the hospital's paperwork. I don't understand some of the questions and if I don't fill out the insurance forms, then we'll have to pay for everything ourselves."

Irmgaard's eyes relaxed and she nodded. I led her to the waiting room, collecting the suitcase on the way. Malcolm had gone. A few people were complaining about the sudden drop in temperature. The receptionist asked a janitor where all the fish had gone. Other than a stream of bubbles rising in a tube, nothing moved inside the aquarium.

Had Malcolm set them free? Of course he had.

We sat. "Did you find Grandma's insurance information?" I asked.

She opened the suitcase and took out another purse—my grandmother's daytime purse. I had grabbed the wrong one. She had also collected Grandma's pajamas, slippers, bathrobe, bedside radio, all the medications from the bathroom counter, and a container of homemade soup. I showed her the pile of papers. She opened the purse and pulled out a Medicare card. Then she started filling out the forms.

"Thank you," I said, feeling totally relieved.

Malcolm rushed through the automatic doors, holding his satchel. Before I could stop him, he waved the golden envelope. "You've got to take it," he said.

Irmgaard gasped and dropped the pen, her eyes darting madly. A wall, an aquarium, and an angel blocked her escape. She closed her eyes, then opened them. Closed, then opened, as if trying to wish him away.

"I won't disappear this time," Malcolm said. "I mean you no harm, Irmgaard, but you can't refuse to take a message."

"Malcolm, she doesn't want it," I said. "Can't you see you're upsetting her?"

"I don't mean to cause upset." He looked at the envelope. "All messages are important, but it's becoming a real burden to carry this one around."

"Just put it down," I told him. "We can talk about it later. Right now we've got to finish these forms."

He opened his hand. The envelope floated down through the air, ever so slowly, like a feather. When it landed on the glass table, the table shattered. Those sitting nearby leaped from their seats. The receptionist called security.

"You try to carry that around," Malcolm said snippily. "She needs to take it before it gets any heavier."

Then Irmgaard did something that totally surprised me. I'd never seen her get angry before. She believed

Malcolm to be an angel, but she glared at him, her eyes blazing. Holding her neck straight, looking right into his sparkling eyes, she folded her arms and refused to take that envelope.

He threw his hands in the air. "What am I supposed to do? Do you have any idea the kind of trouble I'm in?"

She shook a piece of glass from her shoe, then turned her back to him, continuing to work on the papers. Her defiance was shocking. Wouldn't a nun be afraid of some sort of heavenly wrath?

"Irmgaard, do you want me to read it?" I asked.

"You can't," Malcolm said. "I can't even read it. Only she can." He picked up the envelope and slid it back into his satchel. "You two are the most perplexing women I've ever met." The automatic doors slid open and Malcolm, his kilt swishing with each angry step, stormed off into the night.

Twenty-three

The rest of Sunday passed in a blur. At 6:00 a.m., the nurse let me peek in to say good-bye to my grandmother, but she was fast asleep. Malcolm didn't come back. I waited for a while in the hospital parking lot, even whispered his name, but he didn't show up. After driving the old Buick home, I fed Ratcatcher, then fell into a stupor, sleeping right through the afternoon. I woke up and made a peanut butter sandwich, called Elizabeth, then fell back into bed, swallowed up by the dreamless sleep of the comatose.

Monday morning felt heavier than usual and not just because Ratcatcher was sleeping on my chest. As I opened my eyes, my new reality descended like a pillow smothering my face. Grandma was in the hospital and sometime that day, I'd have to tell Mr. Darling that we were surrendering.

The shower didn't perk me up like it usually did. I stood there for a long time, watching streams of soap slide down my skinny legs. The dull razor nicked my shin twice, which I took as a sign that I should have stayed in bed. I put on my usual jeans and favorite red sweatshirt, then ate a bowl of Cheerios. I had promised my grandmother that I wouldn't miss school, even though I wasn't prepared for any of my classes. How could I have done homework with all the chaos in my life? Considering the situation, maybe my teachers would give me an extension. At least winter vacation began on Wednesday, which was also the day the health inspector would return. It didn't seem to matter if he found rat turds or not. The doors to Anna's Old World Scandinavian Coffeehouse would close forever.

I brushed my teeth, then stared into the mirror. Was I really going to the Solstice Festival with an angel? How do you wrap your head around something like that? There are so many stories about girls dating vampires and fairy kings, but those are dark stories, dangerous stories where the simple act of falling in love puts the girl's life at risk. Malcolm didn't seem one bit dangerous. Angels are supposed to be pure and sinless, so it would be a pure and sinless date. I didn't have a problem with that. It was kind of a relief that I wouldn't have to fend off blood-sucking or an enchantment on our first date.

Which would probably be our *only* date.

But was I good enough to go on a date with an angel? Didn't you have to be . . . perfect? Sure, my skin was pretty good and my eyelashes were long, even though they were blond and you couldn't see them. If I pulled my hair up I'd look older, but never perfect. One of my bottom teeth was crooked and my lips always got chapped in the winter. And I'm pretty sure that angels didn't have to deal with morning breath. Or sweat. Or a myriad of other human conditions. Malcolm always smelled . . . perfect.

I'd never really thought about angels before. I'd seen

It's a Wonderful Life, that movie about the angel who wants to get his wings. And I'd been to church enough times to hear the stories about Gabriel the archangel and Satan the fallen angel. But that's what they were to me, stories. Improbable, fantastic stories.

And yet, even if I convinced myself that the little white wing had been a hallucination, brought on by the blinding hospital lights and the psychological torture of waiting, I couldn't deny all the other stuff.

Without Grandma's radio, an eerie quiet floated through the apartment. Downstairs was worse. Without the hum of the percolators, the coffeehouse felt lifeless. I sat on the bottom step with Ratcatcher. "Don't worry," I told her, scratching between her black ears. "Grandma will be home soon." But where would home be after we had closed? Would we have to leave Nordby and live in some retirement community like Mr. Darling's mother? Retirement Universe wouldn't look too good as a return address on my college applications. I'd end all my application letters with: *Help, get me out of here*.

"Meow."

I poured Ratcatcher some kibble. She sniffed the nonpastry breakfast, then walked away, and that's when it caught my eye. I hadn't turned on the coffeehouse lights. so I wasn't sure what I was looking at. A puddle of blue sat on the corner table, sparkling. As I walked toward it, Ratcatcher leaped onto the table and sniffed the puddle. I reached out expecting liquid but found velvet. The blue fabric slid softly beneath my hand. "It's a dress," I whispered, picking it up. Little pearl buttons dotted the front, just like my grandmother's dress. I held it at arm's length. It couldn't be my grandmother's dress because it was way too long for her, but perfect for me. A little tag in the back read: *Made Exclusively for Katrina.* I held the dress to my face and inhaled the Highlands.

It was the nicest gift ever.

The school bus passed by. I quickly hung the dress in my room, zipped up my parka, and grabbed my backpack. But just as I was about to leave, someone knocked on the front door. A group of Japanese tourists stood outside, pressing their faces against the window.

"Yes? May I help you?" I asked, opening the door.

One of the tourists shook my hand. "Ratcatcher? Ratcatcher live here?"

"Ratcatcher!" another cried, pointing. She sat on the corner table, cleaning one of her paws, oblivious to her fans.

"Um, we're closed," I said.

They pushed their way in. "We take picture with famous cat?"

"I'm sorry," I said, "but we're closed. I've got to get to school."

"We take picture." And they started taking pictures, posing with Ratcatcher, smiling and laughing, totally thrilled by the moment. One of them held up a little rubber rat, but Ratcatcher ignored it. I let them do their thing for a few minutes. How often does a person get to meet the most famous cat in the world?

"I have to go," I told them, pointing at the clock. They nodded and filed out. One of them handed me a twenty-dollar bill, then bowed. I tried to give it back, but he just kept bowing. "Money for the photos. Thank you."

Storm clouds rolled across the sky. There wasn't time to

walk, so I jumped into the Buick, which took forever to warm up. Up the hill I drove. The road was still wet from last night's rain. Sometime during the weekend, the old Java Heaven billboard had been replaced by a spanking new Java Heaven billboard, this one shaped like a big coffee cup that had Vincent's face on it.

Coffee and a Hometown Hero, a Match Made in Heaven— Java Heaven.

What did it matter anymore? Mr. Darling had won. He was supreme. He had taken our business and my best friend. He should get an award or something.

On my way to Monday assembly, lots of students asked me about Ratcatcher—kids I'd never spoken to before, which narrows it down to just about everyone. A few of them wanted her autograph—a paw print, I guessed. They wanted to take a picture with her to put on their blogs. She was still all the rage on the Internet. I said I'd get back to them. I told them I'd set up a time when they could come down to see her. Maybe not. We'd probably be Florida-bound by then.

Elizabeth sat in the usual spot on the bleachers, her shoulders hunched, an orange hat pulled over her eyebrows. "How's Anna?"

I squeezed in next to her, setting my backpack between my feet. "I'm going to call her at break. She's supposed to have more tests this morning. Why are you sitting like that?"

"I don't want him to see me."

"Face?"

"He didn't call. He had all weekend to call and he didn't. I hate him." She pulled the hat lower.

"You should just ask someone else."

"Why? So I can get rejected by another loser? Forget it."
She laid her head on my shoulder. "I'll help you at the coffeehouse, like I did last year. I don't need to go to the stupid
festival."

"The coffeehouse won't be open for the festival. Mr.
Darling is going to give us some money to close the business. Then he'll expand Java Heaven."

"Oh, I'm sorry. Well, then we can go to Solstice
together."

"Um, there's something you should know." I couldn't
believe I was about to say what I was about to say. "I kind
of have a date."

Elizabeth sat up straight, as if someone had pinched
her. "What? Who with?"

I lowered my voice. I didn't want any more gossip
crawling around school. "With Malcolm."

"No way." She ripped off her hat. Her hair sparked
with static.

I pressed closer to her. "He has wings on his ankles."

"Oh. My. God."

We huddled. "All sorts of weird things have happened
since he showed up, things I haven't even told you about.
It's not just that Vincent got fortune and Ratcatcher got
fame, but when Lars wanted some dignity he got it and
when a lady at the bus stop wanted coffee, she got that. And
Irmgaard got some kind of message, but she won't open it
and I can't even lift it because it weighs a ton and it's just a
piece of paper. And Grandma wanted me to get a new dress
and there it was, sitting in the kitchen this morning."

"But what about you?" Elizabeth whispered. "You're
supposed to get what you most desire. Remember?"

"He won't give me another bean. Not yet. He said he needs to make sure I ask for what I truly desire or he'll get into trouble. Demoted or something."

"Hey, Coffeehouse Girl," Aaron said, sticking his fat head between us. "Heard you've been serving rat crap."

"Shut up, Aaron." Elizabeth jabbed him with her elbow. Then she leaned over to tie her red high-tops. I leaned with her. "I knew he was an angel the minute I saw him. He's way too handsome to be human. Do you think he'd let me paint him? What are you going to wish for?"

From the center of the gym, Principal Carmichael made some announcements about stuff that wasn't important. When you're contemplating your chance to make a wish that might actually come true, things like locker inspections and parking permits seem totally trivial. Elliott rushed out and dealt with the shrieking microphone. Then, as usual, Heidi Darling had something to say. She quieted everyone with a staccato clearing of her throat. "Okay, so those of you who volunteered to help with the festival decorations, the theme this year is Snowflake Serenade. We have lots of snowflakes to make, so meet Vincent and me at Java Heaven this afternoon at four thirty."

My stomach lurched. His treachery was complete.

Twenty-four

Vincent Hawk, best friend since the fourth grade, might as well have stuck a knife into my heart. Not only was he going to step foot inside Java Heaven that very afternoon at four thirty, he was going to hang out there and do crafts. So what if we were going to close our coffeehouse? He didn't know that. So what if Java Heaven wasn't going to be our competitor anymore? I'd still hate that place and I'd still expect my friends not to be one of its customers. That's not a lot to ask. It's not like you can't buy coffee *everywhere* these days.

"Tell your parents and friends to buy Vincent Mochas, because ten percent goes back to the Nordby swim team," Heidi said, still standing at the microphone. Then she punched the air. "*Gooooooo,* Nordby Otters!"

He broke his promise because of her. So what if she was cute and could swim? How could he stand all that perkiness? How could everything have changed so much in one short week? If I wished for it all to go away, would everything go back to normal? Maybe that's what I most desired.

Heidi bounded back to the bleachers and sat next to Vincent. She was about to plant a kiss on his cheek, but he stopped her and said something. She frowned and said something back. He turned away. What have we here? Trouble in paradise? I savored the moment.

While I avoided Vincent on the way out of the gym, Elizabeth avoided Face. I took a moment to call my grandmother. "You should see all the flowers. It looks like someone died," she said, her words a bit slurred. She was probably on pain medication. "Vincent and his father sent a lovely bouquet. The Boys came in. I haven't seen Irmgaard, though. Poor thing. She's probably upset about having to find another job."

"How are you feeling?" I asked.

"Don't worry about me. Did you talk to Mr. Darling yet?"

"No. I'm going to do it after school."

"Good. Tell him that we'll discuss the details when I'm discharged."

"Grandma—"

"Now Katrina, don't try to change my mind. There's more to this than you realize. It's time to move on."

Mr. Prince had shoved an envelope into my locker. *Katrina, Here are the results of your aptitude test. Come in to discuss.* I stuffed it into my backpack. If I went to his office, he'd ask me about my checklist, which, except for Elizabeth's additions, I had neglected to fill out. I still didn't have anything to put on it, except maybe *Owner of the World's Most Famous Cat*, or *Ex-friend of Nordby's Hometown Hero*. I know what would look really good on the list—*Dating an Angel*.

We had a substitute in World Mythology and she sent us to the library. The librarian cornered Vincent, asking him all sorts of questions about his scholarship. I found an empty aisle at the back and sat on the floor. Maybe I could pass the entire class without having to talk to him. I didn't want to hear his excuse for breaking his promise. He'd say something like, "You're not the boss of me," and I'd say something like, "Oh yeah, well whatever," and it would slide downhill from there.

Elliott wandered into my sanctuary. "This is the business/technology section," he informed me, as if I might be lost.

"Yeah, I know. Maybe I like technology." I pulled a book off the shelf and pretended to read it.

Elliott shrugged, then chose a book and sat on the floor. "I liked your story about the potato farmer." He cleaned his glasses with his striped rugby shirt. "Though I didn't understand the ending. The girl's neighbor bought a new tractor and updated his potato packaging, but why did the girl give up? I'm sure there were ways she could have competed."

I looked up from my fake reading. "Huh?"

"She could have done a marketing survey to find out what types of potatoes the customers preferred. She could have researched the latest hybrids to find higher yielding potatoes, giving her an advantage at market. There are small business loans and—"

"It doesn't matter, Elliott. It was just a stupid story."

"Okay." He put on his glasses. "Hey, can I ask your opinion?"

I'd never had a real conversation with Elliott, even though we'd been in school together forever. He was on the small side, as if puberty hadn't quite caught up with him. He seemed perfectly nice, and since my pool of friends had dwindled down to ONE, I figured it would be a good idea to start talking to more people. "Sure. Ask away."

He pulled out a familiar piece of paper and scooted closer. "Have you filled yours out?"

"Not really."

"Mr. Prince said that even though my grades are stellar, I need to join a few more clubs. So far I have Chess Club, French Club, and Robotics Club. Do you have any suggestions?"

"You're asking the wrong person. I don't belong to any clubs."

"What about your friend . . . Elizabeth?"

"She's not into clubs either. But she takes a bunch of classes at the community center."

"Oh. What about this section, *Skills and Talents*? I wrote: *Computer Programming, Digital Photography,* and *Audio Engineering,* but Mr. Prince said that I need to broaden the list, make it look like I'm more well-rounded. How do I do that?"

"Again, you're asking the wrong person. I'm so clueless he made me take an aptitude test."

"How'd you do?"

"I don't know." I pulled it from my backpack. "I'm kind of afraid to look."

"Why?"

"I probably flunked. I'm not good at anything, really."

"You can't flunk an aptitude test." Elliott held out his hand and wiggled his fingers. Might as well find out. I handed over the results. He slid his thumb under the flap and opened the envelope " 'Results for Katrina Svensen: Entrepreneurial Profile,' " he read. "Wow, that's great."

"Entrepreneurial?"

"That means you'd be good at starting your own business."

I knew what "entrepreneurial" meant. What I didn't know was how that related to me. Had Mr. Prince given me the wrong results?

Elliott continued to read. " 'Enterpreneurs possess the following characteristics: they are creative problem solvers, they have the ability to see possibility, they can make independent decisions, and they inspire, persuade, and motivate others.' "

I took the paper and turned it over to see if someone else's name was on it. It had to be a mistake.

"What classes does Elizabeth take?" he asked. "Maybe I should sign up for one of those."

"She'd be happy to tell you about her classes. Just ask her."

Elliott's cheeks erupted like little cherry tomatoes. He opened his book. "Well, I've got some research to do." He lay on his back and started reading.

I lay on my back and read the test results over and over. What sorts of problems had I solved? Who had I ever inspired? Did I ever see possibility, or was I always looking at my life with a loser mentality?

When the bell rang I made sure that Vincent stayed well ahead of me in the hallway. Between second and third period I ducked into the bathroom to avoid Heidi, and at lunch I had to take the long way to the parking lot to avoid Vincent again.

Elizabeth had beat me to the car. As soon as I shut the passenger door, she burst into tears. "He said no."

"I don't believe it."

"He said he had something else to do that night."

"Like what? Everyone goes to the Solstice Festival."

"He's probably going, he just doesn't want to go with . . . me." Her nose started to run. "I don't blame him. I'm fat and ugly. Who wants to go out with this?" She swept her hands over her purple coat and checkered pants. She threw her lunch bag into the backseat. "I'm not going to eat for a month."

"He's a jerk," I said. I had forgotten to pack a lunch, so I grabbed an apple from Elizabeth's bag, then let loose a flood of unhappiness. "They're all jerks. They want perfect girls. Perfect, sporty, perky girls. And when they get those girls they forget about their friends. Okay, so maybe he didn't hold that cup on purpose during his television interview and maybe it wasn't his fault that Mr. Darling named a drink after him, but he promised he'd never go to Java Heaven and now he's going. Heidi's totally brainwashed him against me. It's all her fault. She's doing this on purpose. She's so mean." I tore into the apple's flesh.

Elizabeth wiped her eyes, leaving a smear of mascara on her sleeve. Before I could spew any more unhappiness she said, "I'm going to be totally honest and I don't want you to get mad."

"What?"

She took a big breath. "Heidi's dad's a real jerk, no argument there, but I've never seen Heidi act like a jerk. Sure, she's an overachiever and totally annoying, but she's not mean to people."

I almost choked. "I can't believe you're saying this. I thought you hated her as much as I do."

"I don't *hate* her. I don't like her because I know she stresses you out and she's just not the type of person I would want to hang out with. I'd always feel like a total failure around her."

"Oh gee, thanks."

"You know what I mean."

"No I don't. You like hanging out with me because I have no goals, because I don't do anything? Because you don't feel like a failure around me?"

"Of course not. Jeez. I hang out with you because you're my friend and I love you. But you've decided to hate Heidi simply based on what her dad does for a living."

"So?"

Elizabeth reached into her lunch and unwrapped her sandwich. "I don't think you're pissed at Heidi because of her dad's coffeehouse. I think it has to do with Vincent. I think you should just admit that you're in love with him."

"What?" A piece of apple flew from my mouth. "I'm NOT in love with Vincent."

"It sure seems like you are."

"What are you talking about?"

"Yes, he's a total idiot for agreeing to go inside Java Heaven to make snowflakes. That's wrong. And we should give him the silent treatment. But—"

"But nothing. I *don't* love him."

We sat in silence for a while. I stared out the window. How could she think such a thing? Was everything and everyone against me?

And that's when they walked by, just like before. Vincent

and Heidi, in their matching swim team sweatshirts. But this time he wasn't just touching her arm, he was holding her hand, their morning argument long forgotten.

I started to cry.

Elizabeth slammed her hand on the steering wheel. "I knew it!"

Twenty-five

I couldn't tell where one feeling ended and another began.

I was worried about my grandmother, embarrassed about closing the coffeehouse, excited about the third coffee bean and the whole angel thing, sad about possibly leaving Nordby, and miserable, angry and confused about losing my best friend. Was love mixed up in there too? Me, in love with Vincent?

It didn't make sense. I'd never thought about kissing him. Okay, maybe once or twice, but that had been curiosity, nothing more. I'd seen him in his bathing suit a million times and I'd never looked at him like *that*. Sure, I liked sitting next to him in the movie theater because I could hide my face on his shoulder if it got scary. And sure, when we studied together on the couch, I liked to stick my feet under his knees to keep them warm. I liked it when he let me wear his coat or his sweatshirt. And I especially liked it when, of all the people in our school, all the perfect and beautiful and overachieving people, he chose to sit next to me in class. Was that love?

I said in the beginning that this was not one of those "I'm in love with my best friend" stories. Suddenly, on that Monday, I didn't know what to think. I didn't know squat.

I drove home. A banner hung across Main Street, announcing the Solstice Festival. Shopkeepers had lined their doors and awnings with little white lights. Displays of gingerbread houses, snowmen, and candy canes filled the shop windows. Festivity floated through the air, but it ricocheted right off me as I drove past our front door. *Closed by the Health Department Until further notice*. The rat was my fault. It had appeared because I had lied to an angel, and then I had let the lie fall from my hand, onto the floor, where my fat cat had eaten it. I couldn't blame everything on Mr. Darling.

I parked in the alley. "Hello, Katrina," Ingvar said, opening the back door. He held a broom. "Your grandfather gave me a key ages ago. I hope you don't mind that we let ourselves in. We've been cleaning."

The coffeehouse smelled like bleach and Pine-Sol. While Ralph mopped the kitchen floor, Odin wiped down the pantry shelves and Lars scrubbed the stovetop. "Hi Katrina," they said.

"What's going on?" I asked.

"We're cleaning the place up before that nincompoop of a health inspector comes back," Lars said.

"Can't have Anna worrying about these things," Ralph said. "Worry is bad for the heart."

Ingvar dipped a sponge into a bucket of sudsy water. "We've cleaned plenty of boats in our day. Kitchen grease is a breeze compared to fish guts. This place will be spotless. That inspector won't find a single rat turd."

If we moved to Florida, I'd probably never see these men again. They were like the uncles I never had. The grandfather I missed. The father who got taken away. I couldn't bear to tell them that my grandmother had decided to close.

"Where's Irmgaard?" Odin asked. "Is she at the hospital?"

"I don't know," I told him.

He handed me a postal box filled with mail. "All this came today. Most of it's for Ratcatcher."

"The phone's been ringing all day too," Ralph said. "Took a bunch of messages. Everyone wants to talk to the cat."

"Lots of people been stopping by too," Lars said.

"Thanks." I carried the box into the office and set it on the desk. I opened one of the cards. A little girl had drawn a picture of Ratcatcher and the rat. They were sitting together, smiling. Ratcatcher had a pink bow on her head and the rat wore a purple bowtie. The girl wanted to know if Ratcatcher would write back. I shuffled through the box and found three more bills, each past due. They came to over four hundred dollars. Grandma had said she had two hundred in her checking account. My backpack slid off my shoulder and fell to the floor with a *thunk*. I felt like falling beside it and curling into a little ball. Honest to God, a sixteen-year-old is not supposed to have so many problems at once.

Ingvar stuck his head into the office. "I told him he could use your shower. I hope you don't mind."

"Who?"

"Your boyfriend. The kid with the skirt."

"Malcolm's using my shower?"

"It was my suggestion. He was soaked to the bone. Said he'd been sitting in the rain all night. If you don't mind my saying, Katrina, he could use some new clothes. Maybe you could lend him some of your grandfather's?"

I smelled him before I saw him, following the scent up the stairs and down the hallway to the kitchen. He sat at the Formica table, eating Cheerios out of the box. His hair was wet and slicked back, his torso perfectly clean and sculpted. That's right, his torso. I couldn't tell since the tablecloth hid his lower half, but he appeared to be naked.

"Uh, hi," I said.

"Hello." He smiled in that nice way, giving me his full attention, as if I were the center of the universe. Then he reached across the table and took an apple from the fruit bowl. "You know, there was a time when this was considered to be a very dangerous piece of fruit."

"What did you do with your clothes?" I asked.

"They're gone." He rolled the apple in his hand.

"You threw them away?"

"I took them off and now they're gone. It's for the best. I'm supposed to blend in wherever I go like a chameleon. It doesn't appear that kilts are popular in these parts, so I might as well wear something more befitting your little corner of the world." He started to get up.

"Uh, don't do that."

"Don't do what?"

"Just sit right there and I'll get you some clothes." While going on a date with an angel might not break some kind of cosmic law, I was certain that seeing one naked would get me sent straight to hell or something. Or many, many years in a psychotherapist's office.

My grandmother was one of those people who had trouble getting rid of things—hence the crowded Closet of Failure. "You just might need those things someday," she always said. So, in the back of her closet, some of my grandfather's clothes still hung, including his police uniform. Some of his other clothes were neatly folded in the bottom drawer of her dresser. Malcolm was tall, like my grandfather, and lean like him too. I found a pair of khaki pants, a navy blue T-shirt, and a pullover white Icelandic sweater. Would he need underwear? I didn't want to have that conversation with an angel, so I grabbed a pair of boxers. "I couldn't find any shoes," I said as I went back to the kitchen.

"I don't need any. I have my sandals. They go everywhere I go."

"Here," I said, closing my eyes as he stood. "You can change in the bathroom."

When he emerged, he looked like a model for Ralph Lauren. And all I could think about at that moment were his broad naked shoulders and his hairless chest—a million times nicer than naked Catering Guy.

"Katrina?" He stood close to me. "What's on your mind?"

Like he didn't know. I stepped back and took a long breath. "Can you give me that bean now?"

"Only if you're ready to be honest."

"I want things back the way they used to be," I said. "I want Java Heaven to never have opened. Then we would still have all our old customers and Grandma wouldn't have gotten stressed out and had that heart attack. And Vincent and I would still be friends and I wouldn't have to go tell

Mr. Darling that we're willing to leave." I sat on one of the kitchen chairs. "I don't want to go over there. I just want Java Heaven to disappear."

At some point while I was talking, Malcolm's hair had dried. It fell in soft waves and was so shiny that if you saw him walking down the street, you'd think, "I wonder what kind of shampoo that guy uses."

"Are you certain that this is what you desire?"

"Yes."

He reached into his satchel and pulled out the coffee bean packet. He dumped the last bean into his hand, then sat on the edge of the kitchen table, right next to me. "Are you certain, Katrina? Because this will change your life."

"I'm certain," I said.

"I hope so, because both our futures are riding on this."

"I am." I hated that place. I wanted it gone. Gone forever. "I'm certain."

Malcolm closed his eyes and everything went quiet, just like before. No cars driving down the street, no Ingvar singing "Blow the Man Down," no Ratcatcher digging her claws into the couch. The clock stopped ticking, the refrigerator stopped humming. One wish would change it all back. Everything would be good again. But for how long? Another coffeehouse would open on Main Street. Malcolm would get another girlfriend. Grandma would have to retire eventually. I'd still have to fill out that stupid checklist.

"Wait," I said.

Malcolm's eyes popped open and the world went back to normal.

"What do you mean that *both* our futures are riding on this?"

"I only have one more chance to make this right. If I mess up again, I'll never get that promotion I want. They'll be sending me away. They'll be demoting me."

"They will?" Who was I kidding? I wasn't any more certain about this wish than about anything in my life. I laid my head on the table. "I don't know what I truly desire. I can't figure it out. It's too hard."

Malcolm returned the coffee bean to its package and tucked it back into the satchel. "Everyone knows what they most desire."

"Do you?"

"I'm not supposed to have any desires."

I sat up. "But you want that promotion."

"Yes. More than you can ever know."

"Then you do have a desire."

"More than one." His gaze swept over me, but this time it didn't feel like a feather duster. It was more like fine sandpaper, like a cat's tongue. It felt great. I wanted to move closer and climb into his arms. I thought about those stories of blood-sucking boyfriends and enchantments. Was I under some sort of angelic spell, or was I feeling this way because he was handsome and interesting and nice and different from anyone I had ever met? "Different" was an understatement—he wasn't even human.

HE WASN'T EVEN HUMAN!

What was I doing? This was crazy. I needed to get out of that room and sort out my feelings.

I looked at the clock. "I've got to talk to Mr. Darling now, or I won't be able to get to the hospital before visiting hours are over."

"I'll go with you," Malcolm said.

"No. I want to do this alone."

I hurried down the stairs, each step taking me farther away from his aura. Without a word to The Boys, I walked out the front door of Anna's Old World Scandinavian Coffeehouse and into the belly of the beast.

Twenty-six

When I was eleven, I went to the county fair with Vincent and his dad. Mr. Hawk, in his usual exhausted state, gave us each ten dollars, then took a nap in the shade. Since we only had enough money for three rides each, we had to compromise. We agreed on the Giant Sack Slide, then I chose the Ferris wheel and Vincent chose the Hall of Horrors.

I didn't want to go into the Hall of Horrors, but we had made a deal. "I did the stupid Ferris wheel," Vincent complained while dragging me across the walkway. The facade on the Hall of Horrors had a giant picture of a vampire, some heads in jars, and a bunch of zombies with blood dripping from their mouths. I got kind of shaky and my palms started to sweat.

This really ugly guy with no teeth took our tickets. "Is it scary?" I asked him.

He just shrugged. "I ain't givin' no refunds if ya puke or nothing."

Great. That sounded just great.

Screams of terror emerged from the black curtained

entryway. Evil laughter beckoned us forward, *if we dared*. Vincent went right in with a big smile on his face, like he was looking for Easter eggs or treasure of some kind. The ugly man told me to move it, 'cause the line was backing up.

I didn't puke, but I closed my eyes and held on to Vincent's shirt sleeve. "Welcome to the Hall of Horrors," a recorded voice said. "Once you have stepped inside, you will never escape."

And that's exactly how I felt standing outside Java Heaven. I'd rather go into a million Halls of Horrors than that place. I'd rather face countless jars filled with brains and contorted faces than the perky bleached smiles of the Java Heaven staff.

Without a sleeve to hold on to, I stepped inside. The place was clean, warm, and friendly. Giant clouds hung from the ceiling. A big poster advertising the new Vincent Mocha hung behind the counter. Voices and trendy music filled the air. My head didn't explode. My body didn't disintegrate. But my soul shriveled.

I scanned the room quickly. Heidi's herd sat at the back tables, cutting foam snowflakes. I didn't see Vincent, which was a relief because I didn't want to explain why I was breaking my own law. Heidi would tell him soon enough. Everyone would know, soon enough.

In order to get to the counter, I had to meander past stands of packaged goodies and all sorts of merchandise stamped with the cloud logo—very clever. Little brown bags filled with Java Heaven Organic Morning Blend and Java Heaven Organic Holiday Blend crowded the shelves.

"What are *you* doing here?" Heidi asked. She held a platter of cookies. "Did you come to help with the snowflakes?"

"I need to talk to your dad."

"No way. That's weird. You never come in here." Up close she was still really pretty, but she had these dark circles under her eyes. Was overachievement finally getting to her?

"Where is he? Your dad?"

"He's in his office. It's over there." She pointed, then delivered the cookies to the work party.

Turning my face away from the snowflake-making students, I walked to the back of the shop. This was the worst kind of Hall of Horrors because the monster wasn't a mannequin or a recorded voice or a robot—the monster was real and he was sitting behind his desk.

He didn't look one bit surprised to see me. "Where's your white flag?" he asked, leaning back in his chair. I guess it was totally obvious that our coffeehouse was foundering. The Health Department's sign was just icing on his victory cake.

"I need to tell you something."

"William, what is this?" An elderly woman stormed into the office, pushing me aside. She waved a piece of paper. "I told you I wanted to fly first-class. This is clearly not a first-class ticket."

"Now, Mother." Mr. Darling stood. He brushed his hands over his navy sweater, smoothing out the folds. "That's the best deal I could get."

"Best deal?" She shoved the ticket into his face. "You're a cheapskate. That's what you are. You've always been a cheapskate. Bad enough that you're shipping me off to Retirement Hell—"

"It's Retirement Universe."

"It's death, that's what it is. You're sending me there to die." She slapped the ticket onto his desk. "If you want to get rid of me that badly, then you'll have to do it first-class. I want another ticket." She looked me over. "I hope your grandmother is feeling better." Then she stormed out.

Mr. Darling straightened his sweater again, then returned to his chair. He didn't seem one bit embarrassed that he, a grown man, had just been yelled at by his mother. "You were saying?"

I steadied myself, my feet wide apart to offset the weight of humiliation. "My grandmother wanted me to tell you that she's willing to take you up on your offer."

"Of course she is." He folded his hands. "But my offer no longer stands."

"What?"

"I'm buying the entire building. I'll be your new land-lord. The deal will close in thirty days. Now that you have a reputation for harboring rodents, I anticipate that you'll be out of business by this weekend. And once your rent is overdue, there will be no need for me to honor your lease. I can legally evict you."

"But you told us you would pay us for our space," I cried.

He stood. "Now I'm telling you that I don't need to." He opened the back door, motioning to the alley that our businesses shared. "I'm sure you'd be more comfortable going out this way."

Is there a word bigger than hate? Despise, loathe, detest. Take all those words and mix them together and that's what I felt. If I had been starring in an old movie, I would have slapped him and called him a scoundrel. But a slap in the real world was called aggravated assault.

Give me that coffee bean. Give it to me right now because what I most desire is not to make Java Heaven disappear, but to make this big jerk disappear!

"But—"

"Good-bye." He pointed out the door.

"But—"

And then something amazing happened. The wind kicked up and blew right into Mr. Darling's office. It rustled across the papers on his desk, sending a few into the alley. Mr. Darling chased after them. Watching him struggle to catch each one, cursing and nearly tripping, was a small consolation. With the last paper retrieved, he glared at me, told me to leave, then slammed the door.

I stood in the alley. If ever there was a time to cry it would have been right then and there. But I didn't cry. Something had caught my eye. A single piece of paper, still held aloft by the wind, floated directly overhead. It fluttered, then landed right in my outstretched hand.

It was a receipt from Acme Supply Company, the same company that we ordered from. The receipt was for the delivery of 280 pounds of generic coffee. Generic coffee? That was even cheaper than the brand we used. According to the billboard and the television commercials, Java Heaven only sold 100 percent organic free-trade rain-forest-preserving coffee, not generic coffee.

Two more items were listed on the receipt—a crate of brown paper bags, and ten rolls of custom printed labels.

Oh, little piece of paper, where have you been all my life?

Twenty-seven

By the time the receipt landed in my hands, Mr. Darling had already closed his back door with a gracious, "Good riddance!"

I could have knocked on that door to return the little piece of paper. I could have.

But I didn't.

Why? Because if ever there was a time to believe in signs, that was it. My hand trembled as I read the receipt again. This was huge. Business Man of the Year wasn't looking too good. Big Fat Liar of the year was more like it.

My mind raced. Should I fax the invoice to the *Nordby News*? Mr. Darling would kill me. He'd hire some kind of assassin and have me shot dead one morning while I was filling jam pots. Okay, maybe he wouldn't go that far, but he'd seek some kind of horrible revenge. I'd have to send it anonymously. Tomorrow's headline would be: *Java Heaven Sells Slave Labor Coffee*. After that: *Owner of Java Heaven Indicted for Fraud*. And then: *Java Heaven Closes Forever*. Elizabeth could post it on her blog and word would spread overnight, just like it had with Ratcatcher.

But then a really sneaky thought occurred to me. Was it more valuable if no one else knew just yet—if I used the invoice as blackmail? I shivered. Did I have what it took to be a blackmailer? That would be an interesting addition to my checklist.

"Guess what I found," I yelled as I rushed into our coffeehouse. No one replied. The Boys had left a note: *Finished cleaning, gone for a snort.* Malcolm was still upstairs. He had found my grandmother's photo album and was sitting on the couch, slowly flipping through the pages. I still wasn't used to seeing him in pants. I kind of missed the kilt.

"Look," I said, waving the receipt.

He leaned over the album, his expression one of awe. "This is you," he said quietly. He pointed to a photo taken at one of those cheap mini-mall studios. Two-year-old me sat on a rocking horse, propped in front of a fall panorama. Two teeth, two ponytails, and two red bows completed the goofy look.

"Yeah, that's me. Look at what I—"

He flipped through a few more pages. "This book is a record of your life. Your first haircut, your first birthday, your first piano recital. I've never seen anything quite like it before."

"Really? Everyone has a photo album."

He shut the album, then ran his hand over the cover. "Not everyone, Katrina. In order to have a record of your life, you've got to have a life."

Was he saying that he didn't have a life? He probably felt like he was too busy to have a life. Vincent had told me to *get a life*. "You're an angel. That's an exciting life. You don't need a stupid photo album."

"It's not the album. It's the life. You see, Katrina, I'm not *alive*."

I sank into my grandfather's worn recliner, trying to absorb that sentence. "But you're breathing. I can see you breathing right now. And you're warm. I can feel you from here. And you eat. What do you mean you're not alive?"

He sighed. "I exist. Clearly I exist. But I don't have a life in the way that you do."

"You mean you don't die? You get to live forever?" That little fact would kill any chance of us becoming a couple. Imagine having a boyfriend who never got any older. I'd be sitting in my motorized wheelchair with gray hair and no teeth and he'd be playing beach volleyball in his kilt.

"I'm not immortal. I'm here for a time and then I'm gone."

"Oh. Then I don't understand."

"I'll exist for as long as I'm needed, but existing is a solitary course, Katrina. I go from one delivery to the next, moving in and out of other lives like a vapor, leaving those lives transformed. Every once in a while I stretch out the visit because I want to know what it's like to swim in the ocean, or ride on a Ferris wheel, or dance at a gathering of the Highland clans. Or what it's like to have a family."

I felt small in my grandfather's chair—insignificant and mortal. A regular person who is born and then dies. Whose life had I transformed? "Do all messengers stretch out their visits?"

"No. I've always been different. Curiosity is a real burden for a messenger." He leaned forward, his forearms resting on his knees. "Most people are too busy and distracted to notice me, unless I purposefully reveal myself to them.

But for some reason that I still don't understand, you saw me sleeping in your alley. You noticed me when it wasn't my intent to be noticed. That's never happened before."

"I noticed you because no one had ever slept in our alley. It was weird."

"It's not that simple." He smiled. "Or maybe it is that simple. Maybe we were simply meant to meet. I've enjoyed meeting you, Katrina. I've enjoyed being a small part of your life. You're very fortunate to have your grandmother and your friends. I wish I could . . ." He stopped, his mood turning serious again. "I wish I could have some of the things that you have."

A powerful surge of emotion rushed through me right then and there. He trusted me enough to share his feelings. What guy does that? Even Vincent didn't open up about his mother or his fear of failure.

He pushed the album aside and stood. "I've got to go. I've got to get that message delivered, once and for all." He picked up his satchel, straining to lift it over his shoulder. Then, without another word, he left

I watched him from the window as he strode up Main Street. From the back he looked like a regular guy in a boring pair of khaki pants and a white sweater. How lonely it must be to be a messenger, handing out envelopes that would change people's lives. I realized, then and there, that I'm one of those "cup-half-empty" people. While I didn't have popularity or talent or a boyfriend, those blank spaces were nothing compared to what I did have—the things he longed for.

I clutched the invoice.

I made it to the hospital with only twenty minutes left

for visiting hours. A husband and wife who owned a Main Street gift shop were just saying good-bye as I hurried into my grandmother's room. "Yak, yak, yak," my grandmother complained after they had gone. "Just because I'm a prisoner in this bed doesn't mean I want to hear all about the refinancing on their house. For heaven's sake, I'm a sick woman." She held out her arms. "But I want to hear all about *you*."

She wore her blue floral pajamas and bathrobe. Her little radio was plugged in next to the bed. The IV was gone, but she was still hooked up to a monitor. Four more bouquets crowded the counter.

"Look at this," I said, shoving the invoice at her.

"I don't have my glasses. What is it?"

"It's a receipt from Acme Supply Company." I bounced on my toes like a little kid. This would be the best news she'd heard in a very long time.

"It's not a bill, is it?" She laid her arm across her forehead. "I really can't think about that right now."

"No, it's not a bill. It belongs to Java Heaven. I found it in the alley."

"What's the matter with you? Do you need to use the bathroom?"

"No." I stopped bouncing and read the invoice. As if delivering a commencement speech, I said each word clearly, precisely, hoping to inspire. Grandma Anna didn't say anything, so I read it again. Her expression stayed blank. "Don't you see? He's not selling organic coffee. He's selling the cheapest stuff he can get and then labeling it as organic freetrade rain-forest-saving coffee. He's been lying to everyone." I waved the receipt.

She folded her hands, resting them on her round belly. "It doesn't surprise me one bit. He's always been a scoundrel." Her voice lacked the excitement that pulsed through me.

"If we give this to the newspaper, or maybe even to Officer Larsen, Java Heaven will go out of business. And then our old customers will come back. We can save the coffeehouse."

She shook her head. "The Health Department hasn't agreed to let us reopen."

"They will. You know they will. We don't have rats living in our coffeehouse."

My grandmother took a deep breath and turned her face toward the window. Darkness pressed against the panes. When she looked back at me, her eyes had filled with surrender. "We won't do anything with that receipt."

"What?" Was this some sort of drug-induced fog? I had thought she'd be all over the invoice, ready to make photocopies and plaster the streets with it. Maybe she was secretly afraid of Mr. Darling, of what he might do to an old woman who had turned him over to the authorities. Maybe the heart attack had made her feel vulnerable. "But this will solve everything. It's like an answer to our prayers."

"It's not an answer to *my* prayers." She patted the bed. "Come, sit down."

I sat.

"Katrina, the coffeehouse hasn't gone into debt because of Mr. Darling. It's easy to blame him, but I have to look to myself. I didn't keep up with the changing times. I refused to try new things, and that's suicide for a business owner."

"But it's not too late."

"I'm not going to gain success by stepping on someone else. Even if that someone else is a crook."

"But people have a right to know."

"Yes, I suppose they do, but they're not going to hear it from us. You're not supposed to have that invoice—it's private property. He could accuse you of stealing."

"But—"

"What he has done is his own affair. He's made his bed. And he's the one who has to lie in it."

What was that supposed to mean? His bed was full of money. He'd lie in it all day if he could. "Grandma, you don't understand. He said he's going to buy the entire building. He said that as soon as we failed to pay rent, he would evict us." That should have changed her mind, but it didn't.

"Then it's time for us to move on. I don't want to spend one day with Mr. Darling as my landlord." She squeezed my hand. "Don't take it so hard, Katrina. Change comes to everyone. Years ago I would have felt ready for a fight, but I'm tired. I've struggled with the coffeehouse for so long. I can't do it anymore. But I won't be responsible for the downfall of another business, no matter how conniving Mr. Darling is. He has a family. I wouldn't be able to sleep knowing I had brought them ruin."

She was such a good person. I felt a rush of shame that I had been so ready to expose Mr. Darling—so eager to celebrate his downfall. But still, how unfair. The bad guy is not supposed to win. It had seemed like the perfect answer.

"Get rid of that invoice. Stop worrying so much about the coffeehouse. You should be thinking about your schoolwork and the upcoming festival. You should be thinking about all the fun you're going to have with that handsome boy."

"Does this mean we'll have to move?"

"Yes."

"To Retirement Universe?"

"Heavens no. I have a bit of money in a CD that I'll cash. We'll find a place to rent and we'll be just fine. Your grandfather's retirement check supported the coffeehouse. Now it can support us. We won't be rich, but we'll make do. However, there's someone else I'm worried about."

"Irmgaard?"

"Yes. She loves the place as much as I do. She'll have a difficult time adjusting. I don't know where she'll get a job making soup."

The nurse poked her head in to tell me that visiting hours were over. Grandma pushed herself up the pillows. "Katrina, there's something you should know about Irmgaard."

"That she's a nun?"

"How did you know that?"

"She gave me a book and it said *Property of Sister Irmgaard*."

"She used to be a nun. She left the abbey."

"Why?"

"It's better left in the past. What I want you to know about Irmgaard is that I consider her to be a part of our family." Grandma Anna yawned. "I'm very tired. Go on home now. Drive carefully."

I hugged her. She settled back and closed her eyes. Then, just as I was leaving, she mumbled, "Always remember that to forgive is to set someone free."

I crumpled the invoice and threw it into the backseat. Once a shining beacon of hope, now just a stupid piece of paper.

Why had my grandmother mentioned forgiveness? Did she actually expect me to forgive Mr. Darling for buying the building and kicking us out? No way. I'd return his invoice, but it would be a cold day in hell when I stopped loathing him. Maybe that makes me a bad person. Or maybe that makes me a normal, average person, with normal, average feelings.

I ate three bowls of cereal that night because I didn't feel like cooking anything. The box claimed that one serving met all the day's requirements of vitamins and minerals, so if Grandma asked if I'd been eating healthy, I could say yes. The answering machine flashed, full of messages for Ratcatcher. I listened to a few, then turned it off.

Would Malcolm come back? I wandered to the window. As usual, Main Street had emptied of people and cars, except for the few cars parked outside the pub and a few more parked outside Java Heaven. I watched the end of the street, wishing for Malcolm to appear around the corner. Hopefully he'd be smiling because Irmgaard had finally taken the envelope. But something else appeared—a small white light. It emerged from the place where the streetlights ended, gliding closer like a little fallen star. I pressed against the window to get a better view. The light grew as it floated closer. It was a bicycle light. The rider stopped across the street and slid off his seat.

Vincent didn't wave. I didn't wave either. He held on to his handlebars and stared up at me. I didn't open the window and yell, *Hey, come on up*, like I would have, just one week ago. The span of road that separated us felt like a chasm. My feelings were still hurt. I know that people break promises all the time, but it was my *only* promise and my *only* best guy friend.

To forgive is to set someone free.

Being mad at someone is like a huge weight hanging around your neck—like that sinking feeling I got after swimming the second lap at the Nordby High pool. Forgiveness would set me free, but forgiveness seemed impossible.

We stared, neither of us moving. Then he swung his leg over the seat and pedaled off.

On the night my parents died, when I lay in my bed, I probably felt terribly lonely. I'm just guessing because I don't remember that night. But the night Vincent rode away was lonelier than I could bear.

Twenty-eight

Tuesday was the last day of school before winter break. Usually it would have been a morning of excited anticipation, but I could barely drag myself out of bed.

The coffeehouse remained closed. Malcolm didn't show up, nor did Irmgaard. The pop of the toaster, the rhythm of Irmgaard at the chopping block, the sound of Odin and Lars arguing—that was my sound track. But it had faded like an echo.

"Oh, Katrina." Mr. Prince waved at me from his office as I tried to sneak by. "We should discuss those aptitude results. Very promising, don't you think?"

I shrugged, eyeing the Java Heaven cup he held. Honest to God, I wanted to rip it from his hand and stomp on it.

"You should take those results seriously, Katrina. Think about going to business school. Maybe even pursuing an MBA. Get some business experience. Every entrepreneur needs business experience. Have you ever held a job? Do you know anyone who could write you a letter of recommendation? You could join the Future Business

Leaders of America. Heidi Darling runs the group. Do you know her?"

Oh God, if I have to stand here one more second, I'm going to scream!

He took a sip from the peppermint straw. "Have you tried the Vincent Mocha? It's delicious."

I fled.

In World Mythology I grabbed the empty chair next to Elliott. Mr. Williams sat at the edge of his desk like he always did. "Today we'll finish up our good deed chapter. Please open your books to the next section, called 'The Damsel in Distress.'"

I knew that Vincent was over by the window. I knew that the ends of his hair were dripping onto his sweatshirt, and that he was chewing on his pencil. But I didn't look at him.

"Who can give me an example of a damsel in distress in a fairy tale?" Mr. Williams asked.

Brianna's hand shot up. "Sleeping Beauty."

"Go on."

"Well, she can't wake up until the prince kisses her. He has to hack his way through those vines to get to her."

"Okay, any other examples?"

"Snow White," Ashley said. "She's dead in that glass coffin, but then the prince comes and kisses her and she wakes up."

Mr. Williams nodded. "Thanks to Walt Disney, you are all familiar with damsels in distress. This theme is common throughout mythology. The female, traditionally viewed as the weaker of the sexes, and historically the more vulnerable, is placed in some sort of jeopardy. Her survival depends on the heroic action of the male, usually a prince but sometimes a man of lowly means who is rewarded for his good deed. Often the reward is a kiss, which in a larger context means sexual availability."

Aaron puckered his lips and made some kissing sounds. "Where can I find a damsel in distress?"

I stared at the chapter illustration of a girl looking out a window that was set high in a tower. Her long blond hair framed her sad face. She leaned against the panes, watching, waiting for the prince to rescue her. I stared hard until my vision blurred and her face morphed into mine. Last night I had looked out my own window, waiting for Malcolm, hoping he'd show up with his magic bean to make everything right again. Waiting to be rescued.

And wasn't that what I had always expected from Vincent? Calling him whenever I needed something, relying on him to take me to the movies and to go places with me if Elizabeth couldn't go. To show up if I got scared because I found a stranger lying in my alley. To be the one person I could call any time of the day or night.

Holy crap! I was just like that stupid girl in the tower.

"Mr. Williams?" I raised my hand, interrupting his reading.

"Yes?"

"What about the stories where the damsel in distress saves herself?"

"What?"

"When she doesn't wait for the prince."

He laid the textbook on his lap. "The damsel in distress doesn't save herself in these stories, Katrina. She can't save herself because a curse or a magic spell has imprisoned her."

"But maybe she can save herself, if she tries," I blurted. Everyone stared at me. "Um, I've got to go to the bathroom." I grabbed my backpack and rushed from the room.

I was sick of feeling like a loser, like I couldn't do anything right. I was sick of feeling like everything I cared about was about to be taken away. I wasn't the swim team captain or president of the Glee Club. I was the Coffeehouse Girl and I wasn't going to lose that without a fight. Grandma couldn't stop me, because she wasn't home to stop me. If I knew exactly how much we owed, and how much we had coming in, then I could make a plan. Maybe it was pure ignorance on my part, but somewhere deep inside I felt that I could do it.

Get some business experience, Mr. Prince had said. *Every entrepreneur needs business experience*. What better experience is there than saving a business? But was there enough time?

I hurried past the glass display of Heidi's successes. *Good for her*, I thought. *She's not waiting in some tower*. In the library, I went back to the business/technology aisle and found a book called *How to Be a Successful Entrepreneur,* written by this really rich guy from New York. The bell rang for second period, but I stayed in the library. The author wrote that the most important thing to guarantee success is to select an excellent support team.

I rushed to the office. "Ms. Kolbert? What class is Elliott in? Elliott Minor. I need to see him right away."

Ms. Kolbert's fingers clicked on her keyboard. "Elliott Minor is in Trigonometry. Room eighteen."

Waving like a crazy person outside room 18's glass window, I finally got Elliott's attention. He raised his hand, asked to be excused, then joined me in the hall. "What are you doing?"

"Elliott, I need your help." I started pacing. "Do you really understand all that stuff about marketing surveys and small business loans?"

"I think so."

"Well, my grandmother's coffeehouse is going to go out of business unless I do something right away. She owes a lot of money. I need somebody who's good with numbers. We'd work together. I'll pay you, just as soon as I can, if you'll teach me how to set it all up on the computer."

"Why are you asking me?"

"Because I'm supposed to get the best support team I can get, and I think that you're the smartest kid in school." He narrowed his eyes suspiciously. "And I'm going to get Elizabeth for the team too."

The corners of his mouth turned up in a little smile. "When do we begin?"

Elizabeth wasn't in her Biology class. I called her. "What's wrong? Are you sick?"

"I've been in bed all day."

"Why?"

"I just feel so depressed. I hate feeling this way."

"Is this because of Face?"

"Yes. Isn't that pathetic?"

"It's not pathetic. You got your feelings hurt. There's nothing pathetic about that." I leaned against the wall, pressing Elliott's cell phone to my ear. "Face is a moron. So what if he doesn't like you? It's his loss. Now, get out of bed."

"I'm watching this show on insects. Did you know that

the praying mantis eats her boyfriend's head after they mate? I wonder what she does if he rejects her?"

Elizabeth, not-to-be-messed-with artist-extraordinaire, had wrapped herself in a blanket of self-pity. Some stupid jerk who couldn't see past her weird clothes and pudgy face had reduced her to watching television in the middle of the day, which is a pretty bad sign.

"Elizabeth, I know you feel crappy right now, but we both need to stop moping around. Face is history. Vincent is history. And the coffeehouse is going to be history if I don't do something. I need you to get out of bed, get dressed, and meet me down there."

The crinkle of a plastic wrapper filled the earpiece. "Why?" she asked with a full mouth.

"Because you're the most talented person I know. Because you have vision. Because you make everything interesting and beautiful. Because without you, this will never work."

"Really?" She sniffled.

"I need you."

"Okay. I'll meet you there."

Elliott and I left school in the Buick. I pretended to have a stomachache, he forged a note for an allergy appointment. I shared all the coffeehouse details without shame or embarrassment. Grandma Anna would forgive me because facing the truth was the only way forward. I turned onto Main Street. Last night's craft party at Java Heaven had produced hundreds of foam snowflakes. Shopkeepers had hung them in their windows and from their awnings. Ropes of snowflakes dangled across the street and wound around lampposts. We drove past Viking Square, where the blue spruce stood, decked out in snowflakes and lights. Magical. We passed Anna's coffeehouse, the only shop on the street not decorated, unless you consider the *Closed by Health Department* sign a festive addition.

There was no time to worry about snowflakes.

Elizabeth had parked in the back alley and was waiting for us. "What's *he* doing here?" she whispered when Elliott got out of the car.

"You'll see."

Inside, I turned on the heat and lights. Elliott gave Ratcatcher a good scratch while I started the coffeepot. We'd need lots and lots of caffeine. I made a platter of buttered toast and while they ate, I described the plan that was bouncing around in my head.

"We have three days before the Solstice Festival. I think there's money to be made from Ratcatcher's fame. I want to transform this place into the Ratcatcher Emporium. We've got my grandfather's retirement check and about two hundred dollars in my grandmother's checking account to work with and a credit card in case we need it. I've got some cash from tips. What do you think?" I held out my arms and waited for their reaction. They stopped crunching.

"Is this okay with your grandmother?" Elizabeth asked.

"She doesn't know anything about it. She'll still be in the hospital. And anyway, she decided to close down the coffeehouse, so I might as well use the space while I can."

"Won't she get mad if you spend her money?" Elliott asked.

"Probably, but it's our only chance. That money would only pay a few bills and then we'd still be in debt *and* without a coffeehouse."

Elizabeth leaned across the counter and whispered, "Why don't you just get *you know who* to give you the *you know what?*"

"I don't need that third bean. I'm going to do this myself. Everyone still wants to meet Ratcatcher. We can't compete with Java Heaven in the coffee market, so why not do something completely different? Elliott, I need you to work the financial end. Elizabeth, I need you to work the marketing end."

"What about the Health Department?" Elizabeth asked.

"I'm not serving food, so who cares about them?"

"It's a risk," Elliott said, wiping crumbs from his mouth. "But every great endeavor begins with risk."

Elizabeth finally smiled. "The Ratcatcher Emporium. I love it!"

Elliott set up his laptop in the office and I brought my computer downstairs for Elizabeth. Elliott and I went through all the files and drawers. He created a spreadsheet that listed all the money we owed and current and future expenses. Elizabeth and I brainstormed products. We took a photo of Ratcatcher, then e-mailed it to a company that pasted it onto coffee mugs, sticky notes, and cookie tins. We paid for next-day shipping. Elizabeth created a cute logo of Ratcatcher's smiling face and set up a simple Web site, then sent it off to all her blogger friends. She contacted the *Nordby News* and some local radio stations.

I answered the messages, then left a message on the phone letting callers know that the Ratcatcher Emporium would officially open on Friday for the Solstice festival.

Evening came. I called the hospital. Grandma said she'd had way too many visitors and not to worry about stopping by. She hadn't seen Irmgaard and was worried. I called Irmgaard's apartment, but no one answered. I hadn't seen her since the encounter with Malcolm at the hospital. I kept expecting each of them to show up. While I would have welcomed Irmgaard's help, it was probably best not to have Malcolm hanging around, clogging up my brain with all those *feelings*.

"This is going to be an all-nighter," Elliott said. He called his parents. His dad stopped by with a bathrobe and sleeping bag and a bunch of packaged snacks because Elliott had this low blood sugar thing. Elizabeth's mom brought us a chicken and rice casserole, which was great.

I felt energized and it wasn't from the caffeine. Something powerful surged through my veins. Was it confidence? Do confident people walk around feeling like that all the time—like everything will work out? What a great feeling.

"You know what's missing?" Elizabeth said, drinking her third cup of coffee.

I shook my head. My answer would have been Vincent, but I didn't say that. While Elizabeth, Elliott, and I made a great team, it wasn't the original three. Vincent didn't know anything about spreadsheets or marketing, but it would have been nice to have him there. He could have passed out flyers in his calm, friendly way. I should have waved to him when he had looked up from his bike. I should have run out there and hugged him and said, *It doesn't matter. You broke a promise and I acted like a jealous, insecure idiot. And we both said mean things. Let's just forget it and move on.*

"I'll tell you what's missing. The stupid rat is what's missing," Elizabeth said.

"Huh?"

"We need to get that rat back." She pushed her chair away from the desk. "Why did they take it anyway? Seems to me it belongs to you. It was in your shop."

"You're right," I said, suddenly indignant. "Why did they have to take it? People will want to see that rat. I need to get it back." Then I remembered. "But it smelled disgusting."

"You can get the rat stuffed," Elliott said. He was stretched out on his sleeping bag, plugging numbers into his laptop. "My dad went hunting last year and had this client of his clean and stuff the deer he shot."

"That's a great idea." I remembered this place in Seattle called Ye Olde Curiosity Shoppe, full of all sorts of weird stuffed dead things. People love those stuffed dead things. I imagined tourists posing with the massive rodent. "That's a really great idea."

"My dad's an attorney," Elliott said. "I'll call him. I bet he can get the rat back."

We worked through the night, drifting off around 3:00 a.m. I fell asleep on the desk. Elizabeth curled next to Elliott, which didn't surprise me. They'd been working together all day, sharing snacks, talking about art classes. They both snored, but it only woke me up twice. Ratcatcher, completely unaware that she was the center of our universe, gnawed her way into one of Elliott's animal cracker boxes. I wished I had someone to curl up next to—someone warm.

The phone woke me up. Expecting another "fan" call, I didn't answer it.

"Katrina?" The answering machine's speaker muffled Officer Larsen's voice. "I've got a young man down here at the station who says he's a friend of yours. Picked him up for trespassing. I can't locate his family and he's refused to make his one phone call. Thought you might be able to clear this up. Says he works as a messenger."

Twenty-nine

The last time I was inside the Nordby Police Station was for a fifth-grade field trip. We were bored out of our minds because the place was nothing like the movies. No guys in striped pajamas and no drug-sniffing dogs. No prostitutes lurking in the hallways saying things like "Hey, girlie, how 'bout gettin' me a cig?" or "My lawyer's gonna sue ya, pig!"

Nordby wasn't the kind of place that overflowed with criminals. Most of the arrests listed in the Police Blotter section of the paper were DWIs, followed by bored teens caught spray painting and blowing up mailboxes. That kind of stuff. As I parked the Buick I thought about the generic coffee invoice, still lying on the backseat. I could accidentally drop it on the police department's floor. Consumer fraud would be an interesting addition to the blotter. But I had already used Grandma's credit card without her permission—I didn't want to break my promise too.

The small brick building sat next to the hardware store. Two police cars were parked outside. Country music drifted down the hall. A secretary showed me to Officer Larsen's office.

"Hi, Katrina," he said. He pulled out a chair, but I didn't feel like sitting. Then he poured himself a cup of coffee from a stained Mr. Coffee carafe. "How's Anna?"

"They're going to discharge her after the weekend."

"Oh, that's good to hear. But too bad she'll miss the Solstice."

"She wouldn't be able to enjoy it anyway. They want her to stay in bed for a while."

"It'll be hard keeping that woman in bed." He sipped. "So, Katrina, how do you know this messenger kid? I can't get any information out of him."

"His name is Malcolm. He just came from Scotland. The Highlands. I met him last week and he's been helping out at the coffeehouse." I fiddled with my coat hem. What else could I say? "He's real nice." Malcolm's satchel sat on the floor. The words *Messenger Service* no longer twinkled. They had turned from gold to gray, as if written in soot.

"He won't give me a last name."

I didn't have a clue about his last name. "Is he under arrest?"

"He was loitering outside Irmgaard's apartment, calling out her name. The manager complained. Said he'd been coming around a lot, especially at night."

"Is that against the law?"

"We have a curfew for minors here in Nordby. Under eighteen and you're supposed to be off the streets after ten p.m.

"Really?" I'd never heard that. Vincent was out late all the time and no one had ever arrested him.

"If Irmgaard's willing to sign a statement saying that he's been harassing her, then I've got good reason to keep him."

"If Irmgaard doesn't sign the statement, will you let him go?"

Officer Larsen set down the coffee mug. "We may have a larger issue. He doesn't appear to have any identification. You say he's from Scotland? Without a visa or a passport, I might have to turn him over to immigration."

Did angels carry driver's licenses, or passports, or labor union cards? "I'm sure he has identification. It's probably back at the coffeehouse. Can I see him?"

Officer Larsen led me down the hall to an honest-to-God jail cell, in which sat an honest-to-God angel. Well, Malcolm wasn't exactly sitting, he was spread out on a bench, his arm flung across his face like the first time I had seen him, which felt like a million years ago. "You can have a few minutes," Officer Larsen said.

I watched him walk back down the hall, then I threw myself at the bars. "Malcolm? What are you doing in here? Why don't you just leave? You *can* leave, can't you?"

"Where would I go?" He lay perfectly still.

"You can come back to the coffeehouse."

"Why? So I can continue to mess up your life? I should have known what you most desired. Any other messenger could have done it with his eyes closed. But I got it wrong with the first bean, and that's why you're not speaking to your best friend. Then I got it wrong with the second bean, and that's why your shop is closed."

I clutched the bars with both hands. "Malcolm, none of this was your fault. Vincent and Heidi would have gotten together anyway, even if he hadn't become a hero. They swim together and she's real . . . cute. And the coffeehouse was losing money long before you showed up. It would have closed even without the rat. Grandma's a great person, but she stinks at business."

"I stink at being a messenger."

As far as I knew, he was telling the truth. He did seem to be having a lot of trouble. I cleared my throat, searching for the right words. After all, it's not every day that you find yourself giving an angel a pep talk. "Look, Malcolm, think of all the other messages that you've delivered. Those worked out, right?"

He said nothing. *Oops.* I tried another tactic.

"Irmgaard's hard to figure out. I mean, she hasn't spoken a word in all the time that I've known her. You've got to be really stubborn to keep a vow of silence, don't you think? That's why you're having trouble with her. When she decides to do something, then forget about changing her mind." But I couldn't come up with an example of Irmgaard's stubbornness, other than the vow of silence. She was usually easy to work with, almost submissive. My pep talk was a dismal failure.

He didn't move or say anything, sinking deeper and deeper into the dark pit that I knew so well. Earlier that morning I would have joined him, and our combined brooding could have been the sulkfest of the century. But I had snapped out of it, so he could too. Angels were supposed to fall out of grace, not into bouts of self-pity. Oh, what did I know? He wasn't anything like a storybook angel. He was himself. I wanted to throw my arms around him and tell him that things would get better.

"Malcolm, let's worry about the message later. I'll talk to Irmgaard. It'll work out. Come on, let's get out of here. Can't you just slip through the wall or something? I could really use your help at the coffeehouse. And you still owe me that third bean, right? So until I figure out what I most desire, you're stuck with me."

Slowly, his face straining, he sat up and looked at me. His vibrant blue eyes had faded to gray. Sweat laced his upper lip. He groaned and leaned against the cell wall.

"Malcolm, are you sick?"

He lifted the hem of my grandfather's sweater. The golden envelope was tucked under his belt. "I hid it from the officer. It's heavier. In a few more hours I won't be able to move."

Won't be able to move? He wasn't sulking. He was in serious pain! "Then get rid of it. Put it on the ground."

"I cannot. It's my burden to bear." He grimaced. "Katrina, I can't be seen like this. I need your help."

He was trapped in that cell. What would happen if the world found out about him? He'd get into serious trouble. I ran back to the office. "Officer Larsen?" I cried. He was doing some paperwork. "I need to take Malcolm back to the coffeehouse. He's sick."

"I can't release him yet."

"Irmgaard's not going to press charges. I'll talk to her. I know she won't. And Malcolm will go back home as soon as he's better. I promise he will."

Officer Larsen stroked his chin. He was a man of rules. I'd never known him to make exceptions.

"Please." I paced in front of his desk. Vincent's and Rat-catcher's media coverage would be nothing compared to the frenzy a real angel would cause. "You've known me my entire life. I promise you that he's not a terrorist or a criminal of any kind. He's just here on vacation, but he's real sick."

"Are you sure he's sick? He didn't look sick when I brought him in. Let's take a look." He unhooked a set of keys from his belt and led me back to the jail cell. "You're right, he sure doesn't look well," which was a total understatement because Malcolm had turned a light shade of green. "Maybe we should get him to the hospital."

"It's just the flu," I said. "It's going around. Maybe you shouldn't get too close. It's very contagious."

Officer Larsen stepped away from the cell. "The flu can bring a man to his knees. Last time I caught it, my fever went to a hundred and three."

"I've already been exposed, so I'll take him back to the coffeehouse and Irmgaard will make him some soup." *Come on, come on, just let him go.* Malcolm's eyes had closed again. I think he was trying to hide his pain. "Please, Officer Larsen."

"Well, I guess until I hear from Irmgaard I have no real reason to keep him. And, as far as I can tell, there's no warrant out for his arrest."

"He can go?"

Officer Larsen nodded. "Consider it a favor to you, Katrina. I appreciate all the times you've helped my father. I have your word that you'll get this boy's passport sorted out?"

"Yes." What else could I say?

He unlocked the gate. I rushed in. It took all my strength and still I couldn't get Malcolm to his feet. "Malcolm," I whispered in his ear. "You've got to help me get you out of here." He opened his eyes, groaned, then stood on shaky legs. "Don't get too close," I told Officer Larsen. Though I could have used his help, how would I explain the fact that Malcolm weighed as much as an elephant? And what if he found the envelope? "Be sure to disinfect this place after we leave."

Malcolm stumbled. I swung his arm over my shoulder, then we hobbled down the hall. "Thank you," I said as Officer Larsen slid the satchel over my arm. Then he held open the front door.

It took forever to get Malcolm to the Buick. Despite the winter wind, I started to sweat. The car tipped when he finally fell onto the passenger seat. The tires went a bit flat, but they held up as we drove off like a car in a cartoon. Malcolm groaned again and doubled over.

"What will happen if she doesn't take the message?" I asked.

"It will crush me," he said quietly.

"Crush you?"

"Like a bug under your foot."

I stepped on the gas. "We're almost there."

We screeched into the apartment's parking lot. It's not easy to maneuver a lopsided car. I'd been to the building a few times, but I'd never gone inside. Irmgaard had never invited us over for dinner or to watch a movie. Her life outside the coffeehouse was a total mystery.

The building sat on a really depressing corner, at the exact spot where the Scandinavian charm of Nordby ended and the strip malls began. Beyond stretched the shared landscape of America—cheap nail salons, fast-food restaurants, and outlet stores. I parked crooked, taking up two spaces. "Wait here." He wasn't going anywhere and there was no way I could get him up the stairs.

Malcolm nodded. His long hair fell over his face.

I didn't want anything to happen to him. He was the only angel I'd ever met—maybe the only one I'd ever meet. He was kind, and honest, and handsome, and I was the only person who could help him. Imagine that.

I ran up the front steps and slipped into the building just as an old guy was leaving. Irmgaard lived in apartment 201. I knew that because I always helped Grandma address our Christmas cards.

At first, Irmgaard wouldn't open her door. "It's me," I said. No response. "Irmgaard, please let me in. Grandma had another heart attack." The door swung open. Irmgaard clutched the knob, her eyes wide with alarm. I flew inside. "Don't worry. She didn't have another heart attack. She's fine. I need to talk to you about the message."

Irmgaard pulled a black shawl around her shoulders. The place was freezing and barren, with only an old thrift store table and one single wooden chair. The only thing that hung on the white walls was a wooden cross. No television, no photographs, no radio. It looked like a convent cell in the middle of nowhere rather than an apartment next to a teriyaki hut. The place gave me the creeps. Why would a person live with no comforts? Like some sort of punishment?

"Irmgaard?" I looked her right in the eyes. "Each day that you don't take the message, it gets heavier and heavier." I pointed to the window. "Malcolm's sitting down there. He can barely move. The message is crushing him. I think he might die. Or cease to exist. Or something like that. It's very confusing."

She pulled the shawl tighter, shrinking beneath its folds.

"Look, if it's bad news I'll help you. Grandma will help you. The Boys will help too. But maybe it's good news. Maybe it's something amazing." I forced a feeble smile, picturing Malcolm doubled over. "There's not much time."

Dark shadows circled her usually beautiful eyes. Her silence didn't feel comfortable or hypnotic. It felt eerie and chilling. She knew he was an angel, but she didn't seem to care. I recognized the tight look on her face. "Irmgaard, why are you so scared? Please tell me. I can't help you and I can't help Malcolm if I don't know. He's in real danger."

She nodded, then motioned for me to sit in the chair, which I did while she went into the other room. What was she doing? I fidgeted and was about to yell her name when she returned with a folder in her hands. She set the folder on the table, then stepped away. I opened it.

Three newspaper clippings lay inside. The top clipping had a photograph of a mangled car. *Local Husband and Wife Killed in Crash*. I'd never seen the article before. Why hadn't my grandmother ever showed it to me?

My heart sped up as I read. According to the article, my mother and father had been driving in unusually thick fog on their way to a weekend stay on the coast. On a curvy stretch, where the highway wound around Lake Crescent, an oncoming van had swerved to avoid a deer and had crossed the center line. My parents died immediately. I scanned the photo for signs of them but only found the aftermath, caught in black-and-white, grainy and fading.

The next clipping had the headline: *Funeral Held for the Svensens*. The funeral had taken place at the Nordby Lutheran Church. A photo showed Grandma, Grandpa, and me holding hands as we left the church. I hovered over the photo, trying to take in every inch that had been me at age three. My Mary Janes, my wool coat buttoned to my chin, my little sad face, my long hair, braided and golden. The only memory I had of that day was that I had to sit very still in the front row of church and that Grandpa kept handing me caramels, one at a time, as my reward for sitting still. I could still see his big calloused hand opening to reveal each sweet cube, as if it had appeared magically. But I remembered nothing more. My three-year-old mind had chosen to save the caramel memory, probably the only happy memory from that day.

I hesitated, sensing that something terrible waited in the third article. *Driver of Van Released from Hospital.*

The unidentified driver of the van that caused the deaths of Mr. and Mrs. Svensen was released today, after two weeks in the hospital for treatment of a punctured lung and three broken ribs. The photo of the van showed its front end, completely crushed. On the side of the van were the words: *Abbey of St. Clare.* The clipping said that St. Clare's Abbey was set in a remote location in the Olympic Mountains, and that the nuns only ventured into the outside world for supplies, which is where the van's driver had been headed on that fateful afternoon.

I looked up at Irmgaard. She stood as rigid as a statue, her arms clutching the shawl. Her face empty of color, her expression filled with anguish.

I didn't want to read any more. I knew what the article would tell me.

I leaned closer to the photo. Two paramedics were bent over a figure laid out on a stretcher. I squinted.

From the stretcher, Irmgaard's face looked back at me.

Thirty

I didn't say a word. I sat back and took a long breath, inhaling the horrid truth.

Irmgaard burst into tears and flung herself at my feet. Numbness spread over my body as if I were watching a movie. How could this be true? The woman who had worked with us each and every day, who had filled our stomachs with wonderful soup, who had filled the shop with the aroma of freshly baked krumkake and had become part of my family, had killed my parents?

This was someone else's life.

"I don't understand," I murmured. But I did. The facts were printed right there in that article—irrefutable evidence. Irmgaard kept crying, her head bowed. Anger rushed through me, intense and physical. I wanted to lash out, to blame her for all that had gone wrong. For an instant I felt true hatred. I admit it. But the feeling left as quickly as it appeared. I looked down at her. Her hair was sheared so short I could see patches of white scalp. Part of her punishment, I realized, along with the nothingness of her apartment and her vow of silence. She hated *herself*.

I held the article in my trembling hand. "Did my grand-mother know about this when she hired you?" I asked.

Irmgaard nodded, her shoulders heaving between sobs.

To forgive is to set someone free, Grandma had mumbled from her hospital bed. This was the person she wanted me to forgive, not stupid Mr. Darling. But how do you forgive someone for causing the death of your parents? I needed time to work it out—it was too much to digest right then. Would this forever change the way I felt about Irmgaard? She was still the same person, the one who had taught me how to cook and how to knit. How to see an angel when I had only seen a homeless guy.

"It was a horrible accident," I said, to her as much as to myself. "Nothing can change what happened. Malcolm can't even bring them back to life."

Malcolm. He was in the car, struggling to breathe. There was no time to work out my feelings.

I slid off the chair and knelt beside Irmgaard. "My parents are dead. But you and me, we're here. And all we can do is to keep going, Irmgaard, to try to make things work with-out them." She stopped crying. The guilt she had carried was as heavy as the message that threatened to crush Mal-colm. "You've got to take that message. I know you're afraid. I went into Java Heaven yesterday and faced Mr. Darling. I was scared to go in there, but I did it. I don't know what that message says, but if you don't take it, something terrible is going to happen to Malcolm. Please take the message, Irm-gaard. If it's bad news, I'll be there to help you. You won't be alone."

She didn't get up. She just knelt there in some sort of trance. What more could I say? How could I convince her to take that message? I hurried to the window. Only a few cars sat in the parking lot. But something had changed. The Buick didn't look quite right. It was still tilted from the weight of the message, but it seemed closer to the ground. Why couldn't I see the tires? Why was the car moving? Oh my God!

I threw open Irmgaard's door, ran down the stairs to the first floor and out the front door. A couple of joggers stood in the parking lot, pointing. "Don't go near it," one of them cried as I ran toward the car. The tires weren't visible because they had sunk into the pavement!

"Get away from there," another jogger said, waving wildly. "It's a sinkhole. I just called 911."

"My friend's in there," I cried, yanking open the driver's door. The air inside the car was as cold as Irmgaard's apartment. No tropical aura, no scent of the Highlands.

Malcolm lay slumped against the passenger window. "Malcolm, get out of the car." I pulled on his arm. He didn't move.

The car shuddered, then sank a few more inches. I slid down the bench seat and wrapped my arms around his waist, but I couldn't move him. I scrambled out of the car and ran to the passenger side. "Somebody help me," I yelled. Because of the car's tilt, the passenger door was partially submerged in the sinkhole and wouldn't open. I ran back to the driver's side, but before I could climb back in, a man grabbed me.

"Are you crazy? The whole thing could cave in at any moment," he warned, pulling me toward the sidewalk. He wore a uniform from the mini-mart. A crowd had gathered. Women with cotton between their toes and foil packets in their hair hurried out of a beauty salon.

"He's stuck in there," I yelled, pulling free of the man's grip. I ran back to the car.

"I'll try." The teriyaki hut's owner climbed in and tried to move Malcolm, but Malcolm stayed slumped against the passenger window. The car tilted even farther. The man panicked and climbed to safety.

"Roll down the window," one guy yelled. "Maybe we can pull him out on this side."

The passenger window was already level with the ground, so I had to move quickly. Sliding down the bench again, I reached across Malcolm and turned the old-fashioned handle as fast as I could. Once the passenger window was open, two men reached in, but still, Malcolm wouldn't move an inch. The ground shuddered. The men fell back as the car sank deeper.

Malcolm seemed to be asleep. "Wake up, Malcolm. MALCOLM!" I shook him and pulled on his arm. Would he get swallowed up? Is that what happens to angels when they get demoted? Would I get swallowed up? Is that what happens to girls who fall in love with angels? "MAL-COLM!" Why wouldn't he wake up? "Please, Malcolm, I want to help you. I want—"

The third bean.

"Malcolm, give me that bean right now. With all my heart I desire that you don't die. You hear me? With all my heart! Give me that bean. Please, Malcolm. I want that bean." I grabbed his satchel from the floor and dumped it upside down, but nothing fell out. No packet, no bean.

My eyes filled with tears. What was I supposed to do? Not even Superman could lift that envelope.

But wait.

There was one other person who could lift it.

"Irmgaard!" I yelled out the window.

"Get out of there," a lady cried from the sidewalk.

The car tilted and the driver's door slammed shut. I pulled myself up the bench seat, rolled down the window, then climbed out of the car. Irmgaard stood on the front steps of her building, terror in her eyes. Terror had invaded my entire body, but at least I was trying to help. "Irmgaard! You're the only one who can save him."

Half the passenger window was below the pavement. I lay on my stomach at the edge of the sinkhole and reached in, taking Malcolm's cold hand. My pulse pounded in my neck. "Malcolm, Irmgaard's coming."

"Katrina," he whispered. "If anything happens to me—"

"She's here. She'll take the message. IRMGAARD!"

"If it hadn't been for this message, I would never have met you." His eyes stayed closed. "I'm glad I met you, Katrina. I'm glad you let me be a part of your life."

Those sounded like dying words. This was not going to be a death scene. No way. I let go of his hand and twisted around. "IRMGAARD!" She was there. She lay down next to me as the window sank lower. "Hurry. Take the envelope. It's tucked in his belt."

She reached in with her slender arm and easily lifted the envelope out of the car.

The change was instantaneous. The sinkhole stopped trembling. A cloud of warm air drifted from the passenger window. Malcolm sat up and looked at me. His eyes went electric blue. YES!

As I got to my feet, he crawled out through the driver's window and stood on the side of the car. The crowd yelled at him to move away from the hole. An ambulance whined in the distance. A police car barreled into the parking lot.

"Get away from that sinkhole," Officer Larsen ordered. Irmgaard and I stepped away. "How'd this happen?"

I didn't know how to answer that question. How could I possibly explain? "It's an emergency," I told him. "This time it's a real emergency."

As Malcolm leaped off the car my eyes got all misty. I rushed to him and threw my arms around his neck. He hugged me back, his arms strong and tight around my waist. My heart slowed. I buried my face in his long hair and inhaled the sweet smell that I had come to love. "Thank you," he whispered in my ear.

Officer Larsen strung yellow tape around the hole. Firefighters arrived. "We've got ourselves a sinkhole," he told them. "Everyone out of the parking lot."

Malcolm and I wandered over to the sidewalk. "I want to thank Irmgaard," he said.

We found her sitting in a cement playground behind the apartment building. The envelope lay in her lap. I sat next to her and put my hand on her rigid shoulder. "It will be okay," I said calmly. "I'm here with you. We're both here."

She nodded. Then slowly, she peeled back the golden flap. She pulled out a little piece of paper. One word floated on the page—one simple word that a person may take for granted, while another may desire it with all his heart.

Live.

As the three of us breathed in that word, the paper and envelope dissolved into nothing.

Thirty-one

The next few days flew by. I basically ran around like a chicken with its head cut off, as my grandmother would say.

On Wednesday morning, Mr. Health Inspector came by. He appeared to be in the same foul mood as last time, scowling and making "hmph" sounds. I made sure Ratcatcher was upstairs while he poked through the pantry, swabbing for bubonic plague. He set some test tubes and eyedroppers on the counter. Finally, he handed me a piece of paper. "You pass. But you must replace the broken dishwasher. Everything else seems satisfactory." What he did not say was: "I'm so sorry to have closed you down unnecessarily."

"Great," I said, holding the door open for him. Passing the inspection was good news, but his visit had totally slowed us down. In order to make enough money to buy a new dishwasher, we needed to get the Ratcatcher Emporium up and running.

When I say "we" I'm talking about Elizabeth, Elliott, Irmgaard, and The Boys. Malcolm had disappeared, again.

Right after the "Sinkhole Incident," which is what the *Nordby News* had called it, Malcolm had grabbed his satchel and hadn't been seen since. But he'd be back. After all, he still owed me a magical coffee bean. And we were supposed to go on that date—not that I was thinking about that. Not at all. Going on a date with an angel to the Solstice Festival was the last thing on my mind. The very last thing. Really.

The sinkhole ended up swallowing three parking spaces. A crane was brought in to lift out the Buick. Except for a few scratches, the car was miraculously undamaged, which was great because buying a new car was not an expense I wanted to add to the list. The city engineer called the sinkhole a natural disaster even though there was nothing natural about it.

That morning at Irmgaard's had changed everything. Now I understood her attentiveness and why she had kept a close eye on me all the time. Her life with us suddenly made sense. She had become a surrogate mother for her own sake as much as for mine. I would struggle with anger and blame, like any normal person. What I learned was that tragedy spreads out in a wide circle, like a drop of dye in a pool, touching many lives. We would work through it together.

Over the days after the sinkhole, Irmgaard started to speak. The first thing she said was: "I'm sorry." People say *I'm sorry* every day. We say it about little things, about unimportant things, but this was the biggest "I'm sorry" I'd ever heard. We hugged and cried some more. Later, when Ralph sat at the counter and bid her good morning, she said, "Good morning." He nearly fell off the stool. But her words were few and carefully selected. Another person might have the opposite reaction to getting her voice back. She might talk about everything, even if it was totally boring. She might sing all day, yell as loud as she could, and yodel from the rooftop. But Irmgaard treated her voice as if it was something precious that shouldn't be wasted. Odin said that if more people acted like Irmgaard and kept their stupid opinions to themselves, the world would be a better place.

Things moved forward for our grand opening. I went to City Hall and got a temporary business license. Ingvar made a sign. Elizabeth painted it with the smiling cat logo she had designed. Odin and Ralph cleared the coffeehouse, stacking all the chairs and tables in the back office. Lars and Elliott set up some shelves that had been gathering dust in Officer Larsen's basement. The merchandise began to show up on Thursday morning. The cutest coffee mugs with Ratcatcher's fat face, plastic cat food dishes with her name, pink headbands with cat ears, black headbands with rat ears—all sorts of silly stuff.

Mr. Darling poked his big arrogant head in about a million times to ask what we were doing. "You need a business license."

"I have one."

"You can't have a cat in a place that serves food."

"I'm not serving food."

"You—"

"Why don't you mind your own business?" I said, right in his face, confidence rushing through me.

He narrowed his eyes, then ran his hand along his thin ponytail. "You won't be able to save this place. As soon as the sale goes through, I'm kicking you out of here."

"You have no legal right to kick us out as long as we pay the rent."

He snickered. "You think that stupid cat is going to help you pay the rent? Ratcatcher Emporium. What a waste of time."

Ingvar and Odin "escorted" Mr. Darling out the door.

I tried to keep the emporium a secret from my grandmother because I knew it would stress her out, but the ladies from the shoe shop told her. "What's going on down there?" she asked over the phone. "I'm stuck in this hospital bed and you're doing I don't know what."

"You said you wanted to close the coffeehouse."

"Yes, but—"

"The coffeehouse *is* closed. But Grandma, we can't ignore our problems or be embarrassed by them. Elliott helped me make a spreadsheet and we've got a lot of debt to pay, so I'm going to take advantage of the Solstice crowds. We're going to make some money. It's going to be great." Why did I feel so excited and giddy? I was risking our last few dollars, but risk feeds the entrepreneur's soul. Risk makes you feel like you've had way too much coffee and are waiting at the very top of a roller coaster, just before the plunge. I liked the feeling.

Each time the front door opened, I expected to see Malcolm. But he stayed away. I wished he'd join us, and I whispered his name when no one could hear me.

On Thursday afternoon, after talking to a local travel agent who wanted to book some Ratcatcher tours, we got the best news of all. Elliott's dad got the rat. Don't ask me how he did it, but he's some kind of attorney god. The taxidermist agreed to stuff it and deliver it Friday morning. I asked him to stand the creature on its hind legs so it would be tall enough for photos. Ingvar and Irmgaard created a pedestal out of an old stool and some red fabric. Ralph suspended a "World's Largest Rat" sign from the ceiling. On the other side of the emporium, Elizabeth and Elliott painted an old wooden chair to look like a throne. Odin hung a "World's Most Famous Cat" sign. The throne was complete when Elizabeth added a velvet pillow from her bed.

On Thursday night, we gathered upstairs to eat Irmgaard's corn chowder. Sitting at the kitchen table, surrounded by friends, I felt happier than I had in a long time. Tomorrow would be an exciting day. I went over everyone's duties, then stood and raised my water glass in a heartfelt toast. "Here's to all of you," I said, feeling suddenly shy as everyone looked at me. "I couldn't have done this alone."

"Don't underestimate yourself," Lars said, his cane leaning against his chair. "You've got a good head on your shoulders."

"If your grandfather were here, he'd be real proud," Ingvar said.

"Thank you." I raised the glass higher. "Here's to old friends, and to new ones." I nodded at Elliott. He sat next to Elizabeth. Funny, but during the past few days, she hadn't mentioned Face at all.

Ratcatcher jumped onto the table and licked my empty chowder bowl. "And here's to Ratcatcher, the World's Most Famous Cat."

"To Ratcatcher," everyone cried. Ratcatcher thought we were yelling at her, so she jumped off the table.

As the meal wound down, I wandered over to the living room window. The Solstice Festival was most fun when it snowed, but not a cloud hung in the star-filled sky. No angel wandered down the street. No best friend rode past on his bike. Happiness is sweetest when shared, my grandmother liked to say. Vincent had always been a part of my happiest memories.

I remembered the word that had floated on Irmgaard's message. *Live*. How many of us need to be reminded that living has nothing to do with trying to be as good as someone else, or trying to fit into some category, or filling in the blanks on some stupid checklist. That it has nothing to do with punishing yourself for past mistakes.

I was stupid to stay mad at Vincent. Who cared if he had gone inside Java Heaven to make snowflakes? Who cared if he had held some stupid cup on TV? The law that I had imposed on my friends, *Thou shalt never, ever partake of Java Heaven coffee*, wasn't important anymore. We were moving forward. I was moving forward.

I picked up the phone to call him. But he didn't answer.

Thirty-two

Friday morning might have felt like any other winter morning in Nordby, except for one thing—the Solstice Festival had arrived.

Winter solstice is the time when the sun's position is at its greatest angular distance on the other side of the equatorial plane, meaning it's the shortest day and longest night of the year. Cultures all over the world used to pay homage to this day, but not so much anymore, making way for religious holidays. But in our little corner of the world, though Christmas and Hanukkah were still a big deal, we kept up the Old World traditions. Even the Suquamish tribe added their tradition by baking salmon on cedar planks. Like Nordby itself, the Solstice Festival was a hodgepodge of cultures old and new. Though Ratcatcher and her giant stuffed rat had nothing to do with the old traditions, I was pretty sure that they'd be welcomed with open arms.

Ratcatcher's Emporium officially opened at 9:00 a.m. The taxidermist wheeled in the rat on a hand truck. Its glass eyes and glossy black hair gave me the creeps. Ratcatcher slept on her throne. Irmgaard stood ready behind the cash register. Elliott, digital camera in hand, stood next to the rat. Elizabeth fiddled with a display of Ratcatcher key chains. Elizabeth had *never* worked before, not even as a babysitter. Working was a big deal for her. Working was a normal deal for me. Except that everything was riding on that particular working day. Everything.

"Where is everyone?" Elizabeth asked. She had painted whiskers on her face and wore one of our rat-ear headbands.

I paced next to the door. I went outside and looked down the street. Orange cones blocked each end, making Main Street pedestrian-only. Foam snowflakes twinkled with morning dew. White lights beckoned from every doorway and window—even ours. A few people with laptops entered Java Heaven. A couple of kids ran around the giant blue spruce. "It's still early," I said, trying to hide the fear in my voice. I had expected a line. Not just any line, a line that would go down in Nordby history. So many people had called. So many e-mails had been sent. I had advertised in the paper. The Boys had handed out flyers with little coupons for 10 percent off a photo with Ratcatcher. Maybe I should have gotten a billboard.

Nervous energy burrowed in my stomach. What had I done? I had spent our last penny, literally. I looked around the transformed coffeehouse. What would we do with all the stuff if no one bought it? There wasn't enough room in the Closet of Failure. Entrepreneur, what a joke. Mr. Prince's stupid aptitude test was a scam. My nervous energy turned to nausea. I went back inside. Ratcatcher, sensing my fear, pawed at my ankles. I picked her up and buried my nose in her black-and-white neck. "Where are they?" I whispered. She purred.

"Hello? We hear you got the rat." A Japanese woman stood in the doorway. Behind her stood the same group of tourists from a few days before. "We try to get here, but giant coffee cup sign fall down and block road. Now all clear."

"Come on in," I said, a big smile bursting out. "The rat's over here." They came in. They laughed and petted the rat. They posed for photos, then bought seven coffee cups, twelve sets of sticky notes, and twenty tins of Rat-catcher Breath Mints.

And things just got better and better and better.

By the time Lars hobbled down the street with his fancy cane, the line stretched right up to Java Heaven's front door, which was about the best thing ever. "Move that line," Mr. Darling bellowed, storming into our crowded shop.

"Why?" I asked. It's so nice when a person doesn't scare you anymore. When you can look right into a face that used to intimidate you and say, "What's your problem?"

"Your line is my problem. It's blocking my customers."

"I seem to recall that your line blocked Anna's customers last year," Ingvar said.

Mr. Darling folded his arms. "I don't know what you're talking about." He sneered at me. "I think those old men are purposefully turning the line toward my door."

"I don't know what you're talking about," I said. Ralph and Odin waved through the picture window. My grandmother would be so proud.

"We'll see about this. I'm calling Officer Larsen."

Mr. Darling knocked over a display of Ratcatcher water bottles on his way out.

I didn't worry about Mr. Darling. Turned out, Elizabeth was really good at pushing merchandise. And Elliott, between bouts of picture taking, kept a running tab on the receipts, filling me in on the good news as the day went on. "He's really smart," Elizabeth said, when Elliott took a bathroom break. "If he got contacts, he'd be real cute. I'm thinking about asking him to a movie or something. Do you think that's weird?"

"I think that's a great idea."

Lots of Nordby High students came in, including Face and his country club herd. I thought Elizabeth would hide upstairs, but she walked right up to him, in front of his friends, and said, "Hello. Can I help you?"

"Oh." He smiled uncomfortably. "Hi, Elizabeth."

"I thought you couldn't come to the festival because you had something else to do."

"Yeah. I'm leaving for Tahoe with my family in an hour. So I can't go to the feast or the dance."

"Tahoe," she said after he had left. "It wasn't because I'm too fat. He's going to Tahoe." She laughed. "I don't know what I saw in him in the first place. He's *waaaaaay* too conservative."

At four o'clock it began to snow—big fat flakes that quickly covered the sidewalk and street. The Solstice crowd had grown each hour. More Nordby High students came into the Emporium. It didn't bother me one bit that some of them carried Vincent Mochas. The first group of carolers strolled by in their Victorian costumes. Kids ran past carrying their peanut-butter-and-birdseed-stuffed pinecones. Elizabeth and Elliott took a break and wandered off to see how the tree decorating was going. When they came back, they brought a bag of warm scones with loganberry jam that a Girl Scout troop was selling. Between working the cash register and answering the phone, I barely had time to think about anything else.

Until he walked through the door.

He was dressed in full Highland regalia, with a red and green plaid kilt and a black jacket with gold buttons, like a character from a movie. I was dressed in jeans, a sweatshirt, and an Emporium apron, like a girl from a shop. Hypnotized, I walked straight into Elizabeth.

"Wow. You look great," Elizabeth told him. "Where can I get a jacket like that?"

"It's formal wear," he said proudly. "I tried a tuxedo, but I think this suits me better."

It did. He looked amazing. Did I have any makeup on? When had I last brushed my hair?

He pushed back his long hair. The copper strands glowed like filaments. "I'm here to escort you to the grand feast."

I tried to act nonchalant. "Oh, I almost forgot about that." I looked at the clock. The grand feast at the Sons of Norway would start in half an hour. The store was still full of customers. "I should stay and help—"

"Oh no you won't." Elizabeth pushed me into the kitchen. Irmgaard followed. "You've got a date and you're going on that date."

"But the shop—"

"We can take care of it," Irmgaard said softly.

Malcolm posed for a photo with a group of old ladies and Ratcatcher. His jacket buttons sparkled. Every light in the room seemed drawn to him.

"You've got a date with an *angel*," Elizabeth said. "For God's sake, Katrina, what are you going to do? Reject an angel?"

I smiled. "I'll be right back."

Thirty-three

You'd have to be some kind of idiot to turn down a date with an angel. I flew around my bedroom like a human hurricane. Put on dress, put on shoes, brush hair, brush teeth, put on makeup, check underarms, check for visible panty lines, turn around a hundred times in the mirror and check to see what butt looks like. It looked pretty good. But what did it matter? He was an angel.

I put on so much lipstick that I looked like a clown. My hand trembled as I wiped some off. Calm down. It's just dinner and maybe a little bit of dancing. And then he'd go off to some other place, to deliver another message, and I'd never see him again. Still, the date counted. I was going out with a guy who wasn't my best friend, so it totally counted.

I took one more turn at the mirror. The final product was not half-bad. The dress fit perfectly and my hair graciously formed a few waves. Walking downstairs, I felt like Cinderella transformed. I hope that every girl can have a moment like that, when she gets to dress up and all eyes are on her.

Odin whistled. "Look what we got here."

"Katrina, you're a sight for sore eyes," Lars said.

"What a beauty," Ralph said.

Ingvar plucked his pipe from his mouth. "Our little girl is growing up."

Then The Boys turned their attention to Malcolm. "What time are you bringing her back?"

"Don't keep her out too late."

"Don't you be doing any drinking."

"Why are you still wearing a skirt?"

"Okay, stop it," I scolded. "You guys are totally embarrassing me." But I appreciated the attention, just the same. When you don't have a grandfather or a father or even a brother, it's good to know someone's looking out for you.

One of the nice things about walking with Malcolm was that I didn't need to wear a coat or boots. Sure, it was snowing outside, and the longest night of the year had already begun, but the minute he took my hand, warmth flooded my entire body.

"Bye," everyone called.

He led me out the door. He could have led me anywhere and I would have followed. Even to that London sewer pipe. Maybe I'd complain a little bit about the sewer pipe, but I'd still follow.

Falling in love is not a rational process. It can't be planned or avoided. It happens—for good or bad it simply happens. I knew he'd eventually leave. I knew we couldn't be together, but I fell anyway. It wasn't just the magic or the good looks—though I'm not going to lie and say that those things didn't matter. They definitely bumped him way ahead of most other Nordby guys. But what also bumped him ahead was that he was kind and attentive. He was honest about his failures and worries. He seemed vulnerable and powerful at the same time. In the end, I would never be able to figure it out.

Trying to make sense of love is like trying to dissect a rainbow.

We walked down the crowded street, passing other couples dressed in their holiday clothes. Women of all ages smiled at Malcolm. The old me would have suspected that they were all thinking: "What's he doing with her?" But I felt pretty and . . . successful. Of course he was with me.

"You look nice," Malcolm said, squeezing my hand. "You smell good too."

"Thanks." I looked down, to hide my blush. "So, where have you been?"

"Doing my job," he said.

"Where's your satchel?"

"I'm not on duty. Tonight, I'm all yours."

All mine. That really sounded weird. And nice.

Heidi Darling stood in the entryway of the Sons of Norway Hall. She looked really beautiful in a long peach gown. "Hi, Katrina," she said, not unkindly. Her gaze fixed on Malcolm.

"Hi," I said.

"That's a nice dress."

"Oh, thanks. Your dress is nice too."

"Are you two here together?" She raised her eyebrows.

"I'm escorting Katrina this evening," Malcolm said.

I looked around. Where was Vincent? I had hoped to see him and smooth things out.

"Tickets?" Heidi held out her hand, performing another one of her volunteer jobs.

Oh crap! The evening's momentum came to a screeching halt. I had forgotten to tell Malcolm that we needed tickets to get in. They sold out every year. My heart sank into my stomach. But Malcolm let go of my hand and reached into his coat. "Here you be," he said, handing over two white tickets.

Heidi tossed them into a basket. "Have fun," she said.

"Hello, Katrina." Officer Larsen blocked our entry to the hall. "Good to see your friend is feeling better. Have you sorted out the passport issue?"

"Yes," Malcolm said. "I'll be leaving tonight."

"I see." Officer Larsen relaxed and stepped aside. "Well, have a safe trip."

It would end tonight. I put on a brave face. *Enjoy the evening*, I told myself. *Remember every second of it.*

Tables stood end to end, stretching the length of the Sons of Norway Hall. The waiter seated us near the musicians, a local quartet, which made it impossible to have a conversation, but I didn't really mind. I was totally focused on not spilling food on my dress. A butter lettuce salad with baby shrimp came first. I worried that I might get a green bit caught between my teeth, so I just nibbled. Malcolm ate everything as if it was his last meal. Our last meal. Our date would end with a *I wish you a long and healthy life, Katrina Svensen*. I'd never see him again. I pushed the inevitable from my mind.

The main course was salmon, prepared by members of the Suquamish tribe. It came with roasted potatoes and green beans. I stopped worrying about my appearance and ate the whole thing. Risking every last cent of somebody else's money works up an appetite. Just as I ate my last bean, I noticed Heidi sitting a few tables down. A guy named Jordan sat next to her. Where was Vincent?

The quartet took a break while Nordby's mayor made a speech. "And we all owe a huge round of thanks to the Darling family and Java Heaven for sponsoring this year's festival." Mr. and Mrs. Darling and Heidi took a bow and Mr. Darling said, "Giving back to the community is what it's all about." Everyone applauded. I didn't even grimace at his hypocrisy because I was having so much fun sharing a heaping bowl of apple streudel with Malcolm.

The waiters stacked the chairs and pushed the tables against the walls to make room for dancing. The quartet came back. The overhead lights dimmed. Ropes of snowflakes, strung across the ceiling, sparkled with little white lights. The dance began with a slow song.

"Would you do me the honor of dancing with me?" Malcolm asked.

"Yes."

YES! YES! YES!

I had avoided school dances ever since middle school, when I'd been the tallest girl and the only boys desperate enough to ask me were total sex maniacs who tried to press their faces into my chest. And the idea of standing in the corner at a high school dance, the tall girl, unwanted, never appealed to me. So I approached the dance floor anxiously. Did I even know how to slow dance? Malcolm took my hand, pressing his other hand against my back, and began to move easily, gracefully. I'm pleased to report that we didn't step on each other's feet. He didn't jab me with his knees or cling to me with sweaty hands. His body melted into mine in all the right spots. His shoulder just happened to be at the perfect height for me to rest my head. His scent made me drowsy.

"Katrina?"

"Hmmm?"

"I stopped in today to see your grandmother. She's looking better."

"That was nice of you to see her."

"I wanted to say good-bye."

I held my breath. Was it going to end right then and there?

"Now that the message is delivered, I can't keep coming back. I've broken all the rules by getting to know you, by meeting your friends and family. I've got to give you that reward and then be on my way." He pulled me closer. "But I don't want to go."

Don't cry, don't cry. You knew this was going to happen.

Of all the things that had happened that week—almost losing the coffeehouse, almost losing my grandmother, the fight with Vincent, facing Mr. Darling, learning the truth about Irmgaard, and risking everything on the Emporium—Malcolm had been a bright spot. He'd been . . . an angel.

I looked into his eyes. "I guess we have to say good-bye."

And that's when it happened. He leaned forward and kissed me. It was the last thing I had expected to happen. And it was my first kiss. And first kisses, from what I've been told, are usually awkward. You have to figure out which way to tilt your head, how not to smack your teeth together, and what to do with your tongue. It's a lot to think about.

But there wasn't time to think about any of that because the moment his lips touched mine, an electric jolt ran all the way down to my toes, as if I had stuck my lips into a socket.

This is not a metaphor. I'm being literal. It was an actual electric jolt. We both jumped. "Ouch," I said, pulling away.

A little thread of smoke rose off his lower lip. He frowned and rubbed it. "I guess I'm not supposed to do that."

"I guess not." I rubbed my lower lip too. "That really hurt."

As the other couples danced around us, we stood there, smelling like singed flesh. My first kiss had nearly liquefied my face. What would happen next? Would the floor open up and swallow us in another sinkhole?

"Katrina," he said sadly.

"I know. You have to go."

We left the hall. Snow was still falling, casting its silent charm on everything it touched. Even the fire hydrants looked magical with their snow hats. St. Nicholas handed us each a candy cane as we walked by the blue spruce, its branches heavy with pinecones and lights. A circle of shoes wound beneath to bring harmony to the town. Malcolm took my hand and we walked to the waterfront park. A caroling group sang in the gazebo. We sat on a bench and looked out over the bay. Snow fell on my shoulders and clung to Malcolm's hair.

"I've got a confession to make." His satchel appeared on the bench, the golden letters glittering once again. He pulled out the little black law book. "There's actually nothing in here. I made it all up."

"Made it all up?"

"The bit about rewarding the good deed. You see, I was sent here to deliver Irmgaard's message. I'm not authorized to grant wishes. But I wanted to get to know the one girl who had noticed me. I wanted to spend a *wee* bit of time with you, to see what your life was like, and then maybe I'd understand why you, of all people, had noticed me. So I made you that promise, to reward your good deed. It's got me in a lot of trouble. I'll be getting—"

"Let me guess," I said. "You won't be getting that promotion."

He smiled. "You've been paying attention."

"So all of this, the fortune, the fame, was just to get to know me?"

"Yes."

A gust of wind whooshed over us, sending our hair into a flying spin. Malcolm reached into his satchel again and pulled out the packet of chocolate-covered coffee beans I had given him, then tipped the last bean into his palm. "An angel never breaks a promise. What you most desire, Katrina. It's yours." He handed me the bean.

"I already got what I most desired," I said. "I found out that I was good at something."

"But you did that on your own. I still need to grant you a wish. Surely you have a new desire?" The wind came again, stronger this time. It nearly knocked me off the bench. The ends of Malcolm's hair whipped against his face.

"Can I wish for you to stay?" I asked loudly, wind roaring in my ears.

"Messengers can't stay," he said. The bench began to tremble. The wind came stronger. Malcolm grabbed my waist to keep me from being swept off. "I've got to be going. Hurry, Katrina. Make your wish now."

I closed both hands around the bean. "What do I do?" I yelled.

"Just wish it. But remember, it will only work if it's what you most desire. Do it now. We're running out of time."

What I most desire. What I most desire.

I looked right into his electric eyes and made my wish. Then I popped the bean into my mouth and swallowed it whole.

For a moment, the world stood still. We sat in a silent bubble, just us two, insulated from the snow and the wind. His eyes widened. "But, Katrina, that wish was supposed to be for you."

"It's what I most desire."

And it was.

The bubble burst. Another gust of wind came, picking up fallen snow as it swept its way toward our bench. It blew over us and before I could say anything else, Malcolm's hand tightened on my waist, and then he dissolved into a swirl of glittering snowflakes.

He was gone.

I reached into the empty space. Cold pierced my blue velvet dress. I'd never see him again.

That's when a voice called out my name.

Thirty-four

Vincent's dad, dressed in his security uniform, walked toward me. "What are you doing out here alone?" he asked. "Hey, you're shivering." He took off his gray coat with its silver badge and wrapped it around my shoulders. Then he sat in the place where an angel had sat only moments before. "Katrina? What's the matter?"

I didn't want to explain. Losing someone is the worst feeling. Loss carves out a deep, hollow pocket. There's no magical way to fill it, no medicine or Band-Aid or surgery to cure it. I suppose that over time you get used to it, the way I had gotten used to not having my parents around. But the feeling never totally goes away. And the more time you spend on earth, the more pockets you'll collect. But it's part of living. It's life. Some of us are lucky enough to be alive.

"Where's Vincent?" I asked through chattering teeth.

"He's on the deck behind the booth, watching the Solstice ships." Mr. Hawk buttoned the top button so the coat wouldn't slip off my shoulders. "How come you're not with him? He's been moping around lately. You two been fighting?"

Moping around? Did Vincent feel as bad as I felt?

"Thanks for the coat, Mr. Hawk," I said, jumping to my feet. Then I ran past the gazebo as carolers sang "Frosty the Snowman." The snowfall had eased. Soft little flakes floated from the sky, glittering like sequins. I ran to the dock. The Solstice ships had lined up in the marina. Colored lights wound around masts and along deck rails. Canned holiday music drifted from the lead boat.

Vincent sat on the bench behind the security booth, looking out over the water. I didn't worry about rejection or embarrassment or pride. I wiped snow off the bench and sat right down. "I didn't want to break our tradition," I said.

He pushed back his knit hat, his eyes widening with surprise. "Uh, me neither."

I took a big breath and looked into his brown eyes. "I'm sorry I got so mad. I went a little crazy. I had no right to tell you not to go into Java Heaven. And it's stupid of me to be mad just because you're dating Heidi. I think I got so used to having you all to myself, I wasn't ready to share you. Which is ridiculous, when you think about it." I blew on my fingertips.

"It's not ridiculous." He took off his gloves and gave them to me. They were toasty warm inside. "I felt the same way. When I saw you with that guy, it made me feel kind of sad." He fidgeted. "Look, Katrina, I never went inside Java Heaven. I want you to know that. Heidi lied at the assembly. I never agreed to help with those snowflakes. And when Mr. Darling put my name on that billboard, I should have complained. I guess I kind of liked seeing my name on a billboard. Weird, huh?"

The bad feelings felt like a snakeskin that I just wanted to shed and leave behind. "You were helping the swim team. And Heidi's your girlfriend. I'm fine with it. Really. I don't care about Java Heaven anymore."

"Heidi's not my girlfriend. She just wanted to be featured in all those interviews I was doing." He sighed and slumped forward, resting his arms on his knees. "She wanted to go out with Vincent the hero."

"I'm sorry it didn't work out." I was. Truly sorry. My best friend had gotten his heart broken and I could feel his hurt almost as deeply as I could feel my own. "Really, really sorry."

He sat back. "It's okay. I'll get over it. She would have killed me, anyway, with all her extra activities. Her dad makes her do all that stuff. He really pushes her hard. I feel sorry for her. What about you? Are you still going out with that guy?"

"No. He left town."

"Oh. I'm sorry it didn't work out."

"Me too." My jaw trembled, partly from the cold, but mostly because sadness was creeping all over me.

Vincent reached under the bench and pulled out a blanket, then draped it over our legs. People gathered along the docks to watch as the ships slowly motored out of the harbor. St. Nicholas waved from the lead boat. For one magical night, all the people of Nordby gathered to pay homage to the season, to remember times past and to dance to the old music. To eat weird Old World food, drink New World coffee, and to pet a giant mutant stuffed rat. The two of us, as it had been for so long, sat on that bench, knowing that it would never be quite the same again. We'd go our separate ways, pulled by our desires like ships sailing out of the harbor. But for that moment, as the festival swirled around us, we could pretend that it would always be the same.

Vincent stretched out his long lean legs. "You know, we're going to have to get used to this."

"To what?"

"To us going out with other people."

"I know."

"It can't always be us two."

"I know." I looked up at the winter sky. "Do you think it's weird that we're not in love with each other?"

"No. I think it's perfect."

"Me too." I scooted closer and rested my head on his chlorine-scented shoulder.

Thirty-five

Well, the story's not quite over. Here's what happened after the Winter Solstice Festival.

A *Nordby News* reporter broke the story about Mr. Darling's generic coffee, calling it a "scandal." Turned out that when the crane driver pulled the Buick out of the sinkhole, a certain crumpled piece of paper fell out the window and landed at the reporter's feet. Yes, indeed. The uproar was huge. The town council voted Mr. Darling off all committees and the police department looked into possible charges of consumer fraud. The Organic Coffee Coalition threatened to sue on behalf of consumers everywhere.

Mr. Darling packed up and left town, abandoning his coffeehouse and his offer to buy the building. Heidi and her mother stayed, however, which was great because Heidi became a changed person overnight. Her father had been the one pushing all those extra activities. She stopped doing all that school spirit stuff and focused all her energy on the swim team. She and Vincent ended up getting back together and I got used to having her around. We solved the whole movie theater thing by having him sit in the middle. You can get used to anything, if you put your mind to it.

Ratcatcher's fame grew. Thanks to Elizabeth's marketing genius and Web connections, Nordby became the Loch Ness of Washington State, with "rumored sightings" of a giant mutant rat that lived in the bay. Some thought it was the dead rat's mourning mate. The Emporium sold tons of custom-made stuffed black-and-white cats and stuffed rats. Elizabeth created a coloring book and Elliott worked an afternoon a week as our accountant. They started going out. Elliott put on ten pounds right away, which is really easy to do if you hang out with Elizabeth.

What about Anna's Old World Scandinavian Coffeehouse? Well, we moved right into Java Heaven's space. We bought some of the equipment from Mrs. Darling, who was happy to get rid of it. Along with fancy organic coffee drinks, we continued to serve the old-fashioned stuff. The laptop crowd shared the space with the retired crowd, and those sardine sandwiches became one of our most popular items.

Irmgaard became the manager and kept making soup and krumkakes. She let her hair grow and though she remained a woman of few words, the words she chose were worthy of a place in this world.

Grandma Anna recovered, but she cut way back on her hours and started some new hobbies. She learned how to play Hnefatafl. She went on a Mexican Riviera cruise with the ladies from the shoe shop. She raised money for the cardiac wing of the hospital by hosting a neighborhood garage sale, which included all the junk from my Closet of Failure. Her heart beat steady and strong.

Me? Well, I focused on my grades at school, because my new goal was to get an MBA, which is a master's degree in business administration. I decided to become a venture capitalist. That's a fancy title for someone who risks their money by helping other people start up businesses. Seemed I had a knack for something, after all.

But that's still not the end of the story. There was a little something to do with that third coffee bean.

What I had desired on that night as the winter wind whipped past, was for Malcolm to get his promotion. But I had no way of knowing if my wish had come.

Until I took out the recycling one Saturday morning in March.

I had a bin of papers from the Emporium that I needed to leave beside the Dumpster. In my part of the world, mornings are still dark in March, so I turned on the yellow alley light. And there he was, sitting on a pile of crates, wearing a khaki kilt and my grandfather's white sweater. His satchel was slung over his shoulder and he grinned like a kid. I dropped the bin. "Malcolm?" I couldn't believe that he was sitting there. I hadn't stopped missing him, had hoped every day that maybe he'd have another message to deliver in Nordby. That maybe he'd show up in the alley again.

He didn't say a word. Just walked right up to me and this is what he did. He slid his arms around my waist and kissed me. My face didn't liquefy. No singed flesh, no smoke. The kiss still felt electric, but in a non-life-threatening way. Then I pulled away. "What . . . ?"

"I got that promotion," he said with a blinding smile.

"You did?" Something had changed. I sniffed. Where was that Highland smell? Where was that cloud of tropical air? I put my hand to his cheek. It felt cool.

He held out his satchel. The words *Messenger Service* were gone.

"You got that promotion." I said the words slowly, the truth filling me with fear. "Oh no, this is my fault. I did this to you with my wish. I'm so sorry, Malcolm." I stepped away.

"Why are you sorry?"

He was mortal. I had made him mortal. "I didn't realize that the promotion meant you'd become . . . Oh God, Malcolm, will you ever forgive me? Because of me you're going to—"

"Live. Because of you I'm going to live." He smiled again and held out his arms. "It's exactly what I longed for, Katrina. It's everything I always wanted. It's the highest honor an angel can achieve."

"It is?"

He pulled me close. "Do you know where I can get one of those photo albums? So I can start a record of my life?"

"We have some in the Emporium, if you don't mind one with a giant rat on the cover."

We went into the coffeehouse, and as the busy morning flew around us, customers finding seats, engaging in conversation, clicking on laptops, milk being steamed, coffee being ground, people starting their day, Malcolm and I shared a krumkake at the corner table as if the world had actually stopped. He stared into my eyes and just like before, that feather duster feeling swept over my entire body.

So go ahead and take a picture of that and stick it on a postcard.

ACKNOWLEDGMENTS

Nordby is based on the quaint town of Poulsbo, Washington, not far from my home. If you get the chance to visit Poulsbo, you won't be disappointed. It's a delight. I wrote much of this book there, while sitting in one of my favorite coffeehouses, Hot Shots Java. I'd like to thank its staff for supplying me with great coffee and the perfect place to write. And those little dark chocolate sticks are always appreciated.

And again, I'd like to thank my writers' group for their fastidious attention to the first draft: Anjali Banerjee, Carol Cassella, Sheila Rabe, Elsa Watson, and Susan Wiggs. I'm still blessed to have my agent, Michael Bourret, and my editor, Emily Easton. Thanks to the entire staff at Walker Books for Young Readers.

I always love to hear from my readers, so please write to me. You can visit my Web site at www.suzanneselfors.com.